CLASH OF

In London, after the war, widowed Pandora White remarries and imagines her secret safe. Only three close friends know that Alexis Dolkov, an escaped Russian prisoner whom she nursed back to health in Jersey during the German occupation, is the father of her son Bird.

But Alexis's brother Vladimir, an officer in the KGB, discovers the boy's existence and targets him as a potential recruit. He is patient and thorough, preparing for the day when Bird is old enough to learn his true parentage, and work for his father's country.

Bird's identity is still a mystery when we later meet two brilliant young men at Oxford. Richard Kent and David Windfield are friends and rivals, high-fliers destined for careers in the Foreign Office. But something happens which will shatter that idyllic summer and set Richard and David on different paths. Palma Harcourt keeps us guessing right to the end: which of the two, Richard or David, is Bird, and who is working for which side in the intelligence game?

Clash of Loyalties is the story of two men and the opposing ideologies they serve. And of Julia Manville, the beautiful woman they both love. From the hardships of wartime to the sophisticated world of the diplomatic corps, Palma Harcourt's touch is sure in this intricate and absorbing new novel.

PALMA HARCOURT

Clash of Loyalties

COLLINS
8 Grafton Street, London W1
1988

William Collins Sons & Co. Ltd
London · Glasgow · Sydney · Auckland
Toronto · Johannesburg

First published 1988
Copyright © Palma Harcourt 1988

BRITISH LIBRARY CATALOGUING IN PUBLICATION DATA

Harcourt, Palma
Clash of loyalties.
I. Title
823'.914[F]   PR6058.A62

ISBN 0-00-223318-5

Photoset in Linotron Plantin by
Rowland Phototypesetting Ltd
Bury St Edmunds, Suffolk
Printed and bound in Great Britain by
Robert Hartnoll (1985) Ltd, Bodmin, Cornwall

For Colette and Bill

Contents

Prelude

The Channel Islands were still occupied by the Germans at the beginning of 1945, the last year of the Second World War.

The Jersey Evening Post *had continued to function under German rule, and the following notice appeared in its births column:*

INGRAM. On 15th February, to Pandora, née White, and the late John Ingram, a son.

Only a very few Islanders knew that the announcement was not strictly accurate. John Ingram was not the father of the child to whom his wife had given birth. The boy had been fathered by one Alexis Dolkov, a Russian prisoner of the Germans, forced to work in Jersey for the dreaded Todt Organization.

This fact was to have repercussions which, in the decades that followed, would affect the lives of many individuals . . .

PART ONE

The Forties

1

Moscow, Winter 1948–9

The snow fell thickly from a leaden Moscow sky, great fat flakes that failed to melt as they landed. It had been snowing all morning, and the army of women street cleaners could no longer keep it under control. The city was covered, except for some patches of gold on the distinctive onion-shaped domes. Though the December afternoon was scarcely under way, darkness was already beginning to descend to conceal the depression that pervaded the Soviet capital, and the many scars that still remained three years after the end of the Second World War.

Inside the building on the corner of Dzerzhinsky Square, where Vladimir Dolkov worked, lights had come on in one office after another. Dolkov's had been among the first. In spite of the continuing shortage of electricity, he reasoned that if he couldn't see to read there was little purpose in remaining.

Dolkov sprawled in a chair, his feet on the desk in front of him, his officer's jacket undone. He was sweating gently. Though fuel was scarce for the populace, the steam heating system in the Headquarters of the MGB – the Ministry for State Security, a few years later to be absorbed with the MVD into the all-powerful KGB – was working overtime. In spite of the biting cold outside, the office was excessively warm, and Dolkov, a tall, big man, heavily-built, felt the heat.

He threw down the American periodical he had been reading, and stretched himself vigorously. What fools the Western Allies were, he thought. They were happy to publish almost anything. If one knew where to look – especially in specialist magazines and learned journals – one could, almost casually and with a minimum of effort, gather basic information on so many topics, from service statistics to research and development and strategic thought and argument. Even the foreign popular press could provide items of scandal that became grist to the intelligence community's mill. Really, intelligence work these days was becoming child's play.

Dolkov took his feet off the desk, and began to turn over the sheaf of English newspapers that had arrived in the diplomatic bag. He read a long feature article in *The Times* of London about the development of atomic power in Britain and its possible application to the development of an entirely British bomb. He made some notes, and turned the page. His lips curled derisively. He was a staunch communist, like all who worked for Beria, and his faith had not been dented even by some of Stalin's excesses, which were then beginning to be rumoured. He wondered why anyone – apart, of course, from a recruiter – should be interested in the Court Circular, the public appointments, the social news, the announcement that one upper-class twit was about to marry another.

Then a name caught his eye, and suddenly he was absolutely still. He re-read the announcement. Pandora White, widow of John Ingram, had married again; the new husband was a member of the British Parliament. Surely, Dolkov thought, there couldn't be more than a few people in Great Britain with the unusual name of Pandora, and he half remembered Alexis, his brother, mentioning someone called John Ingram as a man who had been kind to him in Jersey. He remembered other things too – the emotional family reunion that had greeted Alexis's return, the dramatic story of his escape from the island, and the fact that it had taken all his father's not inconsiderable influence to save Alexis from the fate that normally awaited those Russians who had been captured by the Allies and, however unwillingly, spent time in the West. Alexis had been particularly vulnerable once he had admitted he had actually lived as a Westerner – albeit in a territory occupied by the Germans. Vladimir shook his head; it was better not to think like this. Better to treat it as fortunate that their father had still been alive when Alexis finally reached Moscow towards the end of 1944.

Vladimir Dolkov leaned back in his chair, considering. He hadn't before thought Pandora White of any consequence; as far as he was concerned she had served her purpose by sheltering Alexis and caring for him after he had escaped from the brutal Todt Organization. Now he reassessed the situation. Vladimir had a devious mind – almost a requirement for service in his Directorate of the MGB – and he could imagine some interesting possibilities.

But he was short on facts. He wished he could recall more of the nuances of his brother's account of his enforced stay in Jersey, and he wondered if Natalia might help. Natalia, his own plump and pretty wife, had been close to Alexis – closer perhaps than he himself had been after the long wartime separation. And she had nursed Alexis through the bitter bout of influenza which had culminated in his death the previous winter; there was some likelihood that during that period he had confided in her snippets of information that could prove useful.

Eager as he was to question his wife, Vladimir made himself concentrate on his work until it was time to leave the office. Even when he reached home, he was forced to restrain his curiosity. The Dolkovs were lucky enough to have a three-roomed apartment not far from the University. This was luxury in Moscow in 1948, and only due to his position in the MGB. Nevertheless, it had to accommodate not only Vladimir and Natalia, but their two daughters and their *babushka*, who managed the household while Natalia taught at the local kindergarten. All in all, there was little genuine privacy.

Vladimir waited until he and Natalia were alone in their small bedroom before he showed her the page he had illegally extracted from his office copy of *The Times*, and brought home with him in defiance of all regulations. Natalia read it, but showed no more than mild interest.

'I don't understand, Vladimir. What's this to us?'

'It's the same woman, isn't it? Alexis's woman from Jersey?'

'Oh yes. There can't be much doubt about that. She seems to have married the sick friend, Ingram – you remember, Vladimir, Alexis told us the man was dying – and now he's dead she's married this other man. That's what it says, isn't it? I've not misread the English?'

'No, that's what it says, Natalia.'

His wife frowned. 'So?'

'I've just realized we know nothing about this Pandora White.'

'We know she was a nice girl, kind, ordinary, not too clever, but brave. And, according to Alexis, an innocent in bed.' Natalia laughed as she snuggled close to her husband, but for once he didn't immediately respond to the invitation. 'What more should we know about her?' she asked.

'Was she rich? Her family, I mean – or influential?'

'No.' Natalia shook her head. 'It was a fine Jersey house she lived in, Alexis said, but it belonged to her aunt, and the aunt's son – I think he was in Canada – would inherit it. The girl herself was English, and her father just worked in a bank there. Why do you ask, Vladimir?'

'I was just wondering, Natalia – about her marriage, for example.'

'Perhaps she was sorry for him. Perhaps she was lonely after Alexis left her. Perhaps she was going to have a child and wanted to give it a father.'

A child! Vladimir tensed. He realized that Natalia had misunderstood him, and was talking about Pandora White's first marriage, to the sick John Ingram. He had been interested in the second marriage – the one reported in *The Times* – the one to the Member of Parliament. But Natalia had a point. Why *had* the girl married a man who didn't have long to live? Was it possible Alexis had made her pregnant? After all, they had shared the same house for many months – and Vladimir knew his brother.

'Natalia, think carefully. Did Alexis ever say anything to suggest that this Pandora was going to have a child?' Vladimir propped himself up on one elbow so that he could look down on Natalia, but it was too dark to see more than an outline of her face.

'Well, I've never told you before, but he did say once he guessed she might be. I asked him why. He said because she was often sick in the mornings, and he thought she was thickening a bit around the middle.'

'But she never mentioned it to him?'

'No. Nor did he. He didn't dare. He was afraid she might make it an excuse to persuade him to marry her and stay in Britain. I've sometimes wondered if that wasn't why he was so keen to cross to France instead of waiting till the end of the war.'

'I see.' Vladimir paused. 'Anyway, she let him go, then married this Ingram, knowing the marriage would be only temporary.' He spoke ruminatively, thinking aloud. 'She *did* have a child, Natalia! She bloody well did! I'd bet on it! It's the only explanation that fits the circumstances. And it was Alexis's child – Alexis's son, perhaps.'

In his excitement Vladimir had permitted his voice to rise, and there was a sudden burst of coughing from the adjoining living-room. Vladimir swore softly. The walls of the apartment were paper-thin, and he had disturbed the *babushka*, who slept next door, beside the stove. He reminded himself that she was a little deaf. They had been speaking softly, and it was most unlikely she could have overheard anything of importance. Nevertheless, until he had made his plans – if he decided to make plans – he must be careful.

He put a hand between Natalia's legs and began to caress her. 'You understand, my love, you mustn't breathe a word of what we've been talking about – not to anyone? You realize it could be dangerous – very dangerous – for all of us?'

'I do,' she whispered, 'and I'll remember. And you, Vladimir, don't you forget it either.'

★

For several weeks, Vladimir Dolkov took no action. Naturally, when he had first heard of Pandora White's new marriage, he had thought in terms of recruitment: a possible opportunity to blackmail Pandora, or her husband, or both, into working, wittingly or unwittingly, for the Soviet Union. The obvious first step, he reflected, would have been to take the idea to his superiors, and obtain their permission to prepare an outline operational plan.

But Dolkov was under no illusions about the uncertainties of life, working – however remotely – for Beria. Every day he heard of examples of what happened to those who made mistakes, or tried to be too clever – or were just unlucky. He himself had no intention of becoming a victim. And the possibility – the near certainty – that somewhere in England there was a child whom Alexis, his own brother, had fathered could be sufficient to place himself and his whole family under suspicion; an approach to his superiors was out of the question. Certainly he must keep what he had learnt from the authorities, at least until he knew more. But the difficulty of learning more – of making inquiries, discreet inquiries, without arousing undesirable interest – was immense, and he remained content to brood.

Gradually the situation began to obsess him; he realized that he had to understand all the circumstances, so that he could assess the position with certainty. And then chance intervened, providing his opportunity. Sergei Basnov was posted as a Counsellor to the Soviet Embassy in London. Basnov, accompanied by his wife, was to leave in two weeks' time, and Anna Basnova, as she was known, was close to Vladimir and Natalia.

For Anna had been born Anna Dolkova. She was Vladimir's first cousin, the only child of his uncle, and had been brought up with the three Dolkov brothers. Almost inevitably she had married Boris, the eldest boy, who had been killed at Stalingrad. A practical woman, Anna hadn't remained a widow for long; after the war there were far too many widows in Russia. She had remarried a man considerably older than herself, but one who could offer her a comfortable and privileged life, and it was proving a good marriage. Most importantly from Vladimir's point of view, she was someone he could trust.

On the Saturday before she was due to leave Moscow, Anna Basnova came to say goodbye to the Dolkovs. Vladimir had suggested that she should arrive early in the afternoon, and plan to spend the rest of the day with them; Sergei could join them later. She was surprised to find Vladimir alone. It had in fact been hard to arrange. The two girls had been happy to go skating; they knew they wouldn't miss seeing their Aunt Anna. Natalia, however, had objected; she was unwilling to go out on a cold winter's day to queue for some inferior shoes that she wasn't prepared to buy. She had only finally given way to Vladimir's insistence when he told her – not altogether untruthfully – that his work was involved. But she might return unexpectedly, and it was best for her to know nothing of his hopes, his plans.

'Where is everyone?' Anna demanded, only half in jest. 'Don't any of them care about me?'

'We all care about you,' Vladimir assured her. 'But the two girls wanted to go skating, so their *babushka* has taken them, and Natalia has gone to buy a pair of shoes. She was told a queue for them was forming at some store, and she couldn't miss the chance. They'll all be back later. Meanwhile, Anna, I want a private talk with you, very private – you understand.'

Anna, well-versed in Moscow ways, looked up sharply, then nodded. Vladimir explained the situation as he saw it. He was as brief as possible. When he stopped speaking he looked at Anna expectantly.

She had listened carefully, and was quick to respond. 'Vladimir, that's fascinating news. It would be nice, very nice, to know that Alexis had left a child – perhaps a son. But he would, alas, be an English boy, and I don't understand – '.

'No! With Alexis as his father, under Russian law he'd be a Russian, just like us, Anna.'

Anna was no fool and, as a diplomat's wife, she had some experience of the complexities of international relations. 'In – in a way, yes, I suppose so. But do you think this Pandora would let him go? And even if she were to agree, I'm not sure the British Government would permit it.'

'Anna! Anna!' Vladimir expostulated. 'You said you didn't understand, and you don't. There'd be no question of bringing the child to Moscow. We both know things aren't good here at the moment. But when we've recovered from the effects of the Patriotic War, they'll improve, and then – who knows? We'll have to wait and see.'

Smiling, Anna Basnova shook her head to show she was not deceived. Vladimir Dolkov was a strange man, she thought, a devious man. Determined and ambitious, he would undoubtedly be cruel if he were thwarted. But he was also a romantic, and he was devoted to his family. Anna had no doubt that in his own

19

mind he had already written the scenario in which he hoped Alexis's son would one day play a part.

Vladimir returned her smile; he could guess her thoughts, and he knew she was right. But, 'First things first, Anna,' he said. 'We must keep this to ourselves; that's crucial. You know why, as well as I do. And in any case there may not even be a child. But you'll find out, when you get to London, won't you? You *will* help?'

'Of course. Am I not family, Vladimir?' Anna hesitated. 'You'll have to be patient, though. London will be different from Moscow. I'll have to learn my way around – and I'm not just talking about reading a street plan. It may not be all that easy to make inquiries. I know that as Sergei's wife I'll have certain privileges, but there are restrictions, too. I've been briefed – '

'I appreciate that. Nevertheless – '

'I'll do my best. I promise.'

They talked for a little longer, arranging how Anna might communicate anything she learnt under cover of simple family gossip. Then they were interrupted by Natalia. She had recovered from her earlier bad temper, having ignored the queue for shoes and managed to buy a pretty blouse instead. Soon afterwards the two girls returned with their *babushka*, shortly to be followed by Sergei Basnov.

The day ended happily, in spite of tears of farewell, and Vladimir Dolkov went to bed with his Natalia well pleased with himself and the turn of events.

2

London, Spring 1949

Anna Basnova was a level-headed young woman, and it would be an exaggeration to suggest that London, and the life of a Soviet diplomat's wife in the capital, overwhelmed her. But for some time after her arrival she was absorbed by all that was new and different to see and do and learn. In fact, London fascinated her; it was tremendously exciting, though also disappointing.

She told herself that perhaps she had expected too much. It was clearly a fine city, with splendid buildings of historic interest, broad parks, an abundance of museums and art galleries. There were theatres and cinemas, and opulent restaurants of a kind unknown in Moscow. In spite of shortages of some goods, the shops seemed full of things to buy. And this was true not only of famous department stores like Harrods – so different from Moscow's equally famous GUM in Red Square with its constant displays of unavailable goods and its bureaucratic sales procedures – but also of the host of small boutiques. And there were relatively few of the queues to which she had become so accustomed at home.

Certainly she herself had no need to queue; Sergei Basnov's wife was a privileged person. But with her privileges went some serious disadvantages. A staff car might be forthcoming to drive her about. A 'friend' from the embassy might always be willing to go shopping with her or show her the sights, or accompany her on some semi-formal occasion. And in the evenings, at receptions and dinner parties, Sergei might be more attentive that he had ever been. Anna appreciated all this cosseting, but she was too intelligent not to realize that the paramount concern was not for her well-being.

For she was a Soviet official's wife in a foreign country, a country that had recently been a so-called 'ally', but even then was not really to be trusted. And, in spite of the fact that it now had a Labour Government, it was still a capitalist society where the temptations – real or imagined by the paranoid Soviet authorities – were myriad. Like all other Soviet citizens in similar positions, Anna Basnova, good communist though she undoubtedly was, needed to be safeguarded and protected against any dangerous influences.

Anna accepted the situation: she had no choice. Secretly she was amused, but sad. She was amused when she was purposely driven through the dreariest outskirts of the city, when queues were pointed out to her, when the continued rationing of food and coal so many years after the end of the war were lamented, when the difference in lifestyles of the privileged and the poor was constantly stressed.

She was sad because this continuing indoctrination – if that was the word – was so unnecessary. She was neither blind nor deaf. She could see for herself the bombed sites where there had been no attempt at rebuilding and only wild flowers grew. She could see the houses and shopfronts, neglected and badly in need of paint or restoration. She had studied English at university and spoke it well, and she could read the British newspapers and listen to the radio; she was permitted to do this. She could hear the complaints and sense the discontent of many of those whom she met at parties – especially when they assumed she failed to understand their language. Sometimes she yearned to tell such complainants that the situation was infinitely worse in the Soviet Union.

Nevertheless, Anna remained a Russian patriot; she loved her homeland and was proud of it. If anyone had offered her a choice between spending the next forty years in London or in Moscow, she would unhesitatingly have chosen Moscow. It was where she and her family belonged, and nothing could change that.

Vladimir Dolkov, she knew, shared her feelings and, however greatly her movements in London might be restricted, she was determined to do what she could to search out the child that Alexis might have fathered. Anything more she would leave to

22

Vladimir. If Vladimir planned to use the child in some way, she had no doubt it would be for the benefit of Russia.

Sensibly, in spite of this determination, Anna bided her time, the exemplary wife of a senior Soviet diplomat, enjoying London, but giving no one the least cause for suspicion. She would take no risks until she was no longer regarded as a newcomer, and her presence had begun to be taken for granted.

In itself, the search for Pandora presented no difficulty: there was only one Member of the British Parliament of the right name listed in the London telephone directory – which, to Anna's surprise, seemed to be available to anyone, unlike the Moscow book, the circulation of which was strictly limited. The address was that of a quiet square behind Harrods, a location which could scarcely have been better for Anna's purpose when she decided to act.

By the end of March she was ready, but facing a major problem. If Anna were to arrive unannounced this Pandora might quite simply be out or away. Or she might not be alone, which would make Anna's mission embarrassing if not impossible, especially since time would almost certainly be limited. And Anna doubted whether she could readily create more than one opportunity to pay her visit. Yet, if she warned Pandora – by letter or phone call – that she was coming, Pandora might refuse to see her, or deliberately avoid her. There was no way of estimating Pandora's feeling about Alexis after all this time.

In the end the decision was taken out of Anna's hands. She had been instructed to accompany the Ambassador's wife to an exhibition at the Royal Academy, but at the last moment that lady had felt unwell, and Anna found herself being driven alone from Kensington Palace Gardens eastwards towards Knightsbridge. Here was her chance. She tapped on the glass separating her from the driver, and directed him to Harrods; she could think of some excuse for the change of plan later. For the present she must concentrate on what she had to do.

The traffic in the Brompton Road was such that there was no way the driver could abandon the car – in spite of its CD plate – at the main entrance to Harrods, and suggest he might come with her into the store to carry her purchases. Instead, Anna gave him instructions about where and when she was to be picked up. She nodded pleasantly to the doorman and went inside, turning sharply to the right and then to the left. She tried not to hurry as she made her way through the throng of shoppers to the rear entrance on Basil Street. Now, she knew she was committed. Mouth dry, heart pounding, she walked quickly to her destination.

She was breathing heavily when she reached the house, a tall Victorian building on the corner of the square. Once it had been a gentleman's town residence, suitable for housing his large family and considerable domestic staff. But long ago it had been turned into flats. There was a row of bell-pushes with names and numbers beside them. Anna stared at them blankly. None of them meant anything to her. The directory must have been out of date, or she had somehow come to the wrong place.

Turning away, nearly panicking, she almost missed an arrow painted on the wall, with beside it the number she was seeking. A moment later she found the entrance around the corner in a side street. She rang the bell. Time passed; in fact, less than a minute. Then the door was opened and she saw a woman a few years younger than herself, wearing a tweed skirt and a blue twin-set – the kind of clothes which Anna had come to regard as typically English. The woman smiled at her inquiringly.

'Good-morning.'

'Good-morning.' Anna licked dry lips. 'You – you are Pandora White?'

'I was, yes. Now I'm Mrs – '

'I am Anna – Anna Dolkova.' Hurriedly Anna corrected herself; she had nearly given her name as Basnova. 'I am the sister of Alexis Dolkov,' she lied. 'I need to speak to you, please, privately. Are you alone?'

'Alexis's sister!' The woman's immediate reaction was surprise. Then, 'Yes, I'm alone. That is – except for Bird.'

'Bird? Who is Bird?'

'My son.'

'And the son of my brother, Alexis.'

It was a statement, not a question, and Pandora made no attempt to deny the fact. She had become very pale and took a step backwards, as Anna walked into the hall, shutting the door behind her. Suddenly Anna felt sure of herself, in full control of the confrontation. But she reminded herself of the story she had agreed with Vladimir, and hastened to eliminate any threatening element from her approach.

'Please,' she said, 'you must forgive me coming here like this. I am sorry. But I must talk to you, Pandora.'

Nervous, in the aftermath of the shock she had received at Anna's arrival on her doorstep and almost forcible entry into the flat, Pandora spoke with unaccustomed speed and inconsequence. 'Why not?' she said. 'Come along. We live in what is really the basement, though it's euphemistically called a garden flat. Not that there's much of a garden, just a slip of grass, but it's somewhere for Bird to play outside in the summer.'

Anna, however, was scarcely listening to her. The Russian's attention was focused on a small figure who had appeared at the end of the hall.

Seeing the direction of Anna's gaze, Pandora turned, ran forward and picked up her son. Instinctively, in the seeming face of an obscure danger, she clasped him to her defensively, more closely than was necessary, and the boy cried out, alarmed.

The child's reaction served to restore Pandora's composure. 'Come on!' she said sharply to Anna over her shoulder as, soothing the boy, she hastened down a narrow flight of stairs.

Anna followed her into what was clearly the main room of the flat. It was long and low, comfortably but inexpensively furnished and with a dining table at one end. This was, in fact, the first time Anna had seen the normal post-war living conditions of the professional middle-class English, and she admired the furniture, though it was mostly modern and wartime 'utility'. Momentarily silent, she took a seat on the settee to which Pandora pointed.

'I can't stay long,' Anna said at once. 'But I would be grateful if you would answer some questions for me.'

'Perhaps you should answer some for me first.' By now Pandora was in no mood to be intimidated. 'In the first place, how did you know where to find me?'

'Alexis saw an announcement of your new marriage – '

'Alexis! You – you mean he's alive? He didn't drown on his way to France?' Pandora was incredulous.

'No. He managed to get home, but things were difficult for him. You mustn't blame him.'

'For what? Why should I blame him?'

'You would do nothing to harm him, then?'

'No! Of course not.'

'Ah, that's good.' Anna feigned relief. 'You see, Alexis is about to marry the daughter of someone high up in the Soviet hierarchy – a member of the Politburo – and if it became known about you and the boy the marriage would probably not be permitted. And he might be in great danger.' She spread her hands in apparent helplessness. 'Pandora, my country is not like yours. Please tell me – apart from you, who knows the truth about your – Bird?'

Anna made an attempt to smile at the child, now sitting quietly on his mother's lap. He regarded her, eyes wide and serious, and studiously sucked his thumb. The Russian woman found his gaze disconcerting; it was as if he realized that she was play-acting. Quickly she turned back to Pandora.

'No one,' Pandora said at last. 'At least, no one who would dream of telling anyone.'

'But who – your parents? Your present husband?'

'No. If you really want to know, they believe Bird was John Ingram's son. John married me so that the baby should have a legitimate name – that may not matter where you come from, but it does here. In any case, once back in England I never suggested the child wasn't his.'

'What about in Jersey? Your friends there must have known,' Anna persisted.

Pandora shrugged. 'Dr De Brel, for whom I worked in Jersey, certainly. But he's working in Berlin now. Jeanne Rousset – but she's gone to Ottawa to nurse. And the old parson, Edward Beaufort – he knew but, poor dear, he's in a home for retired clergy in Hampstead. That's all. But why ask? You needn't worry, Anna. Nor need Alexis. No one's going to start gossiping about his sinful past.'

'And you – yourself?'

'Me? What on earth do you mean? My life's now settled – and

so is Bird's. Do you think for a moment that I want to rock the boat?'

'Rock the boat? What is that?'

'Change the situation, of course.'

Anna didn't appreciate – or paid no attention to – the growing impatience with which Pandora was speaking. She was too occupied memorizing the names and places that had been mentioned. But she saw Pandora glance at the clock on the mantel, and realized she had lingered too long in the flat.

'Just one more thing then, please. Do you have a photograph you could give me – for Alexis?'

'A photograph – of me?'

This time Anna could hardly fail to be aware of Pandora's sarcasm. 'Of your son,' she said more gently.

'I'll look and see.'

Pandora lifted the child from her lap and went to a roll-top desk that stood in a corner – one of the two or three good pieces of furniture in the room. The boy toddled along beside her, hanging on to her skirt, but with his head turned towards Anna. Pandora rummaged in a drawer, her back to Anna, who was half expecting her to reply that she was unable to find any suitable pictures.

But, turning, Pandora said, 'You can have these,' and she handed Anna a small sheaf of snapshots.

Anna glanced through them. 'Thank you,' she said, surprised. 'They are wonderful. You are very kind.' She stood up. 'I must go now, and I shall not be able to come again. So this is the last time we shall meet.'

'Oh yes,' said Pandora, making no effort to suggest regret. Then she picked up the child and led the way up the stairs to the hall. She opened the front door and waited for Anna to go. She forced a smile. 'Goodbye, Anna,' she said. But she didn't offer her hand.

'Goodbye, Pandora. Goodbye, Bird.' On the doorstep Anna turned impulsively. 'Thank you once more. You have been generous. Alexis was cruel to leave you when he suspected you were pregnant. It must have been hard for you to lose the man you loved.'

27

Pandora stared at the Russian. The idea was so remote from reality as to be laughable. 'It wasn't love, or anything like love,' she said finally. 'It was circumstance and mutual sympathy, if you like – propinquity, almost, if you know what that means. I was never in love with Alexis. If he told you I was, it was untrue.' Her voice hardened as she added impulsively, 'I loved someone else – a German officer. But he's dead now. His father wrote to me after the war to say he'd been killed trying to keep your people out of Berlin.'

The front door shut quietly before Anna could think of a suitable reply. She stood on the step, staring at the brass letter-box and the peeling paintwork. She thought she heard the sound of a sob on the far side of the door, but she couldn't be sure; a car was passing in the road.

In the distance a clock was striking. It galvanized Anna, and she ran. Later, she promised herself, she would consider her meeting with Pandora White and the child in detail. Now, the factor of overriding importance was to get back to Harrods and the car that would be waiting for her. The driver would undoubtedly report on her absence, but if she were not unduly late it would probably be overlooked.

Anna had been right. Inside her front door, Pandora was sobbing. She was remembering a period of her life she had hoped to forget . . .

3

Jersey, 1944–5

Pandora remembered lying in bed on that particular dark, dank morning, reluctant to get up in her cold room, to wash inadequately, to dress in clothes that were none too clean, to bicycle through the dripping lanes to St Helier and the doctor's office where she worked as a receptionist and secretary. It was all so depressing, and the situation was not improved by the fact that Pandora had just celebrated – if you could call it celebrating – her twenty-fifth birthday. She felt that she was vegetating, growing old while she waited for the war to end.

The alarm clock startled her. She turned it off and pushed back the bedclothes. A tall, athletic girl, she had suffered four years of a diet merely adequate to keep hunger at bay, and felt, like so many others in the Island, a constant sense of lethargy. But now the cold forced her to hurry. Shivering, she went into the bathroom.

Quickly she washed and cleaned her teeth, hoarding both soap and toothpaste – they had become precious commodities – and took a moment to regard herself in the mirror with some distaste. She thought of herself as plain, her brown eyes too widely spaced, her mouth slightly crooked. In fact, Pandora's face, framed by dark shoulder-length hair, might not have been pretty, but it was appealing, especially when she smiled.

She dressed in layers of warm clothing, thankful as always that she and her aunt had been much the same size. Otherwise, she didn't know how she would have survived; she had brought so few things with her. She had expected to be in Jersey for some weeks at most, until her aunt was well again, but events had overtaken her and what had started as a wartime adventure had ended in disaster. Her aunt's condition had deteriorated, and she had died in the autumn of 1940, but by then of course the Island had been occupied by the Germans.

Some day, Pandora supposed, there would be peace. Some day the Allies would launch their attack on Europe. Jersey would be free, and she would be able to go home, back to England. Some day . . . She made herself a cup of ersatz coffee to serve as breakfast, collected her cycle and set off for St Helier.

As usual she found Francis De Brel at his desk. Since the doctor had managed to get his wife and son on to one of the last boats leaving Jersey, and his partner was already in the RAMC in England, De Brel had taken over the house in David Place – Jersey's equivalent of a Harley Street – and moved into the flat above the practice. When Pandora arrived, he was busy with paper work, before setting out on his house calls. A short, square man with fair hair and bright blue eyes, he greeted her warmly, gave her a few instructions and was gone.

There was a lot of work to be done. In any circumstances February is a bad month for sickness, and in Jersey in 1944, with everyone's resistance lowered by poor diet and constant strain, there were many sufferers from coughs and colds and minor ailments quite apart from those with more serious diseases. By two o'clock that afternoon Dr De Brel's waiting-room was already full, and it was late before Pandora thankfully slipped the lock as the front door closed behind the last patient. De Brel had already produced a carefully-hoarded bottle of whisky, three-quarters empty, and two glasses.

'I need this, Pan, and I imagine you do too. It's been a busy day for both of us. And for other people, too.' He poured them each a small tot and added water.

'Pan, did you know that early this morning one of the Russian prisoners-of-war working on some excavations in St Peter's Valley decided he'd had enough. Not surprising, really. The Germans treat their Todt labourers appallingly, like slaves, but as a rule the poor devils are too physically weak or too mentally cowed to protest. Not this chap. He split open a guard's head with his shovel and made a run for it. You can imagine the furore that caused.'

Pandora nodded as De Brel paused to sip his whisky. 'Yes.

One of the patients said that something was going on there. What happened finally?'

'The guard's dead. Which means God help that Russian when they catch him.' Under his breath De Brel added something in *Lé Jèrriais*, or Jersey-French, which Pandora failed to understand. Then he said, 'Time you were going home, Pan. It's a lousy evening.'

By the time Pandora had reached the foot of Trinity Hill it was dark, and the earlier drizzle had given way to a steady rain. In spite of her allegedly waterproof cape she was uncomfortably wet, and the long grind was still ahead of her. She often wished that the Island didn't slope so violently from north to south, or that her aunt had chosen to live somewhere on the south coast.

She got off her cycle as soon as she felt the first sign of strain in her leg muscles. It was easier to walk. Head down, letting the handle-bars take some of her weight, she plodded along until, reaching the summit at last, she remounted automatically.

Another five minutes and she had come to the end of the lane in which stood her aunt's house, overlooking Bouley Bay. Her spirits rose. Thoughts of dry clothes, a small fire and hot soup were enormously encouraging. Then she saw the lights.

A German staff car was parked, together with a half-track, in front of the main door of the house. The vehicles' headlights were blazing, and other lights flickered around the outbuildings as shadowy figures moved. With a stab of fear Pandora realized that the premises were being searched.

'*Achtung! Halt!*'

Pandora nearly fell off her bicycle as a torch was flashed directly into her face, blinding her. She put up a hand to shield her eyes, but caught only a glimpse of a tall, dark shape in a long black shiny rubber raincoat. The beam of light swept her up and down, and she was involuntarily conscious of her appearance – wet, bedraggled, unattractive. Obstinately she lifted her head.

'What do you want?'

To her surprise the man laughed. 'Do you live here?' he asked, ignoring her question.

'Yes.'

When Pandora nodded the man said, 'Good. Then we won't

need to break into the house. You can let us in and, considering the unpleasantness of the weather, I suggest you do so as quickly as possible.' His English was excellent, though heavily accented, and his voice was educated.

'But why? What do you want?'

'To search the place. What do you think, Fräulein? Or is it Frau? What is your name?'

'Pandora White. Miss.'

'Then open the door, "Pandora White, Miss", and let us continue this conversation in a little more comfort.'

In silence Pandora propped her cycle against the wall of the house, unlocked the front door and went through the hall to the kitchen. The German shouted some instructions to his men and followed close behind her, lighting the way with his torch.

Pandora tried to ignore him as she attended to the Aladdin lamp on the table. Her hand was shaking, and to her annoyance she had to use two matches; matches, like everything else, were in short supply. The lamp lit, she hung up her cape in the adjoining scullery and, getting a spill, knelt before the grate and lit the small fire that was laid there. She watched the paper catch, and then the kindling. It would be some time before the fire gave off any heat, but she pulled up a chair and sat as close to it as she could.

The German had been watching her with veiled amusement. Now he perched himself on a corner of the table and remarked, 'The records say there is only one occupier of this house. Is that right? You live here alone, Fräulein?'

'Yes,' replied Pandora. 'Since my aunt died.'

The German took out a packet of cigarettes, said, 'You permit, Fräulein?' and lit one without waiting for an answer. The cigarettes and matches he left on the table. Both the packet and the box were full, and Pandora caught herself staring at them. The difficulty of obtaining cigarettes didn't worry her, but she yearned for the matches.

'Oh, I'm terribly sorry, Fräulein White. I forgot to offer you a cigarette.'

'I don't smoke.'

For the first time, sensing that the German was attempting to rile her, Pandora took a real look at him. Her gaze moved from the muddy boots, which she guessed had been highly polished that morning, past the long shiny raincoat dripping on to the floor, and open to expose an officer's uniform, up to the handsome, arrogant face beneath the peak of the black cap he hadn't bothered to remove. The raincoat concealed any indication of rank.

'It is a big house for one person,' the German said.

This was true, Pandora reflected. Her aunt's house, built of traditional Jersey granite, with its sweeping drive and spacious grounds had once been almost a showplace. But the years of neglect and lack of materials and labour . . .

'Are you Gestapo?' Pandora asked suddenly.

'Gestapo? *Gross Gott*, no! Nothing like that. *Geheime Feldpolizei*. Perhaps I should introduce myself.' He slipped off the table, clicked his heels and gave her a mocking bow. 'Horst von Blunthal. *Hauptmann* – Captain. Really quite junior, but with a certain amount of influence. In charge of the military police here, among other odd jobs. And I'm at your service, Fräulein White. That's assuming, of course, that my men – '

There was a tap at the kitchen door, as Pandora became aware that the house had grown quiet and the clump of heavy footsteps and the banging of cupboard doors had ceased.

'*Herein*,' von Blunthal called, and a soldier came in and spoke rapidly. Pandora didn't understand what was said, but it was soon clear that the search had proved fruitless.

'We must leave. *Auf Wiedersehen*, Fräulein.' Von Blunthal sketched a salute. 'Make sure your house is well locked up tonight, won't you? There's a murderer at large somewhere on the Island – a Russian – and he'll be wanting shelter in weather like this. You understand?'

'Yes,' Pandora said.

She listened to the Germans leaving the house, the slam of the front door, the grinding of vehicles on gravel. At last, sure that they had gone, she permitted herself to relax. The cigarettes, which she would give to Francis De Brel, were still on the table with the matches. But it was the Russian of whom Pandora was

33

thinking. God help him, De Brel had said. And she remembered that the last Todt worker to assault a guard had been shot without ceremony.

★

Five days later, on a Sunday, Pandora had invited a neighbour to lunch. This required planning and ingenuity. She had opened two of her few remaining cans of soup, and was preparing a chicken dish, with potatoes, swedes and onion. Afterwards there would be a small portion of cheese. The vegetables she had obtained from a friendly farmer. The chicken had been provided by Francis De Brel.

'My dear Pan, don't argue,' he had said when she protested. 'I'm giving you this scrawny bird for John's sake, not yours. He deserves a good, home-cooked meal.'

'How is John?'

'Ill, as you know. Desperately ill, in fact. I'd give him another year at most.'

'And there's nothing you can do?'

De Brel shrugged irritably. 'I'm not a miracle worker, Pan,' he said at length. 'All I can do is hope I'll have enough pain-killing drugs to see him through at the end.'

Sadly Pandora recalled the conversation as she waited for her luncheon guest to arrive. She heard his footsteps on the gravel, and ran to open the door, glad for his sake that it was fine and sunny. His cottage was only a short distance further along the lane, and the walk would have been pleasant.

John Ingram was a tall, narrow-shouldered man, made thin to the point of emaciation by the cancer that gnawed him. He was thirty-eight, but looked fifty, his long face lined with pain. He had come to Jersey as a teacher before the war, fallen in love with the Island, and now knew he was never to leave it – a fact that he accepted with cheerful equanimity.

He sniffed loudly as he came into the kitchen. 'What a glorious smell, Pan! Obviously we're going to have a feast. And I've not forgotten my contribution.' He produced a bottle of wine from his coat pocket, and set it on the table.

34

'John! Thanks so much. That's wonderful! French, too. How did you get it?'

Ingram merely grinned. 'Ask no questions,' he replied. 'I've got my contacts.'

She helped him off with his coat, noting how loosely his clothes hung on him. 'Let's open that bottle now and have a drink before lunch,' she said.

'Right,' Ingram agreed at once. 'We'll drink to freedom, shall we? Which reminds me. That Russian prisoner still seems to be free. The Germans haven't caught him yet, as far as I know.'

★

Later in the afternoon, after John Ingram had insisted on helping her with the dishes, Pandora walked back with him to his cottage. She refused to go in. She wanted more exercise, and Ingram was looking tired. It was an hour before she returned home.

She was feeling refreshed and pleasantly relaxed. As she strolled up the drive she noticed that the lilac tree was in bud and there were other signs of approaching spring. Soon the summer weather would come, and in the summer things never seemed so bad. She decided to inspect the back garden before going indoors.

At once she saw that the door of the potting shed, where she kept her bicycle, was ajar. Anger welled up in her. If someone had stolen her bike . . . She strode down the path and flung open the door of the shed, hoping against hope that her guess was wrong. It was. The bicycle was there all right, but lying on the slatted wooden floor was a man.

Pandora's first instinct was to turn and run. This was the Russian, the escaped Todt worker who had killed the German guard and would be prepared to kill again. It had to be him. The filthy rags he was wearing, the bits of old tyres tied round his feet in place of shoes, the gaunt face above the straggly beard, the long, matted hair – and the smell! Pandora took a step backwards, revolted by the stench of stale urine, sweat, and something else she didn't recognize immediately. It was fear.

The Russian was staring at her. His eyes glittered in the

35

semi-darkness, but he made no attempt to move towards her. As seconds passed Pandora slowly realized that he was too tired and weak to move, and as scared of her as she had been of him. She swallowed hard. Her terror began to subside, to be replaced by pity.

'It's – it's all right. I won't hurt you,' she said, and thought what a stupid remark that was in the circumstances. 'Do you – do you understand English?'

'A certain amount.' The words came out as a harsh whisper, as if the Russian's throat was dry and it hurt him to speak.

Pandora forced herself to think. There was now no question in her mind. She must help him if she could. But how? Clearly the first step was to get him into the house, though the idea of touching him in his present state revolted her.

'I am a friend,' she said slowly. 'I will do what I can for you. I won't tell the Germans.'

The Russian nodded his understanding. Then, 'Hungry,' he croaked. 'I'm hungry.'

It was the same harsh whisper, but it reminded Pandora of a child, and destroyed any lingering fear. Trying not to breathe too deeply she slipped into the shed. The Russian had pulled himself into a sitting position.

'Food,' he said. 'Please.'

'Yes. You shall have food, but – if I help you, can you walk?'

The Russian shut his eyes and, close to him, Pandora saw how emaciated he was. Just like John Ingram, she thought irrelevantly, and cursed herself for her stupidity. She should have remembered what everyone in Jersey knew, that the Todt Organization gave its slave labourers the barest survival diet, and anyone who had suffered from its brutal treatment would be in no state to spend five days on the run. That was one reason why so few of them ever tried to escape.

'Wait,' she said. 'I'll be back in a minute.'

She ran. There was soup left over from lunch, and some chicken, but perhaps she shouldn't give him too much to start with. She settled for a mug of milk and the heel of a loaf with butter and jam. But when she brought it to him she was horrified at the way he seized the bread from her and crammed it into his mouth. The milk he had difficulty in drinking. His hands were shaking and she had to hold the mug for him.

Nevertheless, the food seemed to give him a little strength. With a minimum of help he managed to get to the house. Pandora sat him on a stool in the scullery, and brought a towel and a piece of soap. She indicated the sink.

'Take off all your clothes and wash. I'll try to find you something to wear.'

'Thank you. You are very kind.' The whisper was less harsh.

'The water's cold, I'm afraid, but – ' Pandora hesitated, knowing that she could have offered him a hot bath, but not wanting the smell of him in the house.

'Please.' The Russian spread his hands and she saw the blackened, broken nails and the calluses on the palms. 'For me this is – luxury.'

★

Pandora allowed the Russian half an hour. It took her that amount of time to find clothing remotely suitable for him. Her aunt had been a widow for many years, so there were no men's clothes in the house, but there was a pair of slacks that she had once worn for gardening, a possible shirt and a jersey. Shoes were an insoluble problem. Thick socks were the best that Pandora could provide.

The result, when the Russian finally emerged from the scullery and came to sit by the fire in the kitchen, was laughable. He was a tall man, and the short slacks bagged at his buttocks and threatened to slip off his hips, his bony wrists showed three inches below the sleeves of the jersey, and the heels of the socks bunched under his insteps. But he was clean, surprisingly clean – he had even made an effort to wash his hair and beard – and he no longer smelt.

Surreptitiously Pandora studied him. His thinness still reminded her of John Ingram, but he was better-looking than John. In spite of everything, his high Slav cheekbones, aquiline nose and deep-set grey eyes were an attractive combination. She tried

37

to imagine him well and strong and properly dressed and, to her
surprise, immediately visualized him in uniform.

'What are you thinking?' he asked suddenly.

Pandora flushed. 'I – I was wondering about you.'

'You don't regret giving me temporary shelter?'

'No, of course not. But I – '

'We have not been introduced? Allow me? My name is Alexis
Dolkov. And you are called?'

'Pandora White,' she replied, and reflected on the absurdity of
the situation. 'You speak English very well, much better than
you suggested.'

Dolkov shook his head. 'Not – not naturally. I have studied
it, but I have to think hard and when my brain is tired – ' He left
the sentence unfinished, and for a minute or two they sat in a
silence that was almost companionable. Then he said, 'You know
that I attacked one of my guards, and the Germans are looking
for me?'

'Yes, I know. They were here. They searched the house.'

'He was a brute, that guard. In the Todt it's each for himself,
but there was a young boy – a Muscovite like me. He was sick
and he couldn't work. The guard was beating him and I – it was
too much and I lost my temper. I hit the man over the head with
my shovel. Killed him, I expect.'

It was the longest speech the Russian had made, and his voice,
which had been improving, grew hoarse again. Pandora got up.
As she lit the gas under the soup she remembered where the
matches she was using had come from, and for the first time she
faced up to the risks she was taking by harbouring the Russian.

As if he had read her thoughts Dolkov said, 'You are preparing
more food? I would like it – and a coat, if you can spare one. I'll
swear I stole it – and these clothes – if I'm caught. Then I must
go. It is not safe for you that I remain here.'

'But where can you go to?'

'Back to my cave, I think – '

'You've been living in a cave? In the weather we've been
having?' Pandora was horrified. 'And eating what?'

'Berries. Vegetables stolen from the fields nearby.'

Pandora said angrily, 'You can't go back to a cave, not in your present state. You collapsed in my shed from weakness. You must stay here by the fire, for tonight at least.' Pandora was positive. 'Tomorrow, we'll have to see. I have friends whom I can trust, and who will help. At least they'll get you proper clothes – men's clothes – and shoes. And they'll know what's best to do.'

'But it is dangerous for them – and for you.'

Pandora shrugged. 'After all, the Germans are our enemies too,' she said.

★

It was not surprising that Pandora slept badly. At first her brain was over-active, and she lay awake, trying to plan for the next day. Towards dawn, however, she fell into a heavy sleep from which she awoke suddenly, sure that she had heard voices.

She flung on a dressing-gown and hurried down the stairs. When she reached the hall she knew she hadn't been mistaken. There was someone talking in the kitchen, loudly, angrily. But when she burst into the room she found the Russian alone.

Alexis Dolkov was lying in front of the grate, where she had left him the night before. His makeshift bed was scattered around him and he lay, limbs writhing, on the tiled floor. As Pandora stared at him he began to talk again, partly in German and partly in what she assumed was Russian. Close to him now she could see the high flush on his cheekbones and the drops of sweat on his brow. She knelt beside him.

'Alexis!'

There was no response, and she shook him by the shoulder, roughly, because she was frightened. Dolkov opened his eyes. Slowly they focused on her, and to her intense relief he smiled weakly, and whispered her name.

Though he did his best to co-operate it took Pandora time and effort to get him upstairs and into her still-warm bed. She bathed his face with a damp flannel, brought him water to drink and made him swallow four aspirin tablets. He seemed to be resting more easily.

She said, 'Alexis, I shall have to go out. I've got to see a friend,

39

someone who can be trusted to help. I shan't be long. Stay in bed.' Seizing her clothes she ran into the bathroom.

As soon as she was dressed she cycled furiously along the lane to John Ingram's cottage, but there was no answer to her repeated knocking. Puzzled, she returned home. She tried to telephone De Brel but the phone rang repeatedly without answer, and she knew she would have to go into the office. She had a job to do; the Russian would have to take his chance.

When she reached the surgery she found a message from De Brel awaiting her. He had been called to a difficult maternity case, and would go straight on with his rounds. In the event she didn't see him until after lunch, and it was mid-afternoon before she had a chance to confide in him. By then she was sick with fear for the Russian, and for herself.

'You will help, won't you, Francis?' she said, coming to the end of her story. 'I can't cope alone.'

'Of course I'll help, Pan, but we must keep this to ourselves. The fewer people who know, the better, at least for the present. You mustn't tell anyone, not even John. He's back in hospital, anyway. I dropped in to see him yesterday evening, and found him in a bad way.'

'Oh dear! He was fine at lunch. Is there anything I can do?'

'Not at the moment, Pan. We'll have to see. Meanwhile let's consider the Russian. I'd better come and have a look at him, hadn't I? And then – '

Pandora, fearful of what might have happened during her absence, would have been glad if De Brel had suggested going home with her, but he had to visit the hospital first. She cycled up the lane to the house, half expecting to find Alexis Dolkov gone, and the Germans waiting to arrest her. Everything, however, seemed tranquil. She let herself into the house and ran upstairs. Dolkov was lying on the bed asleep, his breathing shallow, his face running with sweat. She was picking up the eiderdown that he had thrown off when she heard a car drive up outside.

She was delighted. She hadn't expected that De Brel would arrive so soon. She hurried down the stairs and flung open the front door, eager to welcome him. Then she froze. The man

40

standing there was not the doctor. It was the officer from the *Geheime Feldpolizei* who had left her his cigarettes and matches. Stupidly she wondered what she should do if he had come to reclaim them.

The German saluted her smartly. 'Fräulein White, I've surprised you? I've turned up at an inconvenient time? My apologies, Fräulein.'

Horst von Blunthal had spoken with exaggerated politeness, and Pandora felt anger well up inside her. This saved her, as her mind began to function once more and she faced the facts that a Todt labourer, wanted for the murder of a German guard, was upstairs in her bed, while standing before her was the enemy – their mutual enemy. If the Russian were discovered he would be executed, and at best she herself would be sent to a concentration camp in Europe. She must act innocently, yet decisively.

'What do you want?' she asked coldly. 'To search the house again?'

'No. No, Fräulein.' Von Blunthal seemed taken aback by her aggressiveness. He gestured with his free hand to the car behind him; in his other hand he held what appeared to be a heavy shopping bag. 'I'm alone, as you can see. I hoped – Perhaps you would invite me in and we could have a drink together? I've just returned from France, and I've brought you some wine and one or two other things which I thought might be acceptable.'

It was Pandora's turn to be disconcerted. Automatically she took the bag that von Blunthal was holding out to her. 'Thank you. It's very kind of you, but – ' She couldn't let the German into the house; Dolkov might wake and decide to go to the bathroom or, hearing her voice, might call out. 'I'm sorry,' she said firmly, 'but I'm expecting a friend.'

Before von Blunthal could reply De Brel's car came up the drive. The German smiled ruefully as the doctor got out. Then he clicked his heels and saluted again. 'Some other time, I hope, Fräulein.' He nodded to De Brel.

'And *Heil Hitler* to you too,' Francis De Brel said as the German drove off. 'What on earth did he want, Pan? Now, of all times?'

'I'm not quite sure,' said Pandora. 'He was the officer who led the search party the other day. But now he's brought me a present.' She peered into the bag in amazement. 'Wine. Canned soup. Pâté. Cheese. Matches. He must be mad.'

De Brel laughed. 'You've clearly made a hit, Pan. But remember the old saying, "Beware of Greeks bearing gifts", especially if you're hiding a Trojan under the bed.'

*

Alexis Dolkov recovered slowly from the effects of malnutrition, exposure and pneumonia. Oddly enough his progress seemed to parallel that of John Ingram. By the time the Englishman was able to leave hospital again and return to his cottage, the Russian was strong enough to move around the house, to carry out small chores, and even to venture into the garden. To all intents and purposes, Pandora's house was now his home.

He owed almost everything to Pandora. It was she who had nursed him through the illness and who, in spite of all the shortages and difficulties, had contrived to build up his health and restore him to something like his normal self. Of course, she couldn't have done it alone. Others helped.

Francis De Brel acquired a faked ration book and identity card for him. John Ingram provided clothes, and later spent a lot of time with him, improving his English. Jeanne Rousset, a nurse at the hospital and a close friend of both Pandora and De Brel, was finally let into the secret, and solved the problem of shoes. She begged a pair of boots, and some leather slippers for indoors, from the Reverend Edward Beaufort, the parish priest of St Brelade, who asked no questions.

There was someone else who also helped, though unwittingly. Horst von Blunthal had taken to calling on Pandora. Fortunately his visits were infrequent; he was often away on duty. And he never came empty-handed. Mostly he brought food and wine and commodities that were in short supply. These Pandora accepted thankfully. Other gifts, more personal, such as perfume or chocolates, were less welcome, but they could always be used for barter.

Nevertheless, though von Blunthal never asked for more than to talk and drink with her, Pandora hadn't needed De Brel's warning or Ingram's doubts to know that her relationship with the German was fraught with danger. The worst thing was the uncertainty, the never knowing when he might arrive. As the weather improved and the evenings drew out, new difficulties arose. It was no longer possible to keep all the curtains drawn, and one of Pandora's nightmares was that if she failed to hear von Blunthal's car he would merely look through a window and see Alexis Dolkov eating the food and drinking the wine that he himself had provided.

Dolkov, too, added to the problems. With the coming of spring, he had become restless. He felt cooped up in the house. He wanted to help Pandora in the garden, go for walks with her at weekends, listen to the wireless that Ingram kept buried in a rabbit hole behind his cottage. All this made the Russian more vulnerable, more liable to surprise.

There was another inevitable consequence of his improved health and strength. One Sunday early in May, which Alexis had claimed to be his birthday, a little drunk after a special dinner Pandora had prepared, she and Alexis became lovers. Usually, after a casual good-night, Dolkov went upstairs first, and Pandora stayed behind to make sure the house was secure and to attend to any remaining chores. Tonight was different. She had known it would be, even before Dolkov pulled her to him and murmured something she didn't understand.

'What was that?'

'I'm sorry. I spoke Russian. I asked if I might come to you and make love to you. You – you are not a virgin?'

Pandora laughed aloud at his sudden anxiety. 'No. There was a boy I met at College who saw to that. But it was a long time ago.'

'No one since? No one in Jersey?'

'No. Why do you ask?'

'The Hun – von Blunthal. He wants you. He's been patient, I know, played what you would call "the gentleman", but – ' Dolkov stopped. 'Ah, let's forget him. Let's forget everyone except ourselves. It has been a long time for me also.'

Too long a time. Although he tried, Alexis Dolkov couldn't contain himself. His love-making was quick and savage and seemed to exhaust him, because immediately afterwards he fell into a deep sleep. Pandora, to whom the episode had given a minimum of pleasure, crept into the bathroom and washed. Then she returned to lie beside him, wide awake.

Her body was unrelaxed, and her mind over-active. She thought how little she knew about the Russian. He was a Muscovite and his father was 'something in the Government' – Alexis had been vague – and his mother taught at Moscow University, where he had been a post-graduate student. She had the impression that his family was well-to-do and influential. Alexis spoke of their *dacha* in the woods outside Moscow, and their holidays by the Black Sea. But this was all before the war. And anyway she knew nothing about Moscow society.

She had never met a Russian before Alexis Dolkov, and had never been near Russia. Nor was she likely to go there. She smiled to herself. She was under no illusions. She was fond of Alexis, and believed he was fond of her, but she certainly wasn't in love with him.

And as she dozed she thought how strange it was that in so many ways she felt closer to Horst von Blunthal, whom she had grown to like, than to the Russian who was now her lover . . .

The sixth of June 1944. D-Day. The Allies had crossed the Channel at dawn and were, after so many unfulfilled expectations, at last attacking mainland Europe. The invasion had begun.

The news, largely gleaned from illicit radios, spread rapidly through Jersey, causing excitement and jubilation. The people rejoiced, taking little care to conceal their feelings from the occupying forces. It wouldn't be long now before they were free again. As soon as the Germans were driven from the French coast around the Bay of St Malo, the enemy would be forced to surrender and the Channel Islands would be liberated. It couldn't be more than a matter of weeks; some even said days. Surely there was every reason for joy.

No one, not even the most pessimistic, predicted the real course of events. No one suspected that the invasion, on which rested so many hopes, would in fact prove to be the prelude to the worst period of the war as far as the Channel Islands were concerned.

Previously during the occupation life had been uncomfortable,

44

depressing, sometimes fearful but, except for individuals, it had rarely been desperate. Now, in the months that followed, cut off from France by the progress of the battle there, and with no indication that the Allies were prepared to risk an attempt at reconquest, the inhabitants of Jersey, including the Germans themselves, found themselves in a state of effective siege.

It's no time to be having a baby, no time at all, Pandora thought miserably. She was half-sitting, half-squatting on the lavatory floor, waiting for the next wave of morning sickness to overwhelm her. When it had passed she dragged herself to her feet and went into the bathroom.

She locked the door, stripped off her gown and nightdress and stood, naked, in front of the full-length mirror. There was, she decided thankfully, only the merest sign of swelling, but soon the baby would show. If it had been winter the layers of clothing that everyone was forced to wear for warmth would have hidden her condition, but the summer weather was no help. She bit her bottom lip hard, to prevent her eyes from filling with tears. It was pointless to be sorry for herself.

There was a tap on the door, and a cautious voice asked, 'Pan! Is something wrong?'

'No, no. Everything's fine, Alexis.' She lied easily. 'Put on the kettle, will you? With the gas pressure so low it takes ages to boil. I'll be down before it's ready.'

Pandora washed and dressed quickly. She hadn't yet told Alexis about the baby. She was uncertain how he would take the news that he was going to become a father, though she realized that his reaction scarcely mattered to her. The child would be hers; to him it would be – must be – an accident, a wartime incident, something to be forgotten once he had reached his native Russia. And she knew how much he yearned for that, how eager he had become, as the war dragged on, to get away from Jersey.

Nevertheless, it came as something of a shock when she learnt that escape was not merely wishful thinking on the Russian's part. It was Dr De Brel who warned her one morning in the surgery.

'Dolkov's becoming a menace, Pan – to himself and to you. Did you know he's taken to wandering around the Island – and

45

asking questions? Stupid, obvious questions,' said De Brel, 'about tides and currents, and the possibility of getting hold of a boat. About anyone who's managed to make it to France. And now people are asking questions about him. A friend told me that some people suspected him of being a German, an *agent provocateur*. And sooner or later, if he goes on behaving like this, someone's going to act on his suspicions and turn him in to the *Feldpolizei*.'

'I see. I didn't realize – ' Pandora sat down heavily, frowning. 'I'll have to warn him it's dangerous, tell him he'll have to stop.'

'You must, Pan. Or there'll be trouble,' said De Brel. He patted her on the shoulder. 'Now I'm off to the hospital. See you later.'

Pandora was glad when he had gone, and she could look forward to a morning undisturbed except by the telephone. She wanted to think about Alexis Dolkov. She hadn't realized that he was seeking some practical means of getting away from the Island. She sighed with exasperation. Here was something else for her to worry about.

The doorbell rang, and she went to answer it, hoping that it wouldn't be some desperate request for the doctor to come at once. The last person she expected was Horst von Blunthal. He stepped into the hall, and shut the door quickly behind him.

'Horst! I haven't seen you for weeks.'

'You are alone? I watched De Brel leave.'

'Yes, I'm alone. But what is it, Horst? You've never come here before.'

'I – I needed to see you.'

'To see me? Look, let's go into the surgery.'

As von Blunthal followed her into the room Pandora suddenly felt faint. It was only momentarily, but von Blunthal put out a hand to steady her. He studied her anxiously.

'*Liebling*, what's the matter? You are very pale. You're unwell?'

It was the first time he had ever offered her any form of endearment, and she was surprised at how her spirits lifted. No one else, she thought bitterly, and unfairly, cared a damn about her.

'I'm fine. A bit tired, perhaps. Worn out.'

46

'You're not getting enough to eat. I'm sorry. I've brought you nothing for ages. It hasn't been easy for me, either. And now – ' Von Blunthal shook his head fiercely. 'This wretched war!'

'It'll be over before too long.'

'Probably. But we shall have lost, we Germans, and God knows what will happen to our country. Hitler has destroyed us.'

Pandora was silent. There was no reply she could make. She was sorry for von Blunthal, but the last thing he wanted was pity. He shrugged impatiently as if to cast such problems aside.

'This evening is impossible. I'll come tomorrow, and I'll bring what I can. But it's for you – not for your friends. Oh, I know in the past you've given food to De Brel and Ingram, and doubtless others. It's different now. The situation here in Jersey is bad, and it may very well get worse. At least let me have the comfort of knowing I've done something for you – and you only.'

'Horst, you're very kind.'

'It's not kindness. You must know by now.' Von Blunthal spoke roughly, almost angrily. 'I love you! I love you! But – *Gott in Himmel* – it's useless! I had my orders this morning. A special aircraft is leaving the Island in a couple of days, and I'm to be on it. Tomorrow – tomorrow will be goodbye, *Liebling*.'

As he took her in his arms and kissed her there was no mistaking his meaning. Once again Pandora found herself unable to speak. She was, in fact, not surprised by von Blunthal's declaration. She had guessed his feelings for her for some time. What did surprise her now were her own emotions. To know, to believe you know, was one thing; to be told in words that couldn't be doubted was another. She was overwhelmed by her sudden surge of happiness.

She spent the rest of the day in a kind of a dream. She was busy, for the phone rang constantly and the surgery was packed. The patients seemed more trying than usual, perhaps because of the hot weather. Late in the afternoon there was an electric storm. It was brief, but the rain that followed the thunder and lighting was heavy. She was exhausted by the time she reached home.

Dolkov was in the kitchen, a nautical chart of the Bay of St Malo spread out on the table. God knows how he got hold of that, thought Pandora; possession of such documents had been illegal for years. But he had it, and he looked fit and pleased with himself. He had made no preparations for supper, in spite of Pandora's request that morning. It was all too much for her. She put her face in her hands and wept.

Alexis Dolkov was contrite. 'I'm sorry, Pan. I'm sorry. I forgot. I've been out most of the day and – '

'Yes, I know. And I know what you've been doing. Probably half of Jersey knows.' She told him what she had learnt, and was touched by his crestfallen expression.

'Then it's a good thing I'm leaving so soon,' he said.

'When? When are you leaving? And how?'

'Please. I intended to tell you this evening, Pan. It was only settled today. There's a young man called Pierre Félard. He has a boat, a sailing dinghy with an outboard motor. It's been repaired, and he's stolen petrol from the tanks of German lorries when they were left unguarded. He used to sail before, so he knows about the currents and the rocks. He's promised to take me to France – it's only about thirty kilometres.'

'Has he? Why should he?' Pandora had forgotten her own worries. 'Alexis, are you sure it's not a trap, that he doesn't plan to hand you over to the Germans?'

'And lose his boat? All the work he's put into it? Admit he's been siphoning off petrol?' Dolkov laughed. 'No. I'm not a fool, Pan. I know my man.'

'I hope so.' She was far from convinced. 'But why should he take you with him? Why not a friend, a relation?'

'Because – ' Momentarily Dolkov was embarrassed. 'Because I spun him a story. I said my old mother was in France, and I'd just heard she was ill, dying. Besides, I'm a good sailor, and there was no one else who wanted to go with him.' Dolkov had regained his confidence. 'Pan, this is my only chance. I must take it. I must.'

Pandora nodded. She couldn't stop him. She didn't want to stop him, she realized. At least his departure solved one problem: now he need never know about the child. But she didn't want him to come to any harm. She blinked the tears from her eyes, blew her nose, washed her hands at the sink and began to scrub potatoes. With her back turned to him, she said, 'You'll be taking a big risk, Alexis. The seas around here are very treacherous. Are you certain it wouldn't be better to wait till we're liberated?'

'Positive. It's my belief the Germans will hang on to Jersey as long as they can. They'll treat it like a fortress. And even when the Allies do free the place I've no papers, no proof I was an officer in the Red Army. There would be so much – so much officialdom that it could take me for ever to get back to Moscow.'

'France is still a long way from Russia.'

'But not so far from Russian troops. We're sweeping across Europe. We'll be in Berlin before the Allies, you'll see.' Dolkov spoke with pride. 'No, once I get to mainland Europe I'll be all right. I'm in good health now, Pan, thanks to you, and I'll be able to cope.'

'When do you plan to go?'

'This weekend. The tides will be perfect and – '

'This weekend? Both of you?'

'What do you mean, Pan? Of course both of us, Félard and me. I don't understand.'

Pandora made no attempt to enlighten him. She hadn't been thinking of Félard. She had been thinking how strange was the coincidence that Horst von Blunthal and Alexis Dolkov, the German and the Russian, who had come into her life at much the same time, should be leaving it almost simultaneously.

★

Pandora prepared carefully for the next evening. Dolkov was packed off to John Ingram's, having been told that von Blunthal was bringing food, and that some might help the escapees on their journey. But von Blunthal was late arriving, and Pandora had almost given up hope when his car swept up to the door and came to a halt in front of the house, spraying gravel to either side of the rear wheels. She opened the door before he could ring the bell and for a moment they stood, smiling at each other. Then she was in his arms again.

He released her slowly. 'I'm sorry for my lateness. It was unavoidable. And I cannot stay long. Tomorrow I leave the Island and there are things to be done.'

'I – I understand.'

'I've brought the food I promised. Two boxes. I stole it from stores. Probably some poor devil will get the blame, but who cares? You need it more, *Liebling*. Though you're looking better today – and very pretty.'

'Thank you.' She had washed her hair and was wearing the best of her summer dresses; she was glad he had noticed.

They carried the boxes into the kitchen together, but Pandora refused to unpack them. She said they could wait. Von Blunthal, however, insisted on extracting a bottle of champagne.

'A present from Herr General,' he said, 'though the old boy doesn't know he's given it to us.'

They took the champagne into the sitting-room. Now that the warm weather had come, and there was no longer any need to huddle over a fire, Pandora had taken to using it. With the dust-covers removed and flowers in the vases it looked much as it had before – an elegant if slightly shabby room, much more comfortable than the kitchen.

'To you, *Liebling*. May you find happiness in the future.' Von Blunthal lifted his glass.

'And to you, Horst. What – what will happen to you when you leave here?'

'I go to Berlin. I hope to see my parents. Beyond that I have no idea. I am still an officer in the *Geheime Feldpolizei*, so I do what I am told.'

'But after the war?'

'God knows! The world will be a different place. I can't imagine it, or a place for me in it – for us – but we Germans aren't meant to be imaginative. What about you?' His smile was sad.

Fleetingly Pandora thought of Alexis Dolkov – and the child. 'Not – not really.' Her voice broke.

'I know,' the German said consolingly. 'It's too difficult. But, *Liebling*, you and I will forget the future together for a while. There's still the present. Yes?'

There had never been any doubt, but the present was too brief. An hour later Pandora was pouring flat champagne down the kitchen sink. As she did, she wept. Horst von Blunthal had gone but, paradoxically, after their joyous love-making, she had never felt so happy. She was, she knew, in love for the first time in her life.

She tried to compose herself, so that her emotions should not betray her. Then, as she had promised, she walked along the lane to Ingram's cottage to collect Dolkov. Ingram opened the door to her.

'Pan, I'm terribly sorry.' He was embarrassed.

'What is it?'

'It's my fault.' Ingram kept his voice low. 'Alexis is tight. I had a bottle of port I'd been saving, and with him leaving us this weekend it seemed an occasion. We had a couple of glasses each, and I left him with the bottle while I went to wash up. He drank the lot.'

'Oh, John!' Pandora had to laugh.

'It's no joke,' said Ingram ruefully. 'Come and look at him.'

Alexis Dolkov was lying on Ingram's settee, his long legs dangling over the end. He seemed to be asleep, snoring heavily, but as they came into the room he opened his eyes. He stared at them as if not quite sure of their identities. Then he remembered.

'Ah, he's gone, our friend the Nazi.' Alexis's voice was slurred. 'Did he bring lots of – what do you say? – of goodies?'

'Some.'

'Good! Good old Horst! *Heil Horst!* Filthy Nazi!'

Pandora dug her nails into the palms of her hands. She reminded herself that Dolkov was drunk, that he had suffered appallingly in the Todt Organization, that he had every reason to hate the Germans, but she could only think of one German – Horst von Blunthal. For a single moment she could have killed the Russian.

Ingram misread her expression. 'Pan, don't worry. He'll have a hell of a hangover tomorrow, but he's not due at the Félards' till the afternoon. He'll be all right. Drunk or sober, nothing's going to prevent him being in that boat when Pierre Félard sets off, you know. He's determined to get away.'

'Yes.' Pandora nodded. She was in control of herself again. 'But what can we do with him now?'

Alexis Dolkov had begun to sing '*Deutschland über Alles.*' When he didn't know the words, which was most of the time, he hummed loudly. It was an absurd performance. Pandora and Ingram looked at each other and grinned.

'Leave him here for the night,' Ingram said. 'I'll take care of him. It was my fault anyway.'

'Thanks, John. That *is* good of you,' Pandora said, and thought as she walked back to her house that she had more to thank Ingram for than he knew. He had solved what would have been a problem. Tonight she could not have borne to sleep with Dolkov, not after Horst von Blunthal, and tomorrow Dolkov would be gone.

In fact, they would both be gone – the German and the Russian. And she, Pandora, would have to start to think seriously about the baby.

★

'Jerrybag! Jerrybag!'

Three small heads popped up over the hedge, and disappeared again. There was the sound of giggling and scuffling. A clod of earth hit Pandora between the shoulderblades. She paid no attention, but walked steadily along the lane.

'Jerrybag! Big, fat Jerrybag!'

It was a final attempt to force her into some reaction and it failed. Pandora continued as if she hadn't heard, and the children ran off, dissatisfied. They had no idea that the woman they were attacking was inwardly cringing at the abuse, and cursing those who were causing her such anguish.

She had been to the farm in the hope of getting a little cream, because Jeanne Rousset was coming to share a meal with her. There had been no cream. 'These days the Germans take everything. They don't ask any more, they just take,' the farmer's wife had said, looking Pandora up and down with such unabashed appraisal that Pandora was tempted to tell her when the baby was due. Instead, she had disregarded the woman's curiosity, just as she now disregarded the children's jibes.

The anonymous note that had been pushed through her letterbox two days ago had been much more wounding. Whoever had written to accuse her in the most pornographic terms of consorting with the enemy had actually named Horst von Blunthal as her lover, and the father of the child-to-be. And this she was unable to disregard; she wished so much that it was true.

She was thinking of Horst von Blunthal as she walked back to the house. It was five weeks since he had left Jersey and she had heard nothing of him – not that she had expected to do so; the only means of communication between the Germans and the Island was the radio. Neither had there been any news of Alexis Dolkov, and all she could do was assume that he had reached France safely. Sometimes she wondered if she would ever hear of either of them again. Her life had returned to its former dreary monotony, except that by now her pregnancy was becoming obvious to everyone.

But, if some were uncharitable and judged her harshly, others went out of their way to be kind. Foremost among the latter group was Jeanne Rousset. Today, when Pandora came up the drive, she found Jeanne waiting for her, obviously worried.

Pandora waited until they were sitting companionably in the kitchen. Then, 'What's wrong, Jeanne?' she asked.

'I've bad news for you, Pan, and, nurse or not, I've never learnt how to break bad news gracefully. It's about Alexis. Pierre Félard's body has been washed up on the French coast. No sign of Alexis yet, but – but it seems they didn't make it.'

'Is it certain?'

'About Pierre, apparently yes. Someone got word to old Ma Félard. I don't know how. About Alexis, I suppose there's still hope, but not much. My dear, I'm sorry.'

'Yes. I'm sorry too. Poor Alexis.' Pandora thought of all the effort that had been made to nurse him back to health, to feed and clothe him, to hide him safely. She was glad that she had told no one that Dolkov had stolen some of her aunt's silver in order to bribe young Félard to take him in his boat. 'What a waste!' she said sadly. 'I did try to dissuade him, Jeanne, but he was determined.'

'You should have told him about the child. Then he'd have stayed. You could have married.'

'Jeanne, for heaven's sake!' Pandora was impatient. 'You don't really believe I wanted to marry Alexis, do you? Because I assure you I didn't. And he didn't want to marry me either.'

'Maybe not, but what do you think your parents and friends will say when you return to England with a little bastard?'

'Bastard? The world will have changed during this war, Jeanne, and I suspect that word will have changed its meaning a bit too. I shan't be the only girl who's had an illegitimate child. There'll be lots of us, and people can say what they like.'

'Don't worry, they will. Things won't have changed that much.'

'It can't be worse than being called a Jerrybag.'

'I suppose not. But think of the child. Whatever people may or may not say, he'll always be a bastard in the eyes of the law. His birth certificate won't lie. When he goes to college, or gets married or applies for a job or – oh, heaps of things – the question of illegitimacy will arise. It'll dog him all his life.'

'Jeanne, shut up!' Pandora's patience had snapped. 'I don't want to quarrel with you, but this is a stupid argument. I'm four months pregnant, and I'm going to have the baby. Alexis, the father – he's gone, drowned. The baby'll be a bastard, as you call him, and there's nothing I can do about it. And I'm still not sure it's going to matter in the way you think.'

Jeanne Rousset would not be put off. She merely paused a moment before she said, 'But there *is*, Pan – there *is* something you could do about it. You could marry John Ingram.'

★

Three weeks later the Reverend Edward Beaufort read the banns, and three weeks after that Pandora Mary White, spinster, became the lawful wife of John Elliott Ingram, bachelor.

It was a church wedding, at Ingram's request. Except that his old friend Edward Beaufort should be told the true circumstances surrounding the marriage, it was his only request. But the idea that, for the child's sake, he and Pandora should marry had been his originally. He should have known better, he said, than to mention it to Jeanne before putting the proposal to Pandora himself.

Pandora, though her first reaction was to treat the suggestion as a joke in bad taste, had been touched when she realized that John Ingram's offer was made out of genuine concern for her and the child. Nevertheless, she had hesitated. She could appreciate all the practical advantages. Jeanne had made them amply clear, and Francis De Brel had supported Jeanne's arguments. But Pandora's love for Horst von Blunthal had held her back. It had needed some brutally plain speaking from Ingram to force her to make up her mind.

'Pan, you'll be marrying me for *my* life, not yours. That means at worst, from your point of view, four to six months of a platonic marriage. Then you'd be a respectable widow – impoverished, admittedly, because all I have to leave will be the cottage and a few hundred pounds – but a widow, all the same. And the child will have a name. I know you think the war will have changed a lot of things, and you may be right. But I doubt if it'll make being a bastard any more fun. So, Pan, what have you got to lose?'

There was only one answer. Nothing – except a girlish ideal of what marriage ought to be. In the circumstances Pandora knew that her dreams scarcely mattered; their abandonment was a small sacrifice in the face of Ingram's generosity. And the advantages when she eventually returned to England with the child would be immeasurable. Finally, realizing that she would be a fool to do otherwise, she had accepted John Ingram's offer with gratitude.

It was a decision she was never to regret. John Ingram was the most thoughtful of men. For Pandora, growing heavier and heavier with child, it was a blessing to return each evening from work to find the fire lit and preparations for supper under way. Sometimes she wondered how she would have coped during these months without John Ingram. Conditions in Jersey had deteriorated appreciably. There was no gas and no electricity; paraffin, like so much else, was practically unobtainable. The Ingrams, as they quickly became known, depended for heat and cooking on the kitchen fire, and it was John who searched for broken branches in the woodlands to supplement their small and carefully hoarded store of coal, John who made soup out of

55

unexpected odds and ends, John who got hold of a couple of eggs or an occasional chicken or pig's trotter from a friendly farmer to add to their meagre rations. Neither was he above bartering some of his own prized possessions to obtain black-market necessities.

Certainly Francis De Brel and Jeanne Rousset did their best to help, and Pandora received at least one surprising gift – an old perambulator which the Reverend Edward Beaufort had found in the attic of his rectory. But again it was Ingram who scraped off the rust and rendered the pram usable. He seemed to have acquired a sudden infusion of energy.

'I don't understand it,' Pandora said to De Brel shortly before Christmas. 'I thought I'd be looking after John by now, but it's the other way round.'

De Brel gave her a long, steady look before he answered. 'It's true, Pan. You and the baby have given him a new lease of life – a reason for hanging on, as it were. But you must face the fact it can't last. He's getting towards the end, and I'm afraid it may be bad for him. Much worse than it need have been, than it should be.'

'You mean because there aren't any drugs left?'

'Yes. Just that. Drugs, anaesthetics, even ordinary bandages. We're out of damn near everything.' De Brel sounded grim. Overwork and the frustration of trying to do his job with inadequate means had taken their toll of him in the last few months. He looked grey-faced and worn. 'And that includes food, as you well know,' he added bitterly. 'What a Christmas and New Year this is going to be. If we don't get help from somewhere soon, Pan, many of us will be starving – literally starving.'

The doctor's fears were shared by many prominent Islanders, and the Bailiff was doing his utmost to prevent the threatened catastrophe. Fortunately he was successful. On 30th December a Red Cross ship – an old Swedish vessel called the *Vega* – having previously visited Guernsey, came on to Jersey, bringing food parcels from New Zealand and Canada. This was to be the first of regular monthly visits, until the liberation of the Islands the following May.

John Ingram was not to benefit. He collapsed on New Year's

Eve, and died forty-eight hours later after some agonizing periods of pain. For most of the time Pandora sat beside him, holding his hand, praying wordlessly. In one of his last lucid moments, Ingram said, 'Look after our son, Pan,' and grinned at her, the grin turning to a grimace as he was convulsed yet again.

In February Pandora gave birth to an eight-pound boy – she wondered if John Ingram had been prescient, or merely hopeful. Personally she hadn't minded whether the child was a boy or a girl, but she was thankful that he was strong and healthy, and that she was able to feed him herself. She had, she realized as the day finally came for her to leave Jersey, a great deal for which to be thankful.

★

It was a beautiful day, with a bright blue sky and warm sunshine, when Francis De Brel drove Pandora out to the airport in St Peter. She had already said goodbye to Jeanne Rousset and the old parson, Edward Beaufort, and promised to keep in touch with them.

As her flight was called she laid the baby on a banquette to hug and kiss De Brel. 'Francis, you've been wonderful to me. I can't thank you enough for everything you've done.'

'Nonsense, my dear. What about all the help you gave me with the practice? Just take care of yourself and young Master Ingram. Try to remember the good things, and forget the bad. Be happy, Pan.'

'I'll try, Francis, and you – I hope – '

It was difficult to know what to say. Jeanne had told her that De Brel had received a letter from his wife in England; five years of separation had been too long, and now she wanted to marry someone else. Sadly Pandora remembered what John Ingram had once said, that the present was always important because it shaped the future. To hide the tears that threatened her she turned quickly and picked up the baby.

'Goodbye, Francis dear,' she said and, some fifteen minutes later, as the little De Havilland Rapide biplane banked over St Ouen's Bay and she looked down on the Island, she added, 'And goodbye, Jersey.'

4

Moscow, Spring 1949

A week or so after Anna Basnova's visit to the garden flat behind Harrods where Pandora lived with her husband and her son, a letter addressed to Vladimir Dolkov at his office in Dzerzhinsky Square arrived in Moscow via the diplomatic bag. It was not the first letter that Anna had written home, but Vladimir knew as soon as he inspected the envelope that this was an important one. There, in the top right-hand corner, was what could have been taken for a smudge of ink.

Recognizing the sign that he and Anna had agreed upon before she left for London, Vladimir read through the letter, once rapidly, the second time with the greatest care. The first paragraph was innocuous; it merely asked after the family, and remarked that she and Sergei were well, were missing Moscow, but were having a reasonably pleasant time in London.

The next paragraph was more interesting. On the surface it was concerned with the weather. 'There is no snow here,' Anna wrote, 'but it rains a lot and the sky is always grey, which is depressing. However, the English don't seem to mind. They go walking every day, even in London. Luckily there are some very big parks here. My favourite is called Kensington Gardens, which (as you can imagine from the name) is close by our Embassy. In it there is a most attractive statue of a boy, called Peter Pan, a character from an English children's play.'

A boy! Their arrangements for communication made Anna's message clear, and Vladimir could hardly contain himself. He rose from his desk and paced his office. Alexis had begotten a son, something that neither he nor Boris had managed to do. Boris's marriage to Anna had been childless, and Natalia had only given him daughters before she had been warned to have no more children. But Alexis had succeeded where they had failed. There would be another Dolkov to contribute to his country, to serve its ideology, and one with tremendous in-built advantages. With proper handling he could represent one of the ideals of every intelligence officer – an agent *born* in place.

Vladimir laughed aloud. His pleasure was genuine, but he was far from being a stupid man. Partly he was laughing at himself. He knew he was day-dreaming. The child couldn't be more than four years old, so there was a long way to go. Indeed, he must face the fact that nothing might come of his hopes for the boy; a great deal depended, for instance, on how his character and talents developed. But he, Vladimir Dolkov, intended to do his best; he would plot and plan as ruthlessly as he was able, and by the time the boy was approaching adulthood, and he himself held a senior and influential position in the MGB, there was a reasonable chance that, with luck, his day-dreams could become reality.

Vladimir returned to his desk and the paragraph in Anna's letter that was puzzling him. She had written. 'There's something of a cult in this country for toy bears, of all things. They are called "Teddies", though I don't know why, and they don't look a bit like our Russian bears, but they are rather sweet. The Ambassador's wife has been kind enough to arrange for me to send a couple of these little stuffed animals home to you for your girls.'

On the surface, the paragraph seemed pointless to Vladimir. Anna couldn't seriously be intending to send the girls these bears as presents; they were no longer babies, and would probably consider themselves much too old for stuffed toys, however 'sweet'; they might well be bitterly disappointed at such gifts from the West. Anna must realize this, so the paragraph must have another meaning. But what? Bears? Teddies? Could the boy's name be Teddy? At first he had wondered if the reference to Peter Pan indicated that Alexis's son's name was Peter. The boy, he thought with some irritation, would at his age probably welcome a stuffed bear himself, but –

Suddenly Vladimir was still. 'What a fool!' he said aloud. 'What a fool!' He could hardly believe he had been so stupid, so slow on the uptake. Of course, Anna's meaning was obvious, once he had thought of it. The toy bears would arrive, stuffed with information about Pandora and the child. They too would come in the bag, and be deliverd to him here at the office.

Vladimir Dolkov shivered. Anna was taking a risk, an enormous risk. If anyone suspected and the bears were slit open, Anna could be in deep trouble, whatever their contents. She and her husband would probably be sent home on the next Aeroflot flight. And the consequences could be equally disastrous for himself and Natalia and the girls. Whatever explanations he offered, his unauthorized attempt at conspiracy would almost certainly mean the end of the successful career he was expecting and the loss of all the family's privileges; it could even mean disgrace and banishment or imprisonment.

Vladimir gritted his teeth. The next few weeks, until Anna's bears had safely arrived, would stretch his nerves. But he must trust Anna. She knew the risks, and she must have considered them carefully, so the prize, if their luck held, must be worthwhile.

★

Certainly Anna had not acted precipitately. She had carefully considered her meeting with Pandora, and had on the whole been pleased with the outcome. True, as soon as she was safely back in the Embassy car, she had thought of several questions she should have asked, but in general she had acquired more data than she had hoped for. And the snapshots of the boy were an unexpected bonus. The problem was how to get all this to Vladimir, without arousing the interest of the Soviet authorities.

Anna pondered the question for several days. She, like Vladimir, had no illusions about the probable results for herself, for Sergei, for Vladimir and his family, if her activities were discovered. But, in fact, no one had raised any question about her decision to go shopping in Harrods rather than to the Royal Academy exhibition, and that was an encouragement. Besides, she sensed that now, months after her arrival in London, she had become less subject to scrutiny. From now on, she thought, surveillance would only be random. But she must still be careful.

It was the Ambassador's wife who unwittingly offered a solution to the problem. She was a typical Russian grandmother, who adored her grandchildren and missed them sadly. Her English was not fluent, and she had taken a fancy to Anna, finding her ability to interpret informally most useful. She lamented the fact that Anna was childless.

'You must make haste, before it's too late,' she said candidly, one day when they were out shopping together. 'Otherwise, no children, no grandchildren – and so much to regret, Anna.'

'Yes. I'm sure you're right.' Anna tried not to sound bored; she had heard the arguments so many times before. 'But I do have my nieces.'

'Of course. And you must keep in touch with them. You must buy presents for them – especially while we are here in this fine store.' The Ambassador's wife smiled wickedly at Anna. 'I will arrange that anything you buy will be sent with mine in the bag.'

'Thank you,' Anna replied. 'Thank you. That is very kind.'

'Choose some things now.'

'I will.' Anna spoke with enthusiasm. She was no longer in the least bored. Here was an opportunity.

The two women were in Regent Street, in Hamley's, that most famous of London's toy shops. The Ambassador's wife had already bought a doll as a present for a grandchild's forthcoming birthday, and was debating whether or not to buy a wooden train. So far Anna had bought nothing. She was normally allowed – indeed, compelled – to send her mail via the bag, but parcels were forbidden; that privilege was confined to the Ambassador and his lady. But here was the chance to send gifts to her nieces – and to Vladimir.

Glancing about, Anna saw a row of toy bears sitting side by side on a shelf. Perhaps they would do. She knew she must choose nothing odd or obvious. Even a privately-addressed package from the Ambassador himself might not be above suspicion.

The salesgirl, who had seen the direction of her gaze, said, 'Are you interested in Teddies, madam?'

'Teddies?'

'The bears. They're called Teddy bears, and they're very

popular with children. Even quite big children – and some grown-ups – like them. In England they're a sort of fetish, you know.'

Anna didn't know. Nor did she understand the word 'fetish', but she could look it up later. Meanwhile she needed to examine the stuffed bears carefully; she might never get another chance to communicate with Vladimir, and send him the photographs of Alexis's son.

The salesgirl collected an armful of the toy bears and set them up on the counter. The Ambassador's wife was distracted from the wooden train. The girl repeated her remarks and Anna, examining the seams and the imitation leather pads of the bears' paws, translated what was being said.

Anna added, 'They are well made and most attractive, if somewhat tame beside our Russian bears. May I really use the bag to send one to each of my nieces? I'm sure they'd love them.'

'Of course, my dear,' the Ambassador's wife assured her. 'I'll arrange it, I promise.'

Anna once again expressed her thanks, and wondered what her companion would have said, had she known the use to which the bears would be put.

*

Vladimir had less time to wait than he had feared. Anna had written to tell him to expect the gifts for his daughters only when she was sure the Ambassador's wife would be able to keep her promise and, in fact, there was a mere week's delay before the arrival of the parcel. But for Vladimir Dolkov even this short time was trying; it was a week in which he constantly feared the worst would happen.

The actual arrival of the package was something of an anticlimax. A fellow officer, whom he knew well, simply walked into his room and planted on his desk a brown-paper parcel that clearly contained a box. 'Goodies from London for you, Comrade. Aren't you the lucky one,' he said mockingly. 'What it is to have friends in high places.'

'For my children,' Vladimir corrected him hurriedly. 'From

62

their aunt, Anna Basnova. Her husband, Sergei, is in the London Embassy.'

'Ah!' With a grin and a wave of his hand the officer was gone, leaving Vladimir to regard the parcel as if it might explode at any moment.

Then, tentatively, he pulled it towards him, and examined it with care. He could see nothing to suggest that the wrapping had been unsealed or opened, but he knew that this meant little; the censors were experts at their job. Still, he reassured himself, they couldn't have found anything incriminating, or he wouldn't still be sitting where he was. All was well.

He yearned now to open the parcel, to discover whatever it was that Anna had sent him. Instead, he pushed it to one end of his desk, where it might be seen by anyone who entered the office, and returned to his work. It hadn't taken Vladimir Dolkov long to learn that a good way to disguise a dubious purpose was to behave as normally as possible.

But it was not so simple to deceive his family. When he got home the two girls clamoured to know what was in the mysterious parcel, and he was forced to silence them sharply. Such unusual severity produced tears, which in turn brought down on him the wrath of the *babushka*. Thankful that this was a day when Natalia had a teachers' meeting and would be late in returning home, Vladimir retreated to their bedroom and locked the door.

Alone at last, he was able to open the parcel, and the Hamley's box it contained. Inside were two toy bears, each about eighteen inches long, lying head to feet. A card read, 'With much love from Aunt Anna'. Vladimir made sure the card was no more than it appeared to be, and then picked up one of the bears.

There was a low growl, and he nearly dropped the thing. He pressed the bear's chest again, this time on purpose, and was rewarded with a second growl. He experimented with the second bear. The sound was similar, though perhaps somewhat more muffled. Vladimir was becoming increasingly excited, and he had to force himself to proceed cautiously.

First, he inspected the bears, looking for some means of getting inside either of them. Hidden in the back of each furry coat he found a long seam from neck to tail. Anna was an excellent seamstress, but she had been unable precisely to duplicate the work of the original machines on the bear with the muffled growl. However, the concealing fur meant that only a very close observer would have any cause for suspicion.

It took Vladimir ten minutes, with the help of a precious razor blade, to unpick the stitches. Several times he nicked his fingers and swore. But he had to be careful not to get blood on the toy, or to damage the material. Natalia would have to resew the seam, and she was much less neat than Anna.

He was sweating by the time he was able to reach delicately inside the bear and extract a packet. Making sure that he had missed nothing, he laid the toy aside. The packet contained a letter, and the snapshots that Pandora had given to Anna.

In amazed disbelief Vladimir stared at the likeness of Alexis's son. This was more, far more, than he had expected or hoped for. He contemplated the pictures for a moment, and then remembered that Natalia would be home soon, demanding to know why he was shut up in the bedroom. He turned to Anna's letter.

Space was limited, and Anna had given facts and ignored impressions, but she did stress her belief that the child's paternity had so far been a secret – and that it was a secret Pandora would keep. 'Pandora is devoted to the boy,' she wrote. 'I'm sure his welfare comes first with her, and that's why she married Ingram and has told no one that Alexis was the father.'

But it seemed that three other people did know the truth, Vladimir Dolkov reflected – three strangers: the doctor in Germany, Francis De Brel, the nurse Jeanne Rousset, now in Canada, and a religious character called Edward Beaufort. Would they keep their mouths shut all their lives? After all, the secret wasn't theirs and, as time passed, its importance might lessen in their eyes. Pandora herself could apparently be trusted, and that was good, for she *had* to be trusted; there was no alternative. But the others were different.

If he could have killed them with a wish, Vladimir would have done so, without a qualm. They represented a threat to the long-term scenario that was becoming more and more clearly defined in his mind. Somehow they had to be eliminated, if Bird's future was to be assured.

Bird? What a strange name for a boy! Vladimir wondered if it were a petname, or a kind of family patronymic; some English names were most peculiar, he knew. He stared at the photographs again. They had all been taken at the same time, and showed a child toddling towards the camera, arms outstretched, or crawling across the grass, or playing with a large rubber ball. It was impossible to tell if the boy bore any resemblance to Alexis.

The sound of Natalia's voice in the next room startled him. Hurriedly he bundled the bears, the photographs and the letter into the box in which they had come, and pushed it under the bed. His daughters' curiosity would have to remain unsatisfied until he could confide in Natalia to the extent that was necessary.

5

London, Spring 1949

'Here! Perhaps this will make you happier.' Sergei Basnov tossed a letter on to Anna's lap. 'I don't know what's been the matter with you recently. You've been moody and irritable, and not easy to live with, Anna.'

Anna glanced at the envelope, and froze. It took all her mental strength to reply in a voice approaching normality.

'I'm sorry.'

Basnov patted his wife on the arm. He was genuinely fond of her, and hated to see her miserable. But he was also a busy man, an important man, and he expected her support and co-operation. 'I know it's difficult for us while relations with the British are so poor, what with the Berlin airlift, as they call it, and all that.'

'That doesn't worry me, Sergei.'

'Well, fair enough to be a little homesick occasionally, then,' he said. 'It's something diplomats and their families have to accept. Remember, it's not just me. You represent our country, too. Be proud of that.'

'I am, Sergei. Extremely proud. And I'm sorry if – '

'It reflects on both of us, you know. People comment.'

'I've said I'm sorry.'

Anna spoke sharply. She could feel herself becoming angry, and dug her nails into the palms of her hands in order to control her temper. She knew that Sergei was right; she *had* been uptight recently. But it was nothing to do with homesickness. It was worry about Vladimir and the Dolkovs, worry about the parcel she had sent to Moscow, and there was no way she could explain any of this to Sergei. She had to prevaricate.

'Darling, it's the rain. I find it so depressing.' She made herself laugh. 'I even miss the snow. Silly, isn't it? Still, summer will be here pretty soon, and meanwhile I'll try to contain my feelings.'

Sergei smiled at her indulgently. 'I'll leave you to read your letter while I take a bath and change. Don't be too long. The reception at the Polish Embassy's at seven o'clock.'

'I shan't keep you waiting.'

As the drawing-room door closed behind Sergei, Anna grabbed the letter from her lap. It was obvious that it had been opened, for there had been no attempt to hide the fact. This, however, did not bother her unduly; random checks were common. What had worried her when she first noticed it was that the envelope was addressed in Natalia's handwriting, and her immediate reaction had been that something must have happened to Vladimir. It was not unknown under the Stalin regime for persons suspected of some crime or deviation simply to disappear, and if the contents of the toy bears had been found . . .

With shaking hands Anna tore open the envelope. At once she was reassured. Natalia was writing because Vladimir had been promoted, and was working harder than ever. However, he sent his love and thanked her for the gifts she had sent the girls. 'Indeed,' Natalia had commented, 'I think he likes the bears as much as the girls do. You wrote they were called "Teddies", and Vladimir says that in English it's an abbreviation for Edward. He'd very much like to know more about "Edward", and how they got the name and so on.'

Feeling sick with relief, Anna continued to read. The rest of the letter was all casual family news. The younger girl had had a bad cough, but her health was improving. The elder was doing particularly well at school. Natalia and Vladimir had been to the Bolshoi to see *Les Sylphides*. Anna skimmed through it, finding nothing to hold her interest.

She went back to the vital paragraph. Vladimir had safely received the information she had secreted in the bear, and he was particularly interested in Edward. Edward? He must mean the old priest Edward Beaufort, whom Pandora had known in Jersey.

Anna frowned. Though she was not fully aware of Vladimir's plans, it was obvious that the three survivors who were privy to the secret of Pandora's son could represent some kind of threat.

But surely an elderly priest 'in a home', as Pandora had said, was the least likely of them to be a danger.

Nevertheless, Edward Beaufort seemed to have aroused Vladimir's curiosity, though if Vladimir thought it would be simple to make inquiries about him, he was wrong. Pandora had said the home was in Hampstead, but she hadn't given it a name.

And now Sergei was calling: he wanted something to eat before the reception. Anna hurried into the kitchen, reproaching herself. In her preoccupation with Vladimir Dolkov's plans, she was forgetting her role as a good Russian wife. And surely she had done enough for Vladimir. As Sergei had pointed out, she had been irritable and bad-tempered recently, drawing undesirable attention to them both, and that wasn't fair to her husband. If she had needed any proof that she was not cut out for a life of intrigue, surely the heart-stopping anxieties of the last few weeks had provided it. She would do no more.

By the next morning, however, Anna had forgotten her resolution. She waited for Sergei to leave for his office, then tentatively looked up Hampstead in the telephone directory. There was everything from the Hampstead Acupuncture Clinic to the Hampstead Youth Club and, hidden among the many entries, the Hampstead Home for Retired Clergymen. The temptation was too great for Anna.

Sergei had told her that telephone tapping was less widespread in England than in the Soviet Union, but that she should nevertheless be careful what she said; after all, he hinted, the British security services were not the only people interested in what Embassy personnel were up to.

Anna had a choice: to be observed making a call from a public phone, or to use the instrument beside her. She decided the latter was the less risky course. Even if the conversation were intercepted, she could surely think of some acceptable excuse for it. She lifted the receiver and dialled.

When the call was answered she said firmly, 'I'd like to ask after Mr Edward Beaufort.' The first thing was to establish that she had found the right place.

'One moment. I'll put you on to Matron.'

There was a long pause, and Anna's courage began to fail. She nearly put down the instrument. Then a crisp voice sounded in her ear, and she repeated her request.

'Mr Beaufort? The Reverend Edward Beaufort? He's much the same. You can't expect any great improvement at this stage, you know.'

'You – you mean he's dying?'

'No, no. He may last for years.' The Matron was a busy woman; she had a right to be impatient. 'Though you never know. He's old and senile. He could go any time. Are you a relative or a friend, Miss – Mrs – ?'

Again Anna had to chose. Was it less suspicious to give her own name or a false one? In the end she avoided the issue by making no direct reply. Instead, she asked, 'Is it possible to visit him?'

The Matron's patience was exhausted, and her mind on other duties, so she failed to pursue the question of the caller's identity. 'Any afternoon between two and five,' she said curtly. 'But almost certainly he won't know you. He has good days and bad days, but he's never really with it.'

'Never with it?' Anna didn't understand the idiom.

'His mind has failed. Often he forgets his own name.'

'I see. Well, thank you.'

Anna quickly put down her receiver. She was surprised it had been so easy. With little effort and, she hoped, a minimum of risk she had learnt all she needed to know. She could assure Vladimir that the old parson was no longer any kind of danger; the secret of Alexis's son was safe in his poor mind. And as for the other two, the doctor De Brel and the nurse Rousset, they were both far away from London, and there was nothing she could do about them. Vladimir would have to be content with what she had learnt.

6

Moscow, Summer 1949

Vladimir Dolkov appreciated Anna's efforts, and accepted that Beaufort offered no threat. But he was not content. De Brel and Rousset might – probably would – return to England at some point; he wished that Anna had discovered if Pandora was still in touch with them.

The weeks passed. The snow melted. Summer came to Moscow. And still Vladimir brooded. He read everything he could get hold of about Berlin and Ottawa. Fortunately he was able to relate this interest to his work, but both places remained inaccessible. He seemed to have come to a dead end.

Then, early one Sunday morning, having been desk-bound all the week and feeling in need of exercise, Vladimir decided to go for a walk in Gorky Park. Already a few chess players were concentrating on their boards and, stopping to watch a game, he suddenly felt a hand descend on his shoulder. He spun round, only to be met with a great guffaw of laughter.

'A guilty conscience, eh? Is that what you've got, Vladimir?'

'Hello, Ivan.'

Vladimir Dolkov swallowed the bile that had risen in his throat. His fear subsided, though it failed to disappear completely. He had known Ivan Kaleskin a long time. They had been at school and university together, but after that they had lost touch, though they knew they both served Beria. Now, exchanging family news and gossip, they left the chess players and walked on, prepared, within limits, to enjoy each other's company.

'And what are you doing at present?' Vladimir asked. 'The last I heard of you, you were in Washington.'

'I was transferred.' Kaleskin beat Dolkov on the back; he was a large, hearty man and Vladimir winced. 'You're behind the times, old friend. I've been in Ottawa for the last six months.'

'Is that so?' Dolkov cursed the Soviet intelligence community, and its preoccupation with often unnecessary secrecy. 'Six months? What are you doing here then, Ivan?'

'I had no leave between postings – and therefore no new briefing, no instructions.'

'I see. And what's Ottawa like these days?'

'As a place it's a small town, culturally pretty dead, but physically attractive, with lots of trees and rivers – and snow. In winter there's good skiing within easy reach of the city centre. Kaleskin stopped speaking, shrugged and made a face. 'But if you're asking the obvious question, Vladimir, the answer is that since the Gouzenko defection it's a damned hard posting for us. No one trusts anybody. Even the Canadians don't trust each other.'

'Tough.'

Dolkov nodded sympathetically and Kaleskin, encouraged by his old friend, began to unburden himself about his problems. Dolkov listened attentively. At the same time he was wondering how he could possibly make use of Kaleskin for his own purposes.

'Between you and me, Vladimir,' Kaleskin said confidentially, 'my stock's not too high at the moment. I won't bother you with details, but I could do with a slice of luck.'

'Couldn't we all?'

Dolkov glanced sideways at Kaleskin, who had found a loose pebble and was kicking it along the path as they walked. The big man was looking unnaturally morose, his shoulders sagging, his mouth set in a grim line. Dolkov made up his mind. They were alone, with only the birds for company and, if any trouble were to result later, it would be his word against Kaleskin's. It was worth the risk.

He said, 'It's possible I might be able to help. I think I could do you a good turn, Ivan.'

Kaleskin gave the pebble a last vicious kick, and stopped walking. He turned to face Dolkov. 'Are you serious?' he asked. 'And, if so, what's in it for you?' he added harshly.

Dolkov pretended not to notice the sudden aggressiveness. 'Ivan, there's a nurse in Ottawa. Her name is Jeanne Rousset.

71

She's apparently recently emigrated from Great Britain. You might find her interesting.'

'In what way?'

'It's conceivable you could turn her. She's thought to be a great admirer of the Soviet effort during the war, inclined to communism and thoroughly disillusioned about life in Britain under a Labour Government. That's why she decided to go to Canada.'

'I see. I suppose you wouldn't like to tell me the source of this information, Vladimir?'

Dolkov laughed. 'Certainly not, Ivan. Nor why we should be interested in a nurse. And it's only a tip. There may be nothing to it, and you may not want to pursue it. But, if you do, let me know. It could be important to us – and there'd be some kudos attached. But keep it quiet – that's vital. Understand?'

'Yes,' Kaleskin said slowly. 'I'll think about it.'

Unhurriedly Dolkov changed the subject, inviting Kaleskin to have supper at his apartment that evening; Natalia, he said, would be delighted. The invitation was gratefully accepted, and it was a good party which everyone enjoyed. Dolkov and Kaleskin parted on the most friendly terms, though the next morning each bitterly regretted the amount of vodka they had drunk.

But this was Vladimir Dolkov's only regret. Later that day he made a point of telling his chief about the meeting with Kaleskin, and repeated much of what his old friend had said. Naturally he didn't mention Nurse Rousset, but he implied that Ivan Kaleskin was perhaps no longer 100 per cent dependable. Then, confident that he had done all he could to cover his back, he waited to see if Kaleskin would take the offered bait.

The result was unexpected. Within a month he received a communication from Ivan Kaleskin in the diplomatic bag. It was a page from the *Ottawa Citizen*, seemingly a local daily newspaper, with a news item sidelined in red. An attached card merely said, 'No luck.'

Dolkov read the story with growing disbelief. Kaleskin was wrong, quite wrong, he thought. He grinned to himself. If he had been a religious man, a superstitious man, he would have said it wasn't luck, but a miracle.

With quiet satisfaction he read the piece again. It wasn't long. It reported that a Miss Jeanne Rousset, a nurse at the Ottawa Civic Hospital, had been killed by a train at a grade crossing just outside the city. Presumably she had not heard the warning clang of the bell, and had driven on to the railroad track immediately in the path of a freight train. Jeanne Rousset, it added, was thirty-two years old, and unmarried. She had only been in Canada nine months, but would be sadly missed, especially at the hospital, where she had been popular with both staff and patients. She had been an excellent nurse.

This was not the first accident of its kind in or near Ottawa, and it seemed they were frequent in other parts of Canada. The rest of the story was a diatribe against unmanned grade crossings.

Vladimir Dolkov didn't bother to read that part. He sat at his desk, thinking that fate had indeed been kind to him. Two of the three people he had feared might upset the nebulous plans he had for Alexis's son had been eliminated. Only this Francis De Brel remained, and he was said to be in Germany. Unfortunately he was almost certainly the most intelligent, and therefore the most dangerous, of the original trio. And it was too much to hope that he would conveniently lose his memory or drive under a train.

7

Moscow and Berlin, Autumn 1949

There was no doubt that Vladimir Dolkov was an ardent patriot and a good communist. This being so, there were a number of views he hardly dared to admit he held. One, for instance, was his relief that American and British air transport had so nullified the blockade of Berlin that his own people had been forced to accept the continued division of the city between the Soviet Union and the Western Powers.

Of course, this was a blow to Russian pride. Dolkov was quick to denounce the West, and express his regret at the outcome of the year's confrontation. Secretly his views were quite different. If the blockade had been successful Dr Francis De Brel would presumably have been compelled to leave Berlin, and any hope of reaching him would have receded. But, given the right excuse, Berlin was not wholly beyond Dolkov's reach.

Nevertheless, by the late autumn of 1949, it had become obvious that unless he took some positive action, Dolkov was unlikely to achieve his aim. It was not enough to study to perfect his German – everyone knew he was a good linguist – or become an acknowledged expert on the Berlin situation. These achievements might help a plan, but first a plan must be devised. He needed to think, and then act, fairly quickly; De Brel was unlikely to stay in Berlin for ever.

Vladimir Dolkov thought to some effect, and decided on a bold throw. If he failed he would be a little worse off, his motive possibly suspect, but if he succeeded his way would be open. He went to his immediate superior and, armed with evidence that he had gone to considerable lengths to assemble, complained about intelligence operations in Berlin.

'Everything – recruitment, quality of material, even security –

everything's deteriorated since we've begun to hand over some responsibility to the new Democratic Republic,' he said earnestly. 'I feel something should be done to improve the position. I'm particularly worried about the flow of intelligence drying up even more, and the opportunities we're undoubtedly missing.'

'So what do you suggest, Comrade?'

Dolkov shrugged. He could see the chasm yawning in front of him. His Chief was a hard-bitten, cynical character, and nobody's fool. But, Dolkov realized, unless he persevered now he would have lost his chance, and it would be very hard to manufacture others.

'It's difficult to judge from a distance. The man on the ground has a different perspective.' Dolkov didn't hesitate, but continued quite dispassionately, as if the subject were of merely professional interest with no personal involvement. 'But I have wondered, Comrade Colonel, if you would consider authorizing a few days' visit to Berlin. It might pay off, if I could talk to our people and our German colleagues and some of our agents in the Western Zone, and try to sense the atmosphere.'

There was no immediate response. Dolkov could feel his heart thudding against his ribs. He was tempted to protect himself, to suggest that another officer should conduct the operation, and he had to bite his tongue to prevent the words escaping. He knew his Chief would make up his own mind.

'All right, Vladimir,' the Colonel said judiciously, at last. 'Why not? You've been working hard. Perhaps you deserve a mission like this and, as you say, it might well pay off.' He paused, then added, 'Just make sure it does.'

'Thank you, Comrade Colonel. I'll do my best.' Dolkov tried not to show his relief.

Indeed, he must do his best, Dolkov thought as he returned to his office. He must both deal with De Brel, and provide a report that would justify his Chief's decision. This was asking a lot of himself in one short visit to Berlin, and might prove impracticable. Dolkov shook his head in irritation. Such negative thoughts were pointless.

His commitments delayed Dolkov's departure for some ten days, and he made the most of the interval. He studied yet again his city plans of Berlin, and planned his tactics as far as was possible from this distance. He managed to obtain a formidable document, giving himself considerable authority to conduct inquiries and to request facilities from the local Soviet and East German authorities. He was almost ready.

One problem remained – how to kill Francis De Brel when, and if, he found him. Obviously, he needed something quick, foolproof and preferably silent. Dolkov cursed his own inexperience. His career had been spent mainly behind a desk, though he had seen men die and been the distant cause of deaths. But he had never before been responsible himself for the direct killing of an individual. The idea didn't worry him; squeamish he was not. What did worry him was the fear that he might bungle the job.

In the end Dolkov settled for a firearm. It was unusual for MGB headquarters officers to carry arms when stationed in Moscow, but the excuse of travel was sufficient to enable him to draw a Tokarev TT-33 from the armoury in one of the sub-surface levels of the building on Dzerzhinsky Square. Once he had the pistol in his hands, it served to steel his purpose.

*

Unfortunately Natalia came upon the box of spare rounds as she was helping him to pack. 'What is this, Vladimir?' she demanded. 'You are to be armed? I knew it. Berlin is a bad place. You are going into danger.'

'Quiet!' Dolkov ordered, gesturing at the thin walls of their room. 'No one is to know where I've gone. No one! Do you understand?'

'Yes, but I'm your wife. You must tell me – '

'I've told you. I'm going to Berlin, but to our part of the city – East Berlin, if you like. I shall be among fellow comrades. There's no danger.'

'Then why take a gun? And why are you taking civilian clothes. You always wear your uniform if you're travelling on duty.'

'Natalia, please!' Vladimir tried to take her into his arms, but she pushed him away. 'The gun's routine, but yes, if you must

76

know, I may have to go across the dividing line into the Western Zone.'

'I knew it. I knew it.' Natalia was now in tears. 'And what will become of me and the girls if you are killed or captured – or just disappear?'

'None of those things will happen.'

Vladimir Dolkov spoke with conviction. But later, as he lay in bed beside Natalia, he admitted that she had some justice on her side. He *was* taking an enormous risk, though not for the reasons Natalia supposed. Something could easily go wrong, and then . . .

He turned on his other side, and tried to compose himself, but his thoughts continued. Perhaps he really was being stupid. After all, the boy – what was it – Bird? An idiotic name – the boy was only four, and who could foresee his future. It would be the best part of fifteen years before he could even be approached, and more like twenty before he was likely to be of any use. So much could happen in that length of time. On the other hand, Alexis's son surely offered a chance that shouldn't be neglected. What was it he had told his Colonel about missed opportunities?

It was four in the morning before Vladimir finally fell into a troubled sleep.

★

In the course of the war – the Great Patriotic War, as the Russians called it, and a war which the Soviet authorities considered to be still unfinished – Vladimir Dolkov had been in Germany, but never in Berlin. The city impressed him, in spite of the devastation. The first morning of his arrival he was driven up the Unter den Linden to view the restoration already in progress on the Brandenburg Gate. He thought of Napoleon and Blücher, and to his colleagues cursed the West for usurping half the city that Russian troops had liberated from the fascists.

But he was not in Berlin to sight-see. He made that clear at once. He demanded that an office be put at his disposal, together with a staff car and a driver, and he insisted on considerable freedom of movement. The authority he carried was sufficiently impressive to prevent any queries from the resident MGB officers. A number of interviews were arranged at his request and, if some of the questions he asked, such as those concerned with hospitals in West Berlin, seemed irrelevant, they were well hidden among acceptable inquiries.

Dolkov learned a great deal in the next day or two, but he found he had underestimated the difficulty of tracing Francis De Brel, though his task was somewhat simplified by the fact that at this time, long before the flow of refugees from East Germany to the West had reached disastrous proportions and long before the building of the wall, border controls were perfunctory, and he could move freely between the Zones, posing as a civilian. But still, it was not until the morning of the third day that he managed to locate the doctor, who was working for a so-called Western 'relief' agency – really a cover for espionage, Dolkov suspected – in a civilian hospital in Charlottenburg, an inner suburb to the west of the city centre.

He had decided on a bold approach, for he had little time for finesse. He insisted on a series of clandestine meets with a selection of Soviet and German agents living in the Western Zone. The first was in a café off the Kürfürstendamm but, in accordance with standard practice, he had his driver drop him some distance away. Then, his meeting finished, he made straight for the café's phone.

When the hospital answered, he asked to speak to Dr De Brel. While he waited, drumming his fingers with impatience, he tried to visualize his victim, but found it impossible.

'Hello,' a voice said at last. 'De Brel here.'

It was their first contact. Vladimir Dolkov drew in his breath and steadied himself. 'Hi, Dr De Brel. You won't know me, but my name's Stefan Wolczak, and I'm a friend of Jeanne Rousset's from Canada.'

Dolkov had chosen his cover with care. The nationality had to fit both his accent and his appearance, and he knew he would never be able to pass as a native-born English speaker. However, the nurse had died in Canada and, if he could pose as a Polish Canadian, he believed he should be able to deceive the doctor.

'A friend of Jeanne's? Here in Berlin?'

'Yes, but just for a couple of days. And I was hoping you'd have a meal with me, tonight or tomorrow. Would either suit you?'

'Well, Mr Wolczak, I'd like to, but I'm very busy and – '

'Oh, please!' De Brel had sounded tired and uncertain, and Dolkov forestalled the refusal. 'I want so much to talk to you about Jeanne. We were close – very close, you know. I had hoped – did she never mention me to you?'

'I've not heard from her since Christmas. And what do you mean – you *were* very close? How is she?'

Dolkov could hardly believe his ears, but he hastened to quash the growing impatience in the doctor's voice. 'You mean you don't know? Dr De Brel, Jeanne's dead. She was killed in a car accident in Ottawa.'

'Good God! No. I'd no idea. Poor Jeanne.'

'Then you'll meet me please? I'll tell you how it happened, and you'll tell me about Jeanne and her family in Jersey.'

'Yes, of course.' This time De Brel didn't hesitate. He said, 'Where shall we meet, Mr Wolczak? And when? I suggest – '

Listening, Vladimir Dolkov smiled grimly, thankful that De Brel couldn't see him. What the doctor was suggesting would suit him admirably. He said goodbye, and replaced the receiver. He was confident, but not over-confident. He was well aware that unforeseen – unforeseeable – circumstances might negate his purpose, and bring him trouble, disgrace, or worse. But, at the thought of what was at stake and what he might achieve in the long term, he went to meet his driver elated at the prospect before him.

★

That same evening Vladimir Dolkov crossed the Zonal boundary once again, having made no secret of the fact that he must visit the Charlottenburg area. This time his meet was to be especially sensitive, for the agent was a White Russian, now a British citizen and a lieutenant in the British Army. This officer had been selling documents for some months, and Dolkov's ostensible aim was to attempt to improve the quality of the material. In reality, Dolkov intended to make use of the man for his own purposes.

Dolkov dismissed his driver near the Schloss Charlottenburg, with instructions to pick him up again in two hours. Then he made his way to a nearby *Kneipe*, where he found his lieutenant at the bar. They took their drinks and snacks to a corner table where they could talk privately. Dolkov was not impressed.

But the man was happy to drive him to the hospital, and to wait while he collected a friend. Controlling his nerves, Dolkov pushed his way through the heavy swing doors. When he had left the car he had run his fingers through his hair, and slipped on a pair of steel-rimmed spectacles. Now, as he approached the inquiry desk, he feigned a noticeable limp. These were the characteristics he knew would be remembered – the limp, the glasses and the untidy hair. Otherwise he would be described as a big man in a raincoat – and there were innumerable big men in raincoats.

'Dr De Brel, please. He's expecting me. Stefan Wolczak.'

'Okay. Take a seat over there.'

Dolkov sat down where she pointed. The girl wasn't interested. She had scarcely glanced at him, and he needn't have bothered to practise what he hoped was a North American accent. But he heard her on the telephone, saying that a Mr Wolczak had arrived for Dr De Brel. He buried himself behind a newspaper that someone had left behind, and waited.

It was a long wait. Dolkov had been punctual, almost to the minute, but it was a half-hour before De Brel arrived; Dolkov could only hope the lieutenant would be patient.

De Brel shook Dolkov's hand warmly, full of apologies. There had been an emergency; one of his patients had suddenly started to haemorrhage. Dolkov nodded his understanding, as he held the heavy door for De Brel, and let the doctor precede him out of the hospital. So far, apart from the delay, all had gone well. But now, instead of making for the car park as Dolkov had expected, De Brel went straight to a Volvo, parked in a privileged place near the brightly-lit entrance. He opened the door for Dolkov, then walked around to the other side of the car and got in behind the steering-wheel.

Dolkov reacted quickly. In spite of the danger of being seen from a window or by someone arriving at the hospital, he drew the pistol from under his jacket, knelt across the front seat and shot Francis de Brel twice in the right temple. The noise of the shots sounded horribly loud, and Dolkov hadn't been prepared for the blood and brains which spattered the window behind De Brel's head. For a moment he was overcome. Then, swallowing the acid which rose in his throat, he thrust the gun into the pocket of his raincoat and forced himself to touch De Brel's body, to extract his wallet and pull off his watch. If the killing could be taken as incidental to a robbery, so much to the good.

*

The British lieutenant was still waiting. Relieved, Dolkov said, 'Sorry to have kept you so long. My friend can't come after all, but we had a chat.'

'That's okay. You told me to keep the evening free, so I have. Where to now?'

'Back to the *Kneipe*,' Dolkov ordered.

Dolkov made a show of relaxing in his seat and behaving normally. He didn't make the mistake of trying to talk. Nor did he brood on what he had just done: there would be time enough for that when he was once more safe across the boundary and in East Berlin. He concentrated on the next step. As they approached the Schloss Charlottenburg he told the lieutenant to stop.

'Do me a favour,' he said. 'I'd like you to go ahead and look in the *Kneipe*, and see if there's a guy with red hair at the bar. If he's not there, I won't bother; I'll be on my way. In any case it might be better if we weren't seen together again.'

He waited only till the lieutenant was out of sight before going through De Brel's wallet. He kept the identity card and the various passes, but replaced the money. Then he got out of the car, wiped the wallet, indistinguishable among thousands, with his handkerchief and slipped it down a convenient storm drain.

It would arouse less suspicion if he waited for the lieutenant's return; he hoped that there was not in fact a redhead in the bar. And when the lieutenant returned with a negative report, he said goodbye quickly and dismissed him. As the lieutenant's car disappeared into the distance, he set off to meet his Russian driver.

★

Three hours later, alone in his room in East Berlin, Vladimir Dolkov opened a bottle of vodka and drank deeply – to his brother Alexis, and to the potential represented by Alexis's son.

Interlude

As the years went by, the boy grew up, physically attractive and showing signs of above average intelligence. He led a happy home life as an only child with his mother and his stepfather, who had legally adopted him and given him his name. He enjoyed school, and made many friends, two of whom were to have important influences on his later life. And in due course, he won an Open Scholarship to Oxford. Here he performed excellently, and seemed assured of a first-class degree. He had every reason to expect a brilliant future.

No one ever told him that his natural father was one Alexis Dolkov, and he had no means of learning that his uncle, Vladimir Dolkov, a senior officer of the KGB, had been following his career with intense interest.

PART TWO

The Sixties

8

Oxford, Summer 1966

Richard Kent and David Windfield had known each other for a long time. Their friendship dated from the day they had arrived at their preparatory school together, and it had survived throughout the years of public school, in spite of intense rivalry between the two boys. Fortunately, when only one could be the winner, the other was a gracious loser, and they seemed to take the roles in turn. On the whole, it was an ideal relationship.

Now they were both up at the same Oxford College, and during the last couple of weeks of the vacation Richard had been staying with the Windfields, who had a country house not far from Charlbury in the Cotswolds. They were driving back to Oxford for the start of the Trinity Term – their last one at the University, for in a few weeks they would be taking 'Schools', as their final examinations were often called.

To some extent the long-wearing nature of their relationship was due to the similarities between them. They came from much the same backgrounds, though David's parents were far better off than Richard's. They were both only children with rather possessive mothers. They were both physically attractive: David was tall with dark hair and brown eyes, Richard an inch or two shorter with fairer hair and grey eyes. They were both academically gifted, high-fliers expected to get excellent degrees, and their mutual ambition was to follow successful careers in the Foreign and Commonwealth Office. They had many other interests in common, and they even tended to like the same girls.

'Pleasant that the College is having a Commem Ball in our last year, isn't it?' said David.

'Extremely pleasant, but I wish they'd made the tickets a little less expensive.' Richard grimaced.

'Oh, come on. It'll be our last fling before we start the horrible business of earning a living. And I've been thinking about it seriously.'

'The living or the Commem?'

'The Commem, of course.'

'Does that need serious thought?'

'But yes. First of all, it's essential to make up the right party. What would you say to – you and me, Julia and Celia, Karl and Eva, and perhaps old Neil, though let's pray he doesn't bring that scrawny classicist from Somerville.'

Richard didn't answer at once, pretending to concentrate on his driving. He had no objection to going to the Commem in a party; to have Julia Manville to himself was more than he could hope for. But he was less than pleased with the obvious pairings David had suggested. Apart from the token dance, he could see Karl Fischer – a German graduate student, who had rooms on the same staircase in College – dancing the night away with his girlfriend, Eva. Neil Grantham, his tutor and David's, would dance with a fellow don, and David with Julia. He would be left with Celia, Julia's young sister. He liked Celia well enough – but she definitely was not Julia.

He said, 'We'll have to consult Julia. She may have other plans. Her parents could be coming. After all, Manville was up at the College.'

'Yes. I'd forgotten that. But I expect he'll be too busy with his politics.'

'Even in Opposition? Remember, Harold Wilson's got a fair majority now.'

David grunted. He wasn't sure of his feelings about Manville; somehow he found the man intimidating. He shrugged his shoulders and, leaning forward, fiddled with the radio until the sound of the Beatles pounding out their latest hit filled the car. Then, 'Step on it, Richard!' he shouted above the music. 'Or we won't get back to College in time for Hall.'

*

They met Neil Grantham as they were carrying their belongings across the quadrangle. He was a man of medium height, and a typical Scot, with a white skin, blue eyes and a shock of red hair. Still in his early thirties, he had an enviable reputation as a historian, and was expected to be offered one of the next Chichele professorships to become vacant in his field.

'Hello David, Richard. Let me help carry.' He relieved them of a couple of bags. 'I see you've brought your tennis racquets.' He grinned. 'There's not going to be much time for games this term, you know. It's to be work, work and more work if you're to get your Firsts.'

They jeered at him. 'And if we don't, you'll lose your job, I suppose. The College'll sack you,' David said.

'Honour, fame and hopes of a Chair all gone,' added Richard.

Neil Grantham responded in kind. 'Excellent reasons for making you work,' he said. He led the way up the stairs, and dumped the bags he had been carrying outside the door of the rooms the two young men shared, 'Come along in half an hour if you've nothing better on. We can have a drink, and discuss what you've done – or haven't done – during the vac.'

'Okay. Thanks, Neil.'

Richard and David were lucky. As scholars, they were entitled to have rooms in this older, and in some senses more desirable, part of the College, but dons and graduate students took priority and there were never enough suites – usually one 'sitter' and two 'bedders' – to go round.

Both Richard and David had a particular, if ambivalent, attachment to their rooms, for they had acquired them in tragic circumstances. Peregrine Manville, brother to Julia and Celia, who had been at public school with them, was one of the previous occupants, but he had been killed in a skiing accident during the Christmas vacation of his second year at Oxford, and the man who had been sharing with him had preferred to move.

With a wave of his hand Grantham ran downstairs to his own quarters on the ground floor of the same staircase. Richard, going ahead of David and ignoring the bags Grantham had abandoned, went over to the window. He let his gaze move slowly about the quadrangle, taking in the eighteenth-century buildings of crumbling Cotswold stone that surrounded a beautifully-kept expanse of grass, the cloisters to one side, the hundred-year-old medlar tree.

'I shall miss this place,' he said ruefully.

'Shan't we all? But think what the great wide world's about to offer us.'

'Third Secretary in some malaria-infested dictatorship that no one's ever heard of because it's just changed its name as a symbol of liberation from British rule.'

David laughed. 'Don't be so damned cynical. What about a posting to Washington or Paris?'

'You must be joking.'

'No, I'm not. You've got to think big, as my dearly esteemed father's always saying. Anyway, Richard, if you really wanted to stay here you could. The College'd be happy to offer you a Fellowship, and you could follow in old Neil's footsteps. He once said we were the most brilliant pupils he's had for a long time – apart from Peregrine, of course – so he'd rejoice to keep one of us.'

Richard turned away from the window and regarded with affection the big, shabby room with its adjoining minute bedrooms. During the vacation the suite had been let to American delegates to an Eastern convention, so it looked bare and forlorn, but it would only take a few minutes' unpacking to re-impose their personalities on it.

'I'd like to believe we were in the same class as Peregrine. Frankly, I don't. We may all be – have been – scholars, but he was a year ahead of us, don't forget,' Richard said.

'So what? Speak for yourself,' David said absently. He was thumbing through the mail they had picked up at the lodge when they entered the College. He opened an envelope and took out a card. 'Invitation from Karl and Eva. Sunday evening at eight at her flat. Drinks and buffet supper. We accept?'

'Of course. Sounds like a good start to term,' said Richard. 'Eva's a great cook.'

★

Eva Krohn opened her door to David and Richard. She was in fact thirty-two, but she admitted to twenty-seven. A refugee from the German Democratic Republic – East Germany – she had neither family nor friends to disprove the age she claimed, and who was there to care? In five years Eva, like many other women in somewhat similar situations, had become an institution.

She was a clever woman, and spoke several languages, but she was not a member of the University. She had a job as a research assistant for an encyclopaedia commissioned by the Church of England, an occupation which conferred on her a certain aura of respectability – totally spurious, as it happened. She lived in a flat off the Woodstock Road, ostensibly alone, though Karl Fischer slept there more often than in his College rooms. And she was famous for her parties.

An invitation to one of these parties was prized by dons and undergraduates alike. A small woman, no more than Venus height, with smooth dark hair and unusual green eyes, she was apt to refer to herself – jokingly, perhaps – as plain as a door, her mouth the letter-box, her big nose the knocker above it. But five minutes in her company, and such defects were forgotten. She was charming, intelligent, entertaining, full of vitality – and considerate. No one ever had an excuse for feeling ignored at Eva's parties.

Naturally she possessed an inner circle of friends, which included David Windfield and Richard Kent, whom she had not seen since the end of the Hilary Term. Now, when she had opened the door and let them into the narrow hall, she embraced them in a single hug, and reached up to kiss each of them on both cheeks.

'Come in! Come in! Lovely to see you again. Did you have a good vacation?' Her English was almost flawless, the trace of an accent adding to its attraction. 'This isn't really a party. Just a few of us. You'll know them all.'

David sniffed appreciatively. 'There's a glorious smell coming from somewhere.'

'That's Karl. He's making a very special *ragoût* for us. Go and say hello to him. The wine's in the kitchen, anyway. Help yourself, and bring me a glass.'

Obediently they went along to the tiny kitchen at the end of the passage. Karl Fischer, wearing a minute frilly apron and a chef's tall white hat, was tasting his *ragoût* with exaggerated care. Quite unlike Eva in appearance, he was a big, blond man who liked to play the clown. But at this moment his audience of one seemed less than amused.

Celia Manville, perched on a stool in a corner of the small room, was pale and unsmiling. Her pretty face was set, and her body tense. She barely acknowledged Richard's greeting, and turned away from David's kiss.

'What's the matter, sweetie?'

'Karl's just been telling the most appalling lies about Peregrine.'

Karl shrugged his wide shoulders and rolled his eyes wildly, 'Celia, my dearest love, you do me wrong.'

'No, I don't! You said, or you meant, that Peregrine was a – a sort of secret communist, that he believed in what they thought and did, even if he didn't admit it. That's what you implied, Karl. What's the point of denying it? I'm not staying here, if that's how you feel.'

Celia slid off her stool. They heard her running footsteps in the passage, and the slam of the front door. Karl sighed.

'Silly child! All I said was that Peregrine once told me that he'd rather be Red than dead, whatever that means.'

Richard laughed. 'So would most people, if the chips were down and they were actually faced with the choice.'

But David was more serious. 'All the same, you don't want to start any rumours. They can't hurt Peregrine, but what about the rest of the family? Think what a paper like *Private Eye* might make of some such story.'

They were interrupted by Eva demanding her wine, and inquiring when the food would be ready. Julia Manville was with her, and they exchanged greetings and vacation news.

Then Julia said, 'Where's Celia? I thought she was in here.'

In the silence that followed Richard saw Karl give Eva a fractional shake of the head. Julia looked from one of them to the other. She was a pretty girl, prettier than her sister, but with the same corn-coloured hair and violet eyes. Two years older than

92

Celia, she was also more intelligent, and far more self-assured.

'Something's happened,' she said. 'What?'

Karl said, 'I'm sorry Julia. I'm afraid I made Celia angry, and she left.' He explained briefly, making light of the matter.

Julia nodded. 'Don't apologize, Karl, please. I know Peregrine used to make left-wing remarks sometimes. I think he did it to needle Dad. But of course Celia would never admit that. As far as she was concerned Peregrine could do no wrong.'

'Well, in my opinion there's very little he did do wrong,' Eva said stoutly. 'Now, come along, all of you. This is meant to be a party.'

It was a good party. Eva had never been known to give a failure of a party. Karl's *ragoût*, with a mixed salad and home-made bread, was excellent. Afterwards there was fresh fruit and an extraordinary assortment of cheeses. Wine and beer were plentiful. There was no hard liquor, and there were no drugs; a graduate student who had once smoked cannabis had been told that he would be unwelcome in future.

'I'm a guest in this country,' Eva said. 'I'm lucky to be here. What people do outside my flat is their business. What they do here is mine. And I obey the laws.'

No such question arose now. All those present were happy to sit around, eat and drink and talk. For many of them it was the beginning of their last term at Oxford, and there was a lot to talk about. Most had already lined up jobs, or at least knew what they wanted to do; in the so-called Swinging Sixties there was no problem about finding employment. But there were plenty of other current questions to be considered. What was to happen to Rhodesia since its declaration of UDI? Was Philby really the 'Third Man' who had warned Burgess and Maclean? Had the Beatles, as they claimed, actually smoked pot in the Buckingham Palace loos before receiving their MBEs? Would Harold Wilson be a disaster as Prime Minister, now he had an adequate majority? And in the background Joan Baez and Marianne Faithfull sang their haunting songs.

Sitting on cushions, one on either side of Julia Manville, Richard and David were both enjoying themselves. Julia was less relaxed, and was the first to suggest leaving.

93

'I'm a bit worried about Celia,' she said.

'Don't be silly.' Richard, not wanting the evening to end, wasn't sympathetic. 'She's a big girl now, Julia. She doesn't need you to be her nanny.'

David was more understanding. He stood up and gave Julia his hands to pull her to her feet. 'I'll walk you home,' he said, and grinned at Richard, who somewhat ruefully accepted that he wouldn't be welcome to join them.

As David and Julia said their goodbyes and left the party, Neil Grantham, who had been watching the little scene with some amusement, leaned across to Richard. 'That wasn't very clever of you, dear boy,' he said. 'If you love one Manville, you have to love them all. You should know that by now. They're a very close-knit family.'

9

It was an idyllic Oxford day, the kind that memory cherishes. The cloudless sky, a deep Mediterranean blue, was reflected in the water. The sun was hot for an English June, but the heat wasn't humid or unpleasant. Every now and then a soft breeze stirred the trees on the river bank, and made the brownish water of the River Cherwell lap against the side of the punt.

Richard found it impossible to work. He came to the end of a page of notes that was meant to help his revision, and realized that he had absorbed nothing. He couldn't care less about the rise of Hitler, the Russo-German non-aggression pact, the causes of the Second World War and the many betrayals that followed. All this nonsense seemed unimportant when Julia was propped up against the punt cushions opposite him, her long bare legs stretched out beside his.

Perhaps he moved. Perhaps she sensed that his gaze was fixed on her. Julia looked up from the book she had been reading and smiled, though with an unexpectedly doubtful expression.

'*Beowulf!*' she declared, making the name sound like an expletive. 'Why ever did I decide to read English?'

Richard returned her smile. 'Perhaps you thought it was a soft option,' he said. He knew that in its context her remark was meaningless – that it was not what she really wanted to say – and for a moment there was a complete empathy between the two of them. Richard caught his breath. Then another punt swept past, so close that their own craft rocked violently and a collision seemed imminent. Shouts of apology and laughter required some response. The moment was gone.

Instead of what he had had in mind, Richard said, 'It's a

delusion that one can do any serious work on the river. Everything's against it. How I wish we'd just come up, and Schools were something in the distant future. Do you remember?'

'Of course,' she replied, turning a page.

He returned to his notes and tried to concentrate, but he was aware that Julia wasn't really reading, but watching him. Yet when she spoke he was startled.

'Richard!'

'Yes?' When she didn't continue immediately he had a sudden premonition that she was about to say something he would rather not hear. With some reluctance he felt compelled to add, 'What is it, Julia?'

'Last night David asked me to marry him – more or less.'

'More or less?' Richard was oddly unsurprised. 'What the hell does that mean?'

'He said that he had recently been giving the question of marriage serious consideration, and what did I think about it.'

Richard paused before replying. 'And what *did* you think about it?' he asked.

'I suppose I replied in the same kind of tone. I said I'd take the matter under advisement.' Without looking at Richard, Julia was dabbling her hand over the side of the punt, and making ripples in the water. 'But I said I'd no intention of marrying in haste and repenting at leisure. Anyway, I'm not sure he wasn't joking or kidding or something. He hasn't mentioned it to you?'

'No.'

'Well, don't you mention it, then.'

'Of course not.'

Richard wondered how Julia really wanted him to respond. Was she seeking reassurance that David wouldn't joke about such a subject? If so, he could give it to her. David, he was sure, had been serious – was serious. David had been sounding out Julia, if that was a suitable phrase for such an approach on such a subject. He hadn't wanted to risk a direct refusal. Richard himself could understand David's feelings only too well. They were identical to his own. He should have made some such move himself, but seemingly he lacked David's courage.

96

'Richard, I think we should go back.' Julia changed the subject, as if what they had been discussing lacked any special importance as far as she was concerned. 'As you say, it's impossible to work on the river. There are too many distractions – and *I* need to work, even if you don't.

'Okay.' Richard spoke lightly. 'Though I doubt whether anything one can do at this stage will make much difference in the end.'

Richard untied the punt, and eased the pole from the mud. Pushing off from the bank, he let the stern swing out into mid-stream. He enjoyed punting. It was a skill easy to learn but, done well, provided an opportunity to demonstrate an indolent elegance that appealed to him. He liked to feel the tall pole sliding through his wet hands, the power of the thrust from the river bottom, the surge of the punt as it sped forward in a perfectly straight line, with no need to spoil the effect by 'trailing' the pole in order to steer.

This afternoon, however, he punted automatically and without conscious pleasure as they returned to the College moorings. The day had lost its sheen, and for once he was glad to say goodbye to Julia. He decided to collect some different books, and go to the library for a couple of hours before his tutorial with Neil Grantham.

He found David in their rooms, packing a bag, discarding one garment, choosing another. Books were scattered around him. He was pale under his light summer tan, and his mouth was set.

'Ah, I'm glad you're back, Richard. All my dates are in the book on the desk. Be a good chap and make a note of what I'm meant to be doing from now till the end of next week, and cancel everything for me.'

'Why? David, what's happened?'

'I've got to go home. Mother's just phoned to say that my father's died.'

'David! I *am* sorry. Of course I'll do anything I can.'

'It's a hell of a shock. No one knew he wasn't perfectly fit. It seems he went for a stroll in the rose garden and collapsed – just like that. As far as I can make out, the doctor said he must have had a massive heart attack.'

Richard nodded his sympathy. 'And you hope to be back at the end of next week?'

'As soon as I can. After all, it may sound brutal, but I have to take my Schools. I can't let this mess up my whole future, can I?'

★

But that was precisely what it had done, David thought bitterly.

It was two days after the funeral. He was returning to Oxford – and by bus. He had been extremely rude to the elderly lady who had sat down next to him and apologized for her many parcels. She had been surprised, given him a reproachful glance and moved to the only other vacant seat. Now, undisturbed by a fidgeting or talkative companion, he was able to savour his plight in private.

He hated buses. He couldn't remember when he had last been in one. The fact that the vehicle was comfortable made no difference. It chugged around the Cotswold villages, picking up and setting down the odd passenger, when he wanted to go straight to Oxford. He positively hated the lawyer who had insisted that they keep but one car, which his mother obviously needed.

Logic told him that it was a common situation. Husband dies with massive debts; widow must sell up to meet debts; widow left with, perhaps not a pittance, but a vastly reduced income – an income certainly inadequate to provide the expected handsome allowance for a grown-up son.

And that wasn't all. Why in God's name hadn't they told him before that Windfield was his stepfather? He'd asked his mother that question, only to receive a ridiculous answer, 'At first you were too young to understand, and later it never seemed to be the right moment.' Well, he knew now.

Gazing out of the bus window he was happy to see that they had reached the outskirts of the city. A few more minutes and they were turning into Gloucester Green. He had seized his bags and was standing by the door ready to alight almost before the bus had stopped. He walked fast and angrily, not caring whom

98

he knocked against, eager to reach the College and the sanctuary of his rooms. He wasn't sure whether he was glad or sorry to find Richard there.

'David! You're back sooner than I expected.'

David dropped his bags on the floor. 'There was no reason to stay.'

'It was bloody, was it?'

'That's putting it mildly.' David sprawled in an armchair. 'For God's sake, give me something to drink. I'm thirsty, and this evening I plan to get well and truly sloshed.'

Richard produced a couple of cans of beer and two tankards. He watched David as he drank, surprised at how strained he seemed. As far as he knew, David and his father had never been particularly close, and he hadn't expected David to be so affected by the older Windfield's death.

'Do you want to talk about your father, David?' he asked doubtfully.

'What father? If you mean Bernard Windfield, he wasn't my father, though no one bothered to inform me of the fact before.' David didn't try to hide his bitterness.

'You were adopted?'

'No, not exactly. I'm not somebody's little bastard. My mother was perfectly legitimately married, but the chap died or was killed in the war or something, and she married Windfield.'

Richard looked at his friend curiously. 'Well, what's so dreadful about that?' he asked. 'I've got a stepfather myself, as you know, David, and I'm very fond of him.'

'I know, I know, Richard!' David banged his tankard down on the table beside him. 'Really it's the fact that no one told me that rankles. Do you see what I mean?'

'Of course, but – '

'Anyway, that's not the main point. I'll tell you. I wasn't going to, but I will. We're broke.'

'Broke?'

'In a manner of speaking. Look, you know my father was a Lloyd's "name" – one of those rich chaps that has to find money on demand to meet claims. Well, a few years ago his syndicate went through a bad patch, and he had to put up a large sum. He didn't tell anyone, but he mortgaged our properties and started gambling with the proceeds to try and recoup. He never had the sense to tell my mother, or reduce our standard of living – or warn me, for that matter. You must realize we've seemed pretty well off. It was a kind of hoax. And all these years I've been expecting a pretty generous allowance to continue when I left Oxford and started working. Now, not on your life! When everything's settled, there'll be about enough for my mother to survive reasonably, but nothing for me. It means that things'll never be the same again. Hell, if I hadn't already bought the ticket for the bloody Commem Ball, I'd be damned if I'd buy it now.'

'That's too bad, David, but as one who never had great expectations – '

Richard found it hard to offer much sympathy. David would get his degree, then go into the FCO as he had intended. Apparently he wouldn't have to help his mother, so his salary should be perfectly adequate.

' – and you'll soon be earning yourself,' he continued.

'What? The pittance they'll pay me to start with? Don't be a fool, Richard. This has messed up all my plans.'

Which included marrying Julia, Richard thought. He said, 'Cheer up! It probably won't be as bad as you think. Do you want me to cancel my date tonight and get drunk too?'

'Who's it with?'

David sounded so suspicious that Richard was tempted not to tell him. Then he grinned. 'No one you know. No one I know, for that matter. An old friend of my mother's rang up to say she was staying at the Randolph, and would I go and have dinner with her. I expect it'll be a bore, but I didn't like to refuse. I could cancel if you – '

'Don't be silly, Richard. I'll be all right. Drink damnation to my father.'

Richard hesitated.He wasn't sure how to deal with David in this mood. Finally, he shrugged mentally. 'See you when I get back,' he said at last.

★

In spite of his words, David was disappointed, even hurt, when Richard disappeared; unfairly he felt that Richard had, in some indefinable fashion, let him down. He wondered what to do with his evening; he no longer wanted to get drunk – especially by himself. Schools were unpleasantly close, of course, but he knew he couldn't settle to work. Neither did he want to dine in Hall. He wanted company, but not a crowd. He tried Neil Grantham, but the don wasn't in his rooms, and neither was Karl Fischer. There was no one in the least congenial in the Junior Common Room.

Finally, he had an idea, and telephoned Eva Krohn. The phone rang for a full minute, and he was about to put down the receiver when Eva answered, her voice husky with sleep. He guessed she had been in bed with Karl.

'Of course, come along David,' she said when he briefly explained the situation. 'You poor boy. There's only me and Karl, but we'd love to see you. Get three or four bottles of wine on the way, will you, love? We're running low.'

'Sure. No trouble.'

It was easy enough to buy the wine from an off-licence. At any other time David wouldn't have thought twice about it, but this evening he resented having to spend a few extra pounds and reached the flat in a bad temper.

His mood was soon forgotten. Though it was clear from their appearance, like cats after a bowl of cream, that Karl and Eva had been making love, they welcomed him warmly. Whereas Richard had been sardonic, almost indifferent, even a little gratified – or so it seemed to David in retrospect after two or three glasses of wine – Karl and Eva couldn't have been kinder or more understanding. And they offered practical help.

'If you're short of cash to see you through the rest of the term, I can lend you some,' Karl said.

'Thanks a lot, but there's no need. Luckily that wretched lawyer agreed that my allowance should continue till I go down. The major problem's going to be to find somewhere to live in London, now the family flat's got to go.'

Karl and Eva exchanged glances. 'We can't promise, but it's possible we might know of somewhere,' Eva said tentatively. 'It's a flatlet, not self-contained, in a friend's house in Hampstead. Would you like us to inquire? It won't be the kind of thing you'd expected, but it could serve for a while.'

'Of course I would. Yes, please.'

And by the time David was walking back to the College, he was feeling distinctly happier. He had drunk a great deal of wine, for which Karl had insisted on paying him, had eaten an excellent supper, and had talked about himself more unreservedly than he could remember. He felt free and unburdened.

There was a light showing under Richard's door and, his earlier vexation forgotten, he considered going in to say good-night. Then he thought that Richard was probably reading, and wouldn't want to be disturbed. He went to his own room and, drifting off to sleep, decided that, in spite of his changed prospects, he would still marry Julia, if she'd have him.

The undergraduates who had spent the past three years reading modern history were like magpies in their black and white subfusc as they flocked out of the Examination Schools in the High Street, their gowns billowing behind them. Most of them – those who had not thrown them away in disgust – clutched the question papers to which, for the past three hours, they had been attempting to respond. This was their last written examination; for them Schools were over, unless they were called back for the dreaded direct confrontation with the examiners that constituted a viva. Involuntarily, they turned to each other to compare notes on their performances.

'What did you think of it?' Richard asked.

'Not bad,' David said. 'Not bad at all. Did you try the question on Winston Churchill?'

'Yes. Which was probably a mistake. He's not one of my great heroes, so I didn't take the conventional view.'

David laughed. 'And you can imagine some old don saying, "I don't like this chap Kent. To me he sounds unpatriotic."'

'Yes. Something like that,' Richard said curtly.

David glanced at his friend quickly, surprised at the manner in which he had spoken, and was about to comment when he saw Julia, who had no examination that day, on the opposite pavement outside Queen's College. He waved his mortarboard furiously.

'There's Julia. Come on, Richard.'

They hurried across the street, dodging cars and buses and innumerable bicycles. Richard, who could have reached Julia first, waited for David. They greeted her together, in front of the curious cupola that surmounted Queen's porter's lodge.

'I'm late,' she apologized. 'I meant to be waiting for you as you came out. Here.' She gave them each a brown-paper bag. 'Cherries. Father says that when he was up friends always brought cherries on the last day of Schools. You're meant to eat them as you walk back to College, and spit the stones into the gutter. Utterly disreputable.'

'But a wonderful idea.'

David put his arm round her, and kissed her cheek. Julia glanced sideways at Richard, but he was apparently busy inspecting the cherries. She asked them what today's papers had been like. Richard spat a cherry stone expertly into a drain as they went past All Saints' Church, and turned up Turl Street.

'Easy enough, I thought,' he said. 'But I'd hate to predict the results.'

'I'm sure you don't need to worry, either of you.' Julia was reassuring. 'Anyway, worrying's quite pointless now. It's all over. What are you doing to celebrate? I've got no papers till the day after tomorrow, so I'm taking the evening off, and Celia and I thought we'd invite you to the latest James Bond movie. Supper afterwards, too.'

'That sounds super,' David said at once.

'You'll have to count me out, I'm afraid.' Richard spoke simultaneously. 'I've already got a date.'

'I see. I'm sorry.' Julia couldn't hide her disappointment.

'For heaven's sake!' exclaimed David, annoyed. 'Can't you cancel it?'

'No.'

It was a flat monosyllable, and Richard made no attempt to elaborate. He knew that if he said he had made a special appointment to see Neil Grantham, David would justifiably demand details, and he wasn't yet prepared to discuss the matter. He was grateful when Julia changed the subject, and started talking about their plans for the Commem Ball.

★

Richard sat by the window, ignoring the open book on his lap, his gaze on the lengthening shadows in the quadrangle below.

He watched David hurry along the path to the porter's lodge, on his way to spend the evening with Julia. Two dons, capped and gowned, walked by, deep in conversation and oblivious of the clicking cameras of a group of tourists who were being shown around the College. There was the sound of a party getting under way in some neighbouring rooms. Two undergraduates, carrying tennis racquets, stopped to chat. It wasn't a bad life, Richard thought.

'But would it be for you?' Hugh Kent, his stepfather, had remarked, when Richard had unexpectedly gone up to London for the day just before Schools to visit his family.

'Would you be happy, darling?' his mother had asked.

Richard had chosen his words carefully. 'Yes, I think so. I'm sure it's a life I could enjoy.' And when, instead of arguing, they accepted what he said, he had added, 'I'll speak to Neil Grantham as soon as the exams are done.'

Richard sighed and shut his book. 'Better get it over,' he said, unaware that he had spoken aloud. He hoped that Grantham wouldn't probe too deeply. He felt tired and jaded, and wondered if he should have postponed what might be a difficult interview. But time was fairly short. Squaring his shoulders, he clattered down the stairs to Grantham's rooms.

'Beer? Sherry? Or a glass of white wine?' Neil Grantham asked, waving Richard to a chair.

'Wine, please.'

Grantham poured them each a glass, then came and sat opposite Richard, regarding him quizzically. 'You look done in,' he said. 'Whey-faced, and dark circles under the eyes.'

'I've written two three-hour papers today, Neil,' Richard excused himself without mentioning that he had also been sleeping badly. 'It's been a tough time altogether. Thank God I shan't have to go through that again.'

Grantham grinned. 'I know you've got something on your mind, Richard. But do I have to ask the obvious question?'

'If you mean, "How have I done?" the answer's no, you don't. I realize there's never any guarantee, Neil, but I'm satisfied. With all due modesty, I expect to get a good First.'

'Well, thanks be for that! You know, you had me worried for

a while. When you asked if you could see me this evening, instead of celebrating with David, I was afraid you might have made a mess of things. Even the best do on occasion.'

'Yes. After the last few days, I can see how it could happen.' Richard sipped his wine. He knew Neil had given him an opening, but he found it difficult to state his case. Then he said in a rush, 'Actually, how well I did in Schools is pretty relevant to what I want to ask you. I – I've been thinking a lot about the future recently, Neil, and I've decided the Foreign Service is not for me. I'd like to stay on here in College, try for a doctorate, do some teaching, hope to get elected to a Fellowship eventually. In short, an academic career. What would you say my prospects might be?'

'I'd say they'd be extremely good. The College would be happy to have you.' Neil Grantham spoke slowly. 'But – are you joking, Richard? I thought you'd set your heart on getting into the Foreign Office even before you came up, and to throw the opportunity away now, when – '

'Of course I'm not joking,' Richard interrupted rudely. He made a vague gesture with one hand, nearly knocking over his wine glass. 'I'm so sorry, Neil. I didn't mean to bite your head off. I – I realize this is unexpected but, as I say, I've been thinking about it for some little while, and I've made up my mind. I'm positive it's for the best.'

'But why, Richard? Why?'

'Pesonal reasons, you might say. We're a close-knit family and, as you know, I'm an only child. My stepfather and I agree it would be especially hard on my mother if I were to be abroad for years on end. It's as simple as that.'

'Nothing is ever "as simple as that", not in my experience.' Grantham was visibly disturbed. He got up and began to pace the room. 'I still don't understand, Richard. Why this last-minute decision? Because it *is* last-minute, even if you've been thinking about it for some time. After all, you've always known what the position would be if you joined the Foreign Office. Your mother's not ill, dying of something, is she?' It was a brutal question, but Richard merely shook his head.

Neil went on, 'It would be more logical in the circumstances if it were David who decided to chuck the FCO, now that his mother's a widow.'

'I'm sure David won't do anything like that.'

Neil glanced up sharply at Richard's tone, but he made no comment. Instead, he asked again, 'But you're determined to?'

'Yes, and don't think it's any great sacrifice on my part. I'll be doing what I want. You must believe that, Neil.'

Grantham's expression showed clearly that he was at a loss to know what to believe. 'What about Julia Manville?' he asked suddenly.

'Julia?' Richard feigned surprise. 'She's got nothing to do with it.'

'I had the impression you were serious about her – serious enough to consider marrying her, perhaps.'

'No. I'm not considering marriage, to Julia or anyone, not at this stage of the game. Don't tell me you're recommending it, Neil?'

Grantham laughed sardonically. 'If you'd ever met my ex-wife, you wouldn't ask that.' For a moment he was silent, then he said, 'Okay, Richard, if you're sure you want to follow in my academic footsteps, I'll do everything I can to help.'

'I'm sure,' said Richard. 'Thanks, Neil.'

★

Once he had survived the interview with Neil Grantham and gained his promise of assistance and support, Richard had expected no further opposition to his choice of an ivory tower rather than an embassy. Surprise, yes, when the decision became known, and a certain amount of discussion, but no persistent questioning of his motives. He was wrong.

David was inexplicably incensed. To Richard's annoyance, he argued and continued to argue, day after day. He seemed to think that Richard was making a martyr of himself for no good reason, and that he himself would therefore be expected to do the same.

'Julia says she impressed,' David said at one point.

'Really? She's no need to be. On the contrary, I could be said to be playing safe. You could end up as a consul in Bongo-Bongo, and die of some unheard-of disease. Whereas I – '

'Whereas you could become – probably will become – head of a College – this one or somewhere else. *What do you bet?*'

It was a challenge they had issued to each other at intervals since school days. And together they chanted the answer, '*I never bet. I know.*' They grinned. They were close again, but only momentarily. They knew that an era had ended, that their relationship would never be the same.

'I still think you're being a fool, Richard,' David continued. 'Julia says – '

'Damn Julia! And damn you, David, and everyone else who insists on interfering.' Suddenly Richard's temper had flared. 'I'm bloody well going to do what I want.'

He banged out of the room and down the stairs. Hurrying along the cloisters he met Karl, but refused to stop. Karl, not content with arguing about his decision for a couple of hours, had even enlisted Eva's help, and she, too, had done her best to dissuade him from giving up the Foreign Service. As if it were any of their business, Richard thought angrily.

He walked rapidly through the mass of science buildings towards Parks, reminding himself that Term was almost over. They would all be coming up again for the Commem Ball, but by then everything would be different. Their rooms would be occupied by strangers on some summer course or other. Later, David would be in London, a lowly servant of the FCO, and, with luck, he himself would still be in College, struggling in new rooms with his new status. Someone else would be occupying the rooms they still thought of as Peregrine Manville's. Celia would be returning in October, but not Julia, and not Karl, who was going back to Germany; Eva's plans were uncertain. It was not what he had expected, what he had hoped for, but it would be a new beginning.

11

As host, Neil Grantham had the chair at the head of the table. He pushed it back, and rose to his feet a little unsteadily and a trifle pompously. 'Ladies and Gentlemen,' he said, 'please stand while I propose the toast to the College.'

His guests did as they were asked. There were seven of them that evening dining in his oak-panelled room before the Commem Ball: David, Richard and Karl, all, like Grantham, resplendent in tails, and the four women, the Manvilles, Eva, and a young don from St Anne's whom Grantham had invited as his partner. Both Eva and the don, whose name was Elizabeth, were wearing green; Julia was in blue, and Celia in white. Altogether, they made an attractive group.

'The College!' Grantham proclaimed. 'Among Oxford Colleges may she continue supreme.'

There was a chorus of, 'The College!' And they all sat again to finish their champagne, to chat and laugh and reminisce, until David suggested that it was time they went and danced.

By now it was dark outside, a lovely summer's evening, warm and balmy, the sky bright with stars and the thin crescent of a new moon. The College's quadrangles had been floodlit, making access to the gardens behind easy. And in the gardens two large marquees had been erected, one for dancing, the other for a late supper. Fairy lights shone among the trees, adding to the splendid unreality of the scene, and music from the band drifted out to those who chose to sit out a dance or walk beside the miniature lake.

As had become the custom at formal balls in the Sixties, modern pop music – to which couples danced or jived apart –

alternated with older and more traditional ballroom pieces; an occasional Scottish or country dance was introduced for good measure. By the time Grantham's party had entered the main marquee and established a base at a table, a slow foxtrot was in progress. With no discussion, as if the pairing were some established ritual, they broke into couples: Neil and Elizabeth, Karl and Eva, David whirling Julia on to the dance floor, Richard left with Celia.

Celia was not a good dancer. She was stiff and unrelaxed, preferring her partner to perform set steps that she could easily follow. Richard was glad when Neil asked her to dance, and he could partner Elizabeth and then Eva, both of whom were more accomplished. There was no sign of Julia, or of David.

In fact, Julia and David were walking, hand in hand, around the lake. They strolled slowly, scarcely speaking till they reached the side furthest from the marquees, where the music reached them only faintly. Here David stopped, pulled Julia to him and kissed her hard.

'I love you, Julia,' he whispered. 'I want you.'

'David, please.' She pushed him away, gently but firmly.

'Haven't you made up your mind yet? It's ages since I asked you to marry me, and you said you'd think about it.'

'I wasn't sure you meant it, that you weren't joking – '

'Of course I meant it.' He sounded indignant. 'Do you think I make a habit of proposing to girls as a – a form of amusement or something?'

'No, David, but – '

'For heaven's sake, Julia, don't be coy. Queen Victoria's been dead for years; people don't go down on one knee any more. And I am asking you to marry me – not just go to bed with me, which might be more fashionable nowadays.'

'I realize that, but – David, if you insist on an answer now, it's got to be no. I refuse to be pressured.'

'Okay.' David sensed that they were on the point of quarrelling, for Julia had spoken with unusual acerbity. 'Darling, I don't want to pressure you, as you call it. I'll wait – for ever, if necessary.' Then, thinking that this sounded a little too much like a snatch of dialogue from a romantic novel, he grinned suddenly and took her by the hand. They walked on together, but in spite of David's effort they were no longer at ease with each other.

Against his will David heard himself saying, 'It's Richard, isn't it? You're in love with Richard.'

Julia was saved from having to reply by the approach of another couple. This turned out to be Karl and Eva, who greeted them happily and ignored their obvious tension. Chatting, the four of them returned to the group of chairs they had earlier earmarked as their own, and rejoined the rest of the party.

'Time for supper,' Neil Grantham announced when Richard asked Julia to dance.

Julia smiled at Richard. 'The first afterwards,' she promised.

They had tickets for the second supper session, and they didn't finish with the traditional strawberries and cream until the small hours. The men lingered over coffee while the women went off to tidy themselves. Karl accused David of being very quiet, but David replied that he was merely sleepy from too much champagne. 'I'll soon get my second wind,' he said.

When the women rejoined them, David at once asked Celia to dance, and Julia held out her hand to Richard. By this time pop had almost entirely given way to nostalgia, and the band was playing oldies from the Thirties: 'Smoke Gets in Your Eyes', 'Begin the Beguine', and so on. Richard held Julia close, trying not to think but merely to enjoy the moment. Julia spoilt it.

She said, 'You know, Richard, David wasn't joking the other day. He does want to marry me.'

'Yes. I remember you told me you weren't sure if he meant it or not.' Richard spoke lightly after only a fractional hesitation. 'And have you accepted? Do I congratulate him?'

'I haven't decided yet. After all, marriage is a serious business. Don't you agree?'

'Personally I haven't considered it, Julia. I expect I'll marry someone some time, but it won't be for ages.' Richard spoke with seeming inconsequence, and whirled Julia around with a flourish as the music came to an end. 'However, whatever you decide, I wish you – and David – every happiness.'

'Thank you.'

Julia's words were without emphasis or expression. She might have been thanking him for holding open a door. She turned away. And minutes later Richard, dancing once more with Celia, saw David and Julia leave the marquee. He continued to dance, automatically, trying not to stand on Celia's feet which, as she clung to him tightly, seemed to have become more wayward than ever.

'Richard, you're not listening to what I'm saying.'

'Yes, I am,' he said absently.

'Then what did I say?'

'Er – something about Peregrine. It's difficult to hear over the band.'

'Nonsense. You weren't listening. You were thinking about Julia, as usual. If Julia marries David, will you marry me, Richard?'

'You wouldn't have me.'

'Maybe not. I wish I could have married Peregrine, so we could have flown away together.'

'For God's sake!'

Richard glanced at Celia in exasperation. Her speech was slurred, and there was a foolish smile on her face. Suddenly she slumped and he felt her full weight in his arms. He staggered a little, bumping into another couple and apologizing. The man grinned his sympathy but the girl, on whose foot Celia had inadvertently trodden, glared at him angrily.

Supporting Celia, Richard glanced quickly round the dance floor. He needed help. Celia certainly wasn't fat, but she was a tall, well-built girl, and he doubted whether he could carry her out of the marquee without assistance. But he had no wish to cause a scene, and it was with relief that he saw Karl and Eva and waved to them.

No explanations were needed. A glance at Celia was enough for them to understand the situation. With Richard on one side and Karl on the other, Celia was half carried off the dance floor and planted on a chair under the trees outside. Eva knelt beside her.

'My poor Celia,' Eva said. 'Do you feel ghastly? The fresh air should do you good.'

For answer Celia turned away and vomited. Eva found some tissues and wiped her mouth. The two men stood, backs turned, shielding Celia from the curious eyes of passing couples.

'Wretched girl,' Karl said softly to Richard. 'At her age she should have learnt to hold her champagne. Do you think we should try to find Julia?'

Richard shrugged. He had no desire to go looking for Julia, who, he was sure was somewhere with David, but he felt responsible for Celia. Eva settled the question.

'It's chilly out here,' she said. 'Celia's shivering dreadfully. We ought to get her somewhere where she can lie down for a while, and be warm and cosy. She'd be all right then.'

'Neil's rooms would be the best place. He told us we could use them when we liked,' Richard said at once. 'His scouts will have cleared up our dinner, and it'll be quiet and private.'

There was no argument. The four of them set off together, Celia between Richard and Karl, Eva carrying Celia's evening bag. They moved slowly for Celia's sake, though she was clearly feeling somewhat improved, and had stopped shivering so violently.

By now the sun was rising. The birds had begun their morning chorus, and the sky was visibly lightening. But the College floodlighting had not been switched off, and the old Cotswold stone buildings surrounding the quadrangles retained their curious air of insubstantiality.

'It's going to be a lovely day,' Karl said suddenly.

'A pity,' said Eva. 'After our return from breakfast I intend to spend it in bed, catching up on my beauty sleep. What about you, Richard?'

'Me? I'll be on my way home, I suppose.' Richard yawned. 'Here we are,' he said as they reached Neil Grantham's staircase.

Their conversation had been at best desultory, and they weren't intentionally quiet as they entered Grantham's rooms. They were half-way into the sitting-room before they realized that they were not alone. There was a murmur of voices from the adjoining bedroom, then soft laughter and the unmistakable sounds of love-making. They hesitated, wondering what to do, and their hesitation was rewarded by a cry of passion from next door.

'David! Oh, David!'

The four in the sitting-room stood, as if frozen, embarrassed. Richard was the first to recover. He turned and fled, banging the outer door behind him, not caring, just wanting to get away. Karl and Eva exchanged hopeless glances.

Then Celia said, 'That's Julia. Julia!'

She started towards the bedroom door, but Karl's reaction was rapid. He seized her by the arm and pulled her back. Celia swung round on him.

'What d'you think you're doing? You're hurting me!'

'For God's sake!' Karl hissed at her. 'Don't be a fool, Celia. Let's go.'

Eva was already moving towards the door, but they were too late. If Julia and David had failed to hear Richard's departure, or thought that whoever had entered Grantham's rooms had left, Celia's cry had disabused them. There were loud, nervous sounds from the bedroom, and in a few moments Julia apeared in the doorway.

She was fully clothed, but dishevelled. Her dance dress was crumpled, her hair untidy, and there were two spots of colour high on her cheeks. Her attempt to appear nonchalant was not a success.

'Hello. Is – is something wrong?'

Eva took charge of the situation. 'Celia's not terribly well, Julia. Too much champagne.' Her face was expressive.

Karl supported Eva. 'Could you get her a duvet or a blanket? If she could lie down on Neil's sofa for a while, she'll be fine.'

'I'm fine now,' said Celia aggressively.

It was David who settled the impasse. He now appeared in the bedroom doorway, with no apparent sign of embarrassment. He wasn't wearing his jacket, and he was re-tying his white tie. He smiled casually at everyone in turn, as if they were guests who had arrived a little early for a party.

'What's happened? Have you run out of champagne?' he asked blithely.

'I felt sick.' Celia eyed David with a mixture of interest and contempt. 'Richard was very kind. He – '

'He brought her out of the marquee so that she could get some air, but it was chilly,' Eva interrupted quickly, too quickly. 'So Karl and I decided to bring her along here.'

'Yes, of course.' David stared past them at the outer door, remembering the bang that had startled them, and he knew that Julia was also remembering it. He did his best to avoid her eyes, and said,'Okay, then. We'll take care of her.'

'Fine, David,' Karl said easily, putting his arm round Eva's waist. 'Eva and I'll try and get in one more dance before the band gives up. We all meet later, as arranged?'

'Sure!'

Eva and Karl had scarcely left when Julia, who had persuaded her sister to come and sit on the sofa, turned on David. 'It was Richard with them, wasn't it? He went when he heard us – me.' The red spots on her cheeks brightened, but her voice was tight, accusing.

'So? It's unfortunate, perhaps, but not as bad as all that. How were we to know anyone would come bursting in on us?'

'Karl and Eva don't matter. It's Richard – '

'Yes, Richard. It's always Richard who matters to you, isn't it?' David felt his temper rising. 'For God's sake, Julia, don't blame me. It was all quite normal. I wasn't raping you. You came to bed with me perfectly willingly, and don't tell me you didn't enjoy it, because I won't believe you.'

'I'm not blaming you, David, but – '

'I know. You wish it had been anyone but Richard who had caught us, don't you?'

Julia didn't answer, and David bit his tongue. He knew he must be careful. He had no wish to quarrel with her, especially at this moment after they had just made love, and he might say something Julia would never forgive. But she was already looking at him with such bitterness that . . .

Celia saved them, as if they were all playing roles in a black comedy. Clamping a hand over her mouth, she stood up. 'I – I'm going to be sick again,' she mumbled desperately.

*

Richard saw Neil Grantham walking beside the lake, deep in conversation with his partner Elizabeth. Hurriedly he avoided them by stepping behind some bushes. He sat down on the ground, where he couldn't be seen from the path, and where no one was likely to intrude.

Even as a small boy, his immediate reaction to something 'bad', some event he disliked, had been to run away and be by himself. He had never sought sympathy or reassurance. He had merely wanted to cry his heart out, alone.

His feelings now were similar and familiar, though no tears came. He sat and stared straight ahead of him to the tiny island in the middle of the lake. One or two ornamental ducks were beginning to wake, to ruffle their feathers, to make ripples on the still water. Richard watched them indifferently.

He knew he had no one to blame but himself. He had as good as told Julia, not in so many words, that he was not seriously interested in her. He had no right to be jealous of David. But that made no difference. He *was* jealous, bitterly jealous. He buried his face in his hands, and his body shook as if with an ague.

After a while he quietened. He lifted his head and, surprised by how much lighter it had become, glanced quickly at his watch. He now had a choice. He could stay where he was, let the others wonder what had happened to him but eventually go off to breakfast without him. Or he could meet them, but plead a blinding headache or make some other excuse to avoid accompanying them. In either case he would cause concern and embarrassment.

There was a third course of action. He could call on all his pride, join the others for breakfast, and behave as normally as possible. 'And why not? Why the hell not?' Richard said aloud. Slowly he got to his feet, brushed himself down and set off for Neil Grantham's rooms.

12

The Commem Ball was over and, as they had arranged, the eight who had made up Neil Grantham's dinner party had reassembled in his rooms, where a tray of coffee had been laid. The atmosphere was charged with tension, the gaiety spurious. Only Elizabeth seemed genuinely and unconcernedly relaxed.

Celia, curled up on the sofa, was merely pretending to be asleep. Julia, sitting beside her, was obviously on edge; she constantly flicked glances towards David who, equally obviously, was a little drunk. Eva and Karl were doing their best to make the gathering seem reasonably normal but they were trying too hard. So was Richard, who had arrived so late that everyone had begun to wonder if he would appear at all.

And, to crown it all, Neil Grantham was angry. When Karl had quietly told him what had happened, he had sworn furiously, apparently feeling that his hospitality had been abused. 'I don't give a damn if or where David and Julia choose to screw, as long as it's not in my bloody bed!' he had exploded.

Now his anger – explicable, but somewhat surprising – was showing itself in an excessive politeness, so excessive as to verge on rudeness. 'I don't want to hurry you, ladies and gentlemen, but if you've finished your coffee I'd be glad if you'd sort yourselves out. As you know, I've got this commitment to the BBC, so I must bathe and change and get up to London.' He turned to smile at Elizabeth. 'My dear – '

'Not to worry, Neil. Karl and Eva are dropping me off at St Anne's.'

'If we can't persuade you to change your mind and come and breakfast with us,' Karl said.

'Thank you, but no.' She shook her head. 'I have work to do this afternoon, and I need to catch up on some sleep first.'

These trivialities eased the tension, and there was immediate action. The men stood up; Elizabeth was already on her feet. Julia fussed over Celia. Within minutes goodbyes and thanks were said to Grantham, and they were on their way.

They went in two cars, David and Richard with the Manville girls in Mrs Windfield's Rover which she had lent to David for the occasion, Karl and Eva taking Elizabeth in their old Ford. They stopped on the Woodstock Road to deposit Elizabeth at St Anne's, then headed for the Swan Inn on the banks of the Windrush, a minor tributary of the Thames, where breakfast would be waiting for them.

David drove fast. He was very competent, but this competence occasionally encouraged him to take risks, and this morning he was not in the best of tempers. He had drunk too much. His head ached. And he was conscious of Julia sitting unhappily beside him. Anyone would suppose they had committed some crime; making love was not a crime, not yet, he thought irritably, and put his foot down hard on the accelerator.

'David, for heaven's sake, slow down,' Julia protested.

'I'm only doing fifty.'

'That's too fast on these winding roads,' Richard said. 'Keep it down, David. Celia and I are rolling around in the back here.'

Suddenly David turned his head and spoke over his shoulder. 'I'm driving, not you. If you don't like it, get out and walk, Richard.'

The attack was unprovoked and unexpected. Richard had spoken mildly. But his intervention had clearly annoyed David who, without warning, swerved the car on to the grass verge, and brought it to an abrupt halt. Celia screamed as she was thrown forwards, only saved by Richard's protective arm from a probably unpleasant bruise.

David leant over the back of his seat, and opened the door on Richard's side.

'If Richard goes, we go too,' Julia said firmly. 'Don't be childish, David.'

By this time Karl and Eva had drawn up behind them. Eva

wound down her window and called to ask why they had stopped. When there was no reply from the car in front, Karl got out of the Ford.

'What's the trouble?' he asked, coming forwards.

'David's driving like a maniac,' Celia said, 'and it's dangerous.'

'Oh, nonsense!' Karl was placatory. 'If he'd been going all that fast my old banger wouldn't have been able to keep up with him.' In fact he had had some difficulty in pursuing the Rover, and Eva had commented on David's driving, but he thought it best not to raise the temperature any further. 'Come on,' he said instead. 'Let's get going, chaps. I need my breakfast.'

The incident might have ended there, as no more than a petty quarrel, if Julia hadn't suggested that Richard should drive. From David's point of view the suggestion was insulting, and particularly hurtful as it came from Julia. He sat, gripping the wheel tightly and staring straight ahead of him, while the others got out on to the grass. He thought of starting the car, driving off and abandoning the whole pack of them. Somehow everything seemed to have gone sour.

He blamed Richard, which was unfair. At that moment Richard was firmly refusing to drive the Rover, in spite of Celia's urging.

'Don't be silly. It's David's car, or rather his mother's, and it's up to him to drive it. Not me.'

'Of course it is.' Eva had emerged from the Ford and joined them. 'This is a stupid argument, if ever I heard one. What's the matter with you two? David's a splendid driver.'

'Not when he's had too much to drink,' Julia murmured unwisely.

Eva shook her head in exasperation. 'Julia, we've had a super party. Don't spoil it now.'

'Oh, all right. But – ' Julia looked at Richard. 'Richard, you could persuade David to – '

' – to let me drive. Julia, I've no intention of trying, I don't want to drive his damned car. Why don't you ask him if you can drive?'

'Forget it,' she replied angrily.

Julia went over to the Rover, and slid into the seat beside David. She tucked her arm under his. 'Sorry,' she said. 'We're all behaving stupidly. I don't know why. Too much champagne and too little sleep, perhaps. Can't we start off again?'

'You and me?'

'Yes. But I can't leave Celia. She's still not feeling too well.'

'Can you leave Richard?'

'Yes. He can go with Karl and Eva.'

David knew that she had purposely misunderstood him, and ignored the wider meaning of his question. 'No,' he said finally. 'We'll go on as we started. Let him come with us.' He leant out of his window. 'Come on, Celia, Richard. Karl's right, let's forget it and get going. See you at the Inn, Karl.'

This time it was Richard who hesitated. He nearly said that he preferred the company of Karl and Eva, but it seemed churlish to ignore the olive branch that David had proffered and prolong the stupid and unpleasant situation. It was, however, with some slight reluctance that he followed Celia and got in beside her, determined that whatever David did he would make no comment.

His resolution proved unnecessary. David drove steadily and circumspectly. Less than ten minutes later, on a straight stretch of road, he signalled that he was about to stop. Once more the Rover and then the Ford drew up. David got out of the car.

'Sorry. I have to have a pee,' he said. 'What about you, Richard?'

Joined by Richard and Karl, David went behind the hedge and relieved himself. When they returned to the cars, it was he who made the suggestion that Richard should drive. It was a friendly, casual offer, but Richard refused, saying he was perfectly happy to be chauffeured.

David shrugged. 'Okay.' He seemed amused, but only Karl noticed his mood. 'It's not far now, anyway.'

The straight stretch was short and terminated in a series of sharp bends, followed by a humpback bridge. A couple of miles beyond stood the famous Swan Inn, its gardens sloping down to the waters of the Windrush.

As they approached the end of the straight, David switched on the car radio. A disc jockey was playing the latest Stones hit, and he turned the volume up very high. Then he accelerated into the first bend. .

There was a scream from Celia, a gasp from Julia, and Richard gritted his teeth as they were suddenly forced back against their seats. The next moment they were hanging on to whatever they could find as David, grinning broadly, swung the car around the winding lane.

The bridge came up sooner than he expected, but he made no attempt to slow. The Rover shot up the steep incline and into space. All four wheels were off the ground for at least the car's length before it dropped back on to the road with a crash of metal. David shouted with joy.

But his pleasure was short-lived. Either he had forgotten the right-angled turn immediately beyond the bridge, or he had lost control of the car and could do nothing to prevent what happened next. He was never to remember which.

Quite simply, the Rover failed to take the corner. It went up on the left-hand verge, brushed along the hedge for a few feet, burst through a gate into a field and crashed into a stout tree.

All four doors flew open as the impact deformed the structure of the car, and Richard and Celia were both thrown out; their bodies arched high through the air and thudded to the ground. Seconds later, with what seemed to be excessive slowness, David rolled sideways from his seat on to the grass. Julia had gone through the windscreen.

*

The reverberation of the crash, of breaking glass and twisting metal, subsided slowly. But the car radio was undamaged and continued to play. Unwittingly appropriate, the Beatles were now doing their ineffable best with 'A Hard Day's Night'. Their song drowned everything else, the chirping of sparrows, the distant barking of a dog, the rustle of leaves.

Karl and Eva were the first to arrive. They had received some forewarning from the appalling sounds of the accident, and Karl had driven cautiously around the bend. In the early morning light they saw the horror that lay outspread among the trees in the field beside the road. Eva caught her breath, and Karl swore.

'Christ!' he said. 'The bloody boy must have been mad. It's a shambles!'

For quite ten seconds they sat together in their Ford and stared at the scene before them. Then, simultaneously they wrenched open their doors and got out into the road. Eva went to one side of the wrecked Rover, Karl to the other. By now David was recovering consciousness. He staggered to his feet and almost fell into Karl's arms. Tears were streaming down his cheeks.

'I've killed them,' he said. 'All of them. Julia – '

'You haven't killed anyone.' Karl shouted harshly over the noise of the radio. He leant into the Rover and switched off the set. 'Come on, David.' He led him a little way into the field and made him stretch out on the grass, his back to the car and the carnage. 'Stay there! I'll be with you in a minute.'

Next, Karl ran to Celia, who was lying on the ground in a strange, unnatural attitude. He took one look at her and turned away. Celia was dead. There was no doubt. She had hit the trunk of a tree head first, and with tremendous force. Her skull was split wide open, and her neck was obviously broken.

Eva was calling. Karl hurried around the wrecked car to her. She was kneeling beside Julia who was unconscious, and seemed to be covered with tiny fragments of glass which had cut or scratched her. Blood was everywhere.

'Give me your jacket. We must keep her warm, but not move her. I think her leg's fractured, too,' Eva said.

Karl stripped off his jacket, making sure to transfer the contents of its pockets to his trousers, and tucked it around Julia, while Eva used her stole to make a pillow for Julia's head. A couple of yards from them Richard lay on his back, his mouth open but his breathing audible as they tended Julia. Karl glanced at him anxiously.

'And Richard?'

'Alive, as you can hear, but badly hurt, I'd say. Karl, we must get help.'

'Yes, of course. You take our car, and go on to the Inn. It's the nearest place. They'll phone for the police and an ambulance and whatever's needed. And Eva, Celia's dead.'

'Oh, God! But what about David?'

'Oddly enough, he seems to have come off best. He's shocked and bruised, but in one piece, as far as I can tell. But – '

Karl put out a hand and pulled Eva to her feet. He gripped her arm. 'Eva!' Usually, even when they were alone, except perhaps when they were in bed together, they spoke English. Now he spoke their native German, fiercely, rapidly, giving her a little shake as if to make her understand the importance of his words.

Eva's eyes widened, then grew thoughtful. 'It's a risk,' she said. 'If Richard denies it, and Julia supports him – '

'Of course it's a risk, but not a great one. And it's surely worth taking.' Karl interrupted her. 'By the look of them they're not going to remember much of what happened, and it shouldn't be hard to persuade them.'

Abruptly Eva nodded. 'Okay. But we must hurry. Even so early and on a quiet lane like this someone may come along.'

*

David took a deep breath, very slowly. He repeated the experiment, grimacing as the pain knifed through him. There was little doubt he had one or more broken ribs, but otherwise he thought he was all right. He had already tried the traditional tests, moving his arms and legs. Clearly there was little wrong with them, except for some minor discomfort in his right arm. He had been incredibly lucky.

The others? Karl had reassured him, and he had recovered from his first panic fear that he had killed them all. But they must be hurt, probably badly hurt. Karl and Eva would be coping, but he must go and see and help. He was getting to his feet, slowly and with great care, when Karl came striding towards him.

'David, listen and listen carefully.' Karl seized him by the arm – fortunately the left arm. 'You were tight when you left the College, and Grantham will remember that. You drove criminally fast, though we expostulated with you. The accident was your fault, and only your fault. Julia and Richard are seriously injured, possibly very seriously. And – Celia's dead.'

'Dead! But – but, before, you said – '

'Forget what I said before. That's the situation. You've killed one of them, and injured the other two – all because of your drunk driving.'

'No – no! It's not like that! Not really. I – I only meant to surprise them, bounce them over that bloody bridge. I've done it before. I – I just forgot the corner came so soon.'

'David, that's no excuse. Can't you understand, there *is* no excuse. You'll be charged with manslaughter and you'll go to prison. The Manvilles will never forgive you. You'll lose Julia and, of course, any prospect of joining the FCO. In fact, I hate to think about your future.'

'Oh, God!' David felt helpless and exhausted. His ribs hurt, even though he kept his breathing shallow. He, too, saw his bright prospects dissolving. He wanted to curl himself up into a ball like a hedgehog, to sleep, to forget. He looked hopelessly at Karl. 'But why tell me all this? There's nothing I can do now.'

'Yes, there is.' Karl paused, to ensure he had David's full attention. Then he said bluntly, 'Let Richard take the blame.'

'Richard! Are you mad?'

'Not at all. Look, after we had our pee, Richard drove. He didn't know the road. He went into the corner too fast. But he wasn't drunk! It was an accident – and he was badly hurt. He won't go to prison, David, and it won't ruin the academic career he's decided on. Richard can get away with it. You can't.'

'All the same – '

David looked about him desperately. Karl had propelled him to what remained of the gate into the field. He saw Celia, her distorted body against the tree, her white dance dress covered with blood, and he saw Julia – he couldn't bear it. A sob escaped him, and he turned away.

Then he said, 'She'll know it was me. Julia'll know.'

'Not if she can't really remember, and we all tell her differently. That applies to Richard too. Come on, David, help me with Richard. We must put him behind the wheel.'

'No! We can't move him. It might – might kill him.'

'Nonsense!' Karl was as tall as David, and a much bigger, heavier man. He took David by the shoulders and shook him, and David screamed from the pain in his chest. 'Don't be a fool, David! It's you or Richard,' he said. 'He may have a bad time, but only briefly. People will be sorry for him; they wouldn't be in the least sorry for you. For you, it would be the end – the end of everything.'

★

The inquest on Celia Manville was held in Oxford about ten days later. David sat on the hard wooden bench beween Karl and Eva. Celia's parents, Sir Hubert and Lady Manville, were further along the row, with Neil Grantham on Sir Hubert's right. Grantham had given evidence about the origin of the party at the Commem ball, and said that, as he had been the host of the preliminary dinner, and because the disastrous drive had in a sense started from his rooms, he felt at least partly responsible for the tragedy.

But of course no one blamed him. In fact, no one publicly blamed anyone, whatever the Manvilles might privately have thought. Under more detailed questioning, Grantham had added that coffee had been served before Richard left the College, that Richard had drunk his coffee black and had been perfectly sober. Karl and Eva had supported this. They confirmed that when Richard took over the driving from David, who was feeling tired, he had driven fast but with care. Asked how, in those circumstances, they would account for the accident, they said that perhaps Richard had seen some small animal run across his path, and tried to avoid it.

David, pale, his right arm in a sling, since X-rays had shown a fracture of his radius, in addition to three broken ribs, could offer no other explanation. He had seen no animal, but he had been sitting in the back of the car, and had been paying little attention. Frankly, he didn't remember much about it.

As the only witness present who had been actually involved in the accident, he received a great deal of sympathy as he spoke hesitantly, but with confidence. His confidence was due to the support of Karl and Eva, with whom he had been staying, in spite of his mother's protests – and to a couple of visits to Julia in hospital.

In addition to innumerable small cuts, Julia had a broken leg and a fractured pelvis, and was also suffering from shock – shock from the accident itself, shock at Celia's death, shock at the element of responsibility she believed she couldn't escape. At first she had maintained that David had been driving but, confronted by Karl and Eva, by the police who had found Richard collapsed over the Rover's steering wheel, and finally by David himself, she had eventually confessed that she couldn't really remember.

And Richard was in no position to contradict anyone. Of the survivors he was the most seriously hurt. He had both head and internal injuries, and for two or three days after the accident had been in a coma in an intensive care unit. Since then his condition had improved, and the Kents had arranged for him to be taken by ambulance to a hospital in Hampstead where he could be near them. Apart from his family he had been allowed no visitors – even the police had been banned, and because of the apparently straightforward circumstances of the accident had not insisted – and he had not yet been told of Celia's death. Nor of course had he any idea of the deception that was being implemented.

Once again David had been lucky. The only possible outcome of the inquest had been an adjournment pending further inquiries, and it seemed probable that the eventual verdict would be death by misadventure. In fact, by now, though his conscience still bothered him, and would continue to bother him – decreasingly – for some time, David was thankful that he had accepted Karl's advice and not taken responsibility for the accident. He felt immense gratitude to both Karl and Eva, a little of which he tried to express as they left the coroner's court together.

'You've been terribly good to me,' he said. 'I can't think why you've been prepared to do so much.'

'Forget it,' Karl said. 'We like Richard, as you know, but frankly, David, we like you more. Actually things have turned out better than we could have hoped. But we knew to start with that Richard's future would suffer much less than yours. For you, it would have been hell; for him, once he's recovered, it'll be an event to be forgotten. What we did was merely an act of friendship.'

'I see,' said David. 'All I can say is – thanks.'

13

London, Summer 1966

Richard lay in his high hospital bed and gazed out of the window. All he could see was the top of a large chestnut tree, blurred by the rain that ran in streams down the pane of glass. The weather didn't worry him. He was warm and comfortable; and finally he knew that his condition was improving.

He knew he looked gaunt, his eyes unnaturally large above hollow cheeks, but that was of no consequence. It was how he felt that mattered. He could easily put on the weight he had lost during the last six weeks in hospital.

Six weeks. Sometimes it seemed for ever. He didn't remember the ambulance journey from Oxford, except as a vague nightmare; every stop and start, every bump in the road, had jolted and distressed him. But he remembered his joy in arriving at this place near to his home, and the peace once he had been put to bed.

Then time had passed, mostly not unpleasant because he was sedated against the worst of the pain, and he had slowly learnt to bear the residual discomfort. At first he saw no one except doctors and nurses, and his mother and stepfather. Other visitors had been forbidden for some time, until an Inspector from the Thames Valley Police had been permitted to visit him.

To interview him, Richard thought, wrinkling his nose in distaste. In fact, the man had been amiable enough. 'Just for the record,' he had said. 'To clear up a few points.' But Richard had distrusted his questions.

Irritated, he had replied, 'Hasn't the doctor told you? I don't remember a damned thing about the accident. I didn't even know there'd been an accident till they told me. The last thing I remember is – ' He had stopped, hearing again the sounds of Julia and David making love in Neil Grantham's bedroom. He passed a hand over his face. 'The last thing I remember is dancing with Celia Manville, and her saying she felt unwell.'

'Ye-es. Memory's a strange thing, of course.' The Inspector had not seemed convinced. 'You've now been informed that Miss Celia Manville was killed in the accident, I know.'

'Yes. They kept it from me initially. I was horrified when they told me.'

'She was your girlfriend?'

'No.' Richard saw no reason to enmesh himself in complex explanations, and volunteered no more. But when the Inspector let the silence grow, he felt compelled to add something. 'We went to the Commem in a party, eight of us,' he said. 'I assume you've interrogated the others?'

'Interrogated? Mr Kent, there's no need to get uptight or worried about this. Yes. I've spoken to everyone concerned, and as far as I can see there'll be no question of prosecuting you, but – '

'Prosecuting *me*?'

'Look, Mr Kent, I'm just making inquiries, as I say. Doing my duty. Every death – even a traffic accident fatality – has to be properly investigated. What's more, Sir Hubert Manville's an important man, as you're aware, and one of his daughters was killed and the other badly injured. You can't expect him not to press for the matter to be taken seriously. And I'll tell you frankly, Mr Kent, though perhaps I shouldn't, Sir Hubert's not very kindly disposed towards you. After all, it's not so long since he lost his son in another kind of accident.'

'He can hardly blame me for that.'

'Certainly not. But for his daughter's death – yes. He does blame you, rightly or wrongly. You were driving the car, Mr Kent. I'm sure you must blame yourself.'

As he reviewed in his mind the conversation with the Inspector, Richard wondered why he found it so disturbing. It was true that he could remember nothing after he had fled from Grantham's rooms, and all he knew about the accident was what his mother had told him. She hadn't blamed him. And, what was more, the Inspector was quite wrong; oddly enough, he didn't blame himself. He had no feeling of guilt whatsoever. Sorrow, yes, of course, naturally. But guilt or responsibility, no.

Richard sighed. As the Inspector said, the mind played strange tricks. The doctors believed that his memory of that morning would probably return to him. Either it would come back slowly and patchily, or perhaps some event or some chance remark would trigger his brain, and everything would become clear at once. Inexplicably Richard felt a tremor of fear. Perhaps it would be better if his memory of those lost hours never returned, he thought. Then he told himself not to be bloody stupid.

He looked about the room, at the flowers and fruit, which his mother kept up to standard – he grinned to himself – and at the collection of 'get well' cards. He had heard from many friends. David had kept in constant touch. Karl and Eva had written and sent gifts. So had Neil Grantham, and even the don Elizabeth, whose last name was something else he failed to recall. But there had been nothing, nothing at all, from Julia – confirmation of what the Thames Valley policeman had said; as a family, the Manvilles were bitter about him.

He was glad when a nurse bustled in, distracting him from his near self-pity. It was time for tea, and he was beginning to enjoy food again, especially now that he was encouraged to dress and sit up in a chair to eat it. Meals were becoming high-spots in his highly regulated monotonous days. And after tea he could look forward to a visit from his stepfather.

Hugh Kent made a practice of dropping in for a few minutes on his way home every evening. He was a solicitor, with a city practice and a wide spectrum of acquaintances, so that he brought news of political life and public affairs – subjects that Richard had once again begun to find interesting. Today Kent arrived earlier than usual, just as Richard was finishing his tea.

'Hello, Richard, and how are you?'

'Pretty good, Dad. Definitely improving.'

'That's great.'

Hugh Kent sat down and put his briefcase on the floor beside him. He was tall and thin, not unlike Richard in appearance, and he was usually taken for Richard's natural father. When, on rare occasions, it became necessary to correct this misconception, he always remarked, I only wish I were,' a sentiment that Richard himself was fully prepared to echo.

'We must get you home soon, Richard,' Kent said.

'The sooner the better as far as I'm concerned.' Richard spoke feelingly. 'I'm tired of this room. I sometimes think my main complaint is hospitalitis. To be home will be wonderful, Dad.'

'Exactly. That's what your mother and I feel, too. And the doctors are in accord.' Kent appeared to hesitate. 'Poppy came in this morning?'

'Ma? Yes, of course. She always does.' Richard was surprised. 'She brought me some roses from the garden, and a couple of books. Why do you ask?'

For answer Kent picked up his briefcase and sat it on his lap. He opened it deliberately, shuffled through the documents inside it, and extracted his office copy of *The Times*. 'I wondered if she'd told you – but clearly she didn't.'

'Told me what?'

Kent leaned forward and passed Richard *The Times*, folded at the Court and Social page. 'There's an announcement in today's paper that will interest you. Perhaps your mother hadn't noticed it.'

Richard took the paper automatically, and as soon as he saw the headline 'Forthcoming Marriages', he knew what he was about to read. 'The engagement is announced between David Windfield of Charlbury, Oxon, and Julia . . .' To Richard's annoyance, tears filled his eyes, and he swallowed hard.

Hugh Kent buried his head in his briefcase for a moment, as if to rearrange its contents. Then he said gently, 'It's not exactly a surprise, is it?'

'No Dad. On the contrary. I was expecting it, but – '

Richard stopped, unable to control the emotion in his voice. He shook his head. He knew his reaction was partly due to weakness, and he found it hard to explain the difference between expecting bad news, and actually seeing it in print.

'I'll have to write and congratulate them,' he said at last. 'Send them a present, I suppose.'

'Of course.' Kent closed his briefcase, leaving Richard the newspaper. 'Incidentally, there's a bit of gossip about Hubert

Manville going the rounds – or perhaps I should say progressing along the corridors of power.'

'Really?' Richard blessed his stepfather for the way he had introduced a tangential subject.

'It's rumoured – mind you, it's no more than a rumour, but it's beginning to carry weight in the London clubs – that Manville's to be offered a senior post in the Shadow Cabinet.'

'That should please him. He's an ambitious man,' Richard said.

'And I'd guess he's likely to fulfil his ambitions – or some of them – if the Conservatives get back in power. I can well imagine him as Foreign Secretary in a few years' time, or – '

Hugh Kent continued to talk, and Richard tried to sound interested, though this evening he found it difficult. His thoughts kept returning to Julia and David.

★

David had stayed in Eva's flat as long as was reasonably possible, but finally he had left, and reluctantly gone home to his mother. He had no intention of remaining there for long. The house, which he had once loved, had become alien to him since his stepfather's death, and it was constantly full of people – lawyers, estate agents, surveyors, men making inventories or valuations. His mother didn't seem to be affected by all this activity; how aptly she was called Hope, he thought. But he himself hated the influx of strangers into what had once been his home – and a home he still considered should rightly belong to him.

He had retreated to his bedroom to write to Richard. It was an impossibly difficult letter, and he had already thrown two attempts into the wastepaper basket. Grimacing, he tried again.

Dear Richard,

Thank you for your letter of congratulations on my engagement to Julia, and for your good wishes. I appreciate them very much.

We intend to get married during the first week in October. I regret to say it's to be a grand affair at St Margaret's, but

131

that's what my in-laws-to-be want and, as they're paying for
it, I can scarcely object.

David stopped writing. This was where he had gone wrong before.
There was no need to tell Richard that the honeymoon was to be a
brief week in Paris, until he was established at the Foreign Office
and due for leave, when Hubert Manville had promised them a trip
to the States. Nor was it necessary to add that Lady Manville was
already looking for a small flat for them or that, before the wedding,
he would be staying at the Manville's town house, and not with
friends of Karl and Eva in Hampstead, as he had intended. He had
no wish to emphasize his good fortune to Richard.
    David recommenced.

    And there's something else I can't object to because, unlike
the idea of a showy wedding, this has Julia's full support. But
I feel very badly about it. I had always assumed that one day
you would be my best man – and vice versa – but it's not to be.
    Richard, there's no way of putting this except bluntly.
Neither Julia nor her parents want you to come to the wedding, and please don't send a present, for they would return
it. The thing is that at the moment they can't forgive you for
Celia's death. I hope in time, as the horror of what happened
fades, they'll change their minds, but until then

Once again David laid down his pen. He stared at the paper in
front of him. 'You bloody hypocrite,' he said aloud. He despised
himself for what he had done. Yet, as he thought of the future,
he couldn't honestly say he wished it undone.
    He dismissed his doubts, as he had done so many times before,
hurriedly completed the letter, signed it and slipped it into an
envelope. He didn't reread what he had written, for he knew that
if he did he might not send it. But he knew too that this was the
best way, the only practical way. There had to be a clean break
with Richard, for Julia's sake as well as his own.

★

132

Richard read David's letter twice, then he slowly tore it into very small pieces. He tossed them into the air, and let them fall on the bed and the floor. If only the paper had been multi-coloured, he thought cynically, the letter would appropriately enough have turned into confetti.

A nurse came into the room. 'Why, Mr Kent,' she said, 'what a mess you've made. Why did you do that, when here I am bringing you lots of good news?'

'You are, nurse? I don't believe it – not today.'

'Believe it or not, it's true. First, you're to be allowed home at the end of the week.'

'I am?' Richard's face lit up. 'That's splendid! Really good news.'

'Also a Mr Neil Grantham phoned to ask if he might come in and see you in about an hour's time. Matron said there was no objection, if you don't mind.'

'Neil. Of course I don't mind. That's great! I shall get up to receive him.'

And when Grantham arrived, Richard was dressed and sitting in an armchair. He still looked pale and drawn, but he was reasonably cheerful. The nurse had cleared up the scattered pieces of paper, and the thought of being home by the weekend had helped to ease the pain of David's letter. Richard was pleased to see Grantham, who was his first non-medical visitor, apart from family and the police inspector, and he greeted him warmly.

'It's super to see you, Richard,' Grantham responded. 'I'd have come before, but you've been very sheltered. Visitors weren't encouraged, apparently.'

'No, the theory was that, while my body healed, peace and quiet would be best for my mind.'

'How is your memory, if I'm permitted to ask?'

'Fine, in some ways. You needn't worry that I've forgotten any of my history, for instance.' Richard grinned. Then he went on. 'The main thing is this wretched gap from towards the end of the Commem till the time I arrived in hospital.'

'I see.' Grantham, who had been sprawled in a chair opposite Richard, got to his feet and started to prowl about the small

133

hospital room. 'I had a talk with your mother before I came here,' he said abruptly.

'With Poppy?' Richard was mildly surprised. 'Why?'

'It's to do with Sir Hubert Manville. He feels very bitter about the accident, Richard, and – '

'He's not the only one!' Richard interrupted. 'Julia feels the same, and this morning I had a letter from David making it clear that now he's marrying into the family it's the end of our long and beautiful relationship.'

'Damn the lot of them!' Grantham said angrily. 'Hell, it was an accident! You weren't tight! You'd not been smoking pot. And I'd be prepared to swear you weren't the kind of chap to play the fool, not when you were driving a car. For Christ's sake, you were nearly killed yourself. Look, even the police and the coroner called it an accident. "Death by misadventure" – you know the verdict as well as I do.'

'Forget it, Neil, it's over, done with.' Richard had no wish to rehash the affair.

'Not completely.'

'What do you mean?'

'Richard, I'm most terribly sorry, but the College has withdrawn its offer of a Fellowship – at least for the present. Perhaps in a year or so's time – ' Grantham shrugged.

'But – but why? I don't understand.'

'It's Manville, of course. Dear Sir Hubert Manville. He's an influential man, Richard, and he's got important friends, including the Vice-Chancellor of the University, and the President of the College. The argument is that you've shown yourself to be irresponsible.'

'That's absurd,' Richard hesitated. 'At least, I suppose it is.'

'Of course it is. Everyone knows it is, but that doesn't alter the position. Richard, I did my best for you. Believe me, I did. I pointed to your absolutely wonderful degree. I said the College would regret its decision. I said that if they didn't want you there were plenty of others who would.'

'Do you really think that's true? With Manville on the warpath?'

'Yes. I *know* it is. Listen.'

Richard listened because he had no choice. At first almost resentful, his interest quickened as Neil Grantham proceeded, producing not only suggestions, but practical possibilities. He was touched by the efforts that Neil had been making, and impressed by the number of people he had approached.

'I expect you know that Karl's going to teach at Bonn University next term. It's my belief that he'd like to get into the foreign service of the Federal Republic eventually, but that's another matter,' Grantham continued. 'He told me he's sure that with your degree you could get a post there. And of course there are always openings at American and Canadian universities.'

Richard was shaking his head. 'No. I don't think – '

'I appreciate you don't want to go abroad because of your mother, but – '

'My mother?' Richard frowned.

'Well, that's why you turned down the Foreign Office, wasn't it?'

Richard sighed. 'Yes, of course. I'm sorry, Neil. I get tired, and that's when I forget bits of trivia. It'll be a while before I'm completely fit again, I'm afraid, and that rules out any job in the immediate future.'

'But it doesn't hurt to consider the situation, Richard.'

'Certainly not, and I'm most grateful for all your efforts on my behalf, Neil. Truly grateful. And at the moment I think the BBC sounds the most interesting.'

'I thought you might favour that. I'll put some pressure on my contacts. But now I'll be off. Goodbye. See you soon.'

Alone, Richard was suddenly overwhelmed by fatigue. He lay down on his bed in his clothes, and was asleep immediately. He dreamed that it was his first day at school, and he had just met David. In his dream Julia was there, too, and they began to fight over her. David was about to kill him when he awoke, sweating and terrified.

PART THREE

The Eighties

14

Paris, Spring 198–

Julia Windfield sat in front of her dressing-table and studied herself critically in the mirror. She knew she was still a most attractive woman; some would have called her beautiful. Her bone structure was good, and that would last into her old age. Her corn-coloured hair, thanks to an excellent Parisian *coiffeur*, was as bright as ever. Her unusual blue-grey eyes had remained unfaded, and could still be described as violet. But, for all its normal vivacity, her face in repose was often sad.

She noted the tiny lines that ran from her nose to the corners of her mouth with its downward droop. In spite of my appearance I'm getting old, she thought, but surely forty-one wasn't so old, scarcely middle-age in fact. She squared her shoulders and lifted her arms to fasten a pearl choker behind her head, causing her small breasts to stretch the satin of the slip she was wearing. At least her neck showed no signs of age, and she had kept her figure, for which she was grateful. She smiled at her reflection, and immediately looked five or ten years younger.

She turned as her husband came into their bedroom from his dressing-room next door. David had put on weight since his Oxford days, but the extra bulk suited him, making him look more mature and dependable, as did the slight greying at the temples. She sometimes wondered if the hair was altogether natural or was touched up by his barber – just like hers. But it was typical of their relationship that she had never asked him.

'Hello,' Julia said.

'Hello, darling.'

David was already dressed. He was wearing his second-best dinner jacket, but he was immaculate, his midnight blue cummerbund matching his perfectly tied tie. As always, he was prepared

– consciously – to make an impression, Julia thought, and at once blamed herself for being critical. After all, for a senior career diplomat – a Counsellor like David – it was an important element in the game to look the part.

'You're wearing green tonight?' David glanced at the long dress that lay on the bed.

'Yes. Don't you think it suitable?'

'It's fine. But why pearls, instead of your emerald necklace?'

Julia bit her tongue to stop the sharp retort that rose to her lips. David's almost military habit, which dated from their posting to Paris a year ago, of inspecting and approving or disapproving what she wore, irritated her immensely. One day, she promised herself she'd turn up in jeans at some official reception, and shock him; but she knew she'd never keep the promise.

She said coldly, 'I'm not wearing the emeralds because we're giving a small, not very formal dinner party, and they'd be extremely ostentatious.'

'Nonsense. Apart from the others, Karl and Eva would love to see them. They've never had a chance before.'

'Obviously not, as we haven't met since Grandma Manville died.' Julia spoke deliberately, knowing that it would annoy David to be reminded that she had inherited from her own family almost all the jewellery she possessed.

'Quite.' David went to a mirror and fiddled unnecessarily with his tie. Then, ignoring his wife's last remark, he said. 'Do wear the emeralds, Julia. They suit you so wonderfully.'

'As you wish.' She really didn't care enough to argue further about such a triviality.

David fetched the necklace, while she took off the pearls. She allowed him to fasten the emeralds for her, and he bent to kiss her bare shoulder.

'You're looking beautiful tonight, darling,' he said.

'Let's hope Karl and Eva agree with you.' Julia was sardonic. But at once she thought, I'm being a bitch. If he wants to impress the Fischers, why shouldn't he? To change the subject, she said, 'You know, I still find it strange to think of Karl and Eva as a married couple.'

David laughed. 'So do I, after they've been lovers on and off for ages. But I suppose lots of such couples marry eventually. Besides, it's probably good for his career. The FRG has had its share of homosexual personnel problems in the past, in all departments of government, and from the highest to the lowest ranks. Long-time bachelors tend to raise doubts in their masters' minds.'

'I hardly think that's an adequate reason for marrying.' Julia stepped into her dress and David did up the back zip. 'Really, David, why did they bother? They're way into their forties, so it's too late for them to think of children.'

'I doubt if they ever wanted any. These days many people don't, you know, darling.'

Julia bit her tongue again. She resented David's patronizing tone. David himself hadn't wanted children, not even a son as most men seemed to. 'Why should I?' he'd said bitterly once. 'To give him my stepfather's name?'

'Your stepfather's name?' Julia had replied angrily. 'You were happy enough to make *me* Mrs Windfield.' For once she had been determined, and the result had been Rosemary.

Julia loved her daughter dearly, though she tried hard to avoid being a doting and possessive mother. If Rosemary was spoiled it was by her grandfather. Sir Hubert Manville was now Her Britannic Majesty's Secretary of State for Foreign Affairs, and an extremely busy man. But he always found time for his sixteen-year-old granddaughter, perhaps because Rosemary had come to bear a striking resemblance to her dead aunt Celia, who had always been Sir Hubert's favourite among his children.

Julia said, 'We'll have to decide about Rosemary's half-term soon. She wants to come to us here in Paris. Why not let her?'

'For a simple reason that you well know. Her half-term happens to coincide with the Western Summit Conference. It's a terribly important week of international talks at the highest level. The PM's coming over, and I shall be dancing attendance upon your father, and up to my eyes in work. You'll be busy entertaining and being entertained. Frankly, Rosemary would be a nuisance at such a time.'

'Well, where is she to go? To your mother, who wouldn't want her? Mine will be here with father.' Julia carefully spaced the last words of the last sentence.

'I'm aware of that. For God's sake, Julia, Rosemary has plenty of school-friends she could go to, or there are your cousins. It's only a half-term break, not one of the long holidays.'

'She'll be disappointed all the same, especially as her grand-parents will be in Paris.'

'Too bad!' David was impatient. He glanced quickly at his watch. 'Are you ready? Our guests are due in about fifteen minutes.'

'Yes, I'm ready, David.' Julia suppressed a sigh. She would try again, choose a better moment; it was a shame to disappoint Rosemary when it really wasn't necessary. 'Shall we go down?'

★

On David's posting to Paris the Windfields had rented a house near the Bois de Boulogne on the rue de Longchamp in Neuilly. It had been Julia's choice and it was in a fashionable area, but David constantly complained that it was a long way from the British Embassy; he maintained that he would have preferred to live in the *Seizième Arrondissement*. But again Julia had been adamant. When she first saw it, she had fallen in love with the house. It stood somewhat back from the street behind a small forecourt, concealed by high metal railings blanked out in typi-cally French fashion with black metal plates. The railings were pierced by a single entrance – double gates, also blanked, giving on to a short drive which led to an imposing front door and an integral garage. Julia had been determined to live there.

In fact, the place was too large for them and, had it not been for Julia's money, too expensive. Inside, it reminded her of a town house the Manvilles had lived in when she and Peregrine and Celia had been children. The rooms were elegant and spacious and excellent for entertaining – an occupation that went with David's job, and which on the whole Julia enjoyed.

The long salon with windows at either end, curtains now drawn against the darkness, always gave her pleasure, and this evening, with bowls of early spring flowers everywhere, it was particularly pleasing. Julia looked about her with approval. The furniture was not theirs, but they had brought with them a wide variety of personal possessions – books, pictures, including a Stubbs of which she was very fond, and some *objets d'art*. With these, the room, indeed, the whole house, looked happily familiar.

'Will you have a drink before our guests turn up?' David asked.

'No, thanks. They'll be here in a minute or two.'

David went to a side table on which was laid out an array of bottles and glasses. Back turned to Julia, he helped himself to a strong whisky and drank it neat before pouring another, which he diluted with the merest splash of soda. Wandering around the room, rearranging a bowl of freesias, Julia saw David's action reflected in the glass covering a Scottie Wilson abstract. She made no comment, but she wondered why David should be so much on edge as to need two drinks in rapid succession before what was, after all, a quite ordinary dinner party.

The doorbell rang. They heard the manservant – as usual, hired for the evening – go to answer it, and voices in the hall. Moments later Karl and Eva were in the salon. Julia found herself enveloped in a huge bear-hug as Karl embraced her.

'Ah, *Liebling*, how super to see you again.' He held her at arms' length away from him. 'You are more beautiful than ever. David must be a good husband.'

Karl laughed aloud, and Julia did her best to respond to his compliments. She was surprised to find that this required an effort on her part. She'd known Karl and his ability to clown for decades, but this evening his greeting had sounded over-exuberant and therefore somehow false. She glanced at David, also laughing as he kissed Eva enthusiastically. Julia told herself not to be stupid; the four of them were old friends, and they hadn't met for at least a couple of years. All these actions and reactions were quite natural. It was she who was out of tune with the occasion.

She forced herself to make an effort, and kissed Eva warmly in turn. 'It's wonderful to see you. How are you? You look marvellous. Marriage clearly suits you.'

They started to gossip, but David interrupted them. 'Look, I'm sorry. I'm afraid this is going to be a bit of a party, when it

143

should have been just us, but there are people I've got to entertain. You must stay behind after the others have gone and then we can catch up on all our news.'

'Sure, that'll be fine,' Karl said. 'Who are the others?'

David replied, 'A French couple. A professor of politics from the Sorbonne and his rather mousy wife. She's some kind of researcher, but he has a great deal of influence in important quarters. What's more, they're friends of Neil Grantham. Then there's a British economist on the staff of OECD – the Organization for Economic Co-operation and Development – with whom I must make a more personal contact before next month. His wife's a great, jolly character. And to make ten we've invited the Military Attaché from our Embassy, with his wife.'

'It sounds an interesting collection,' Karl said. 'Incidentally, do you know how Neil is? We've not heard from him since a card at Christmas.'

David shrugged. 'Neither have we. I'm afraid we've rather lost touch. But I'm sure he's flourishing.'

'I suppose you know – ' Eva began.

She stopped as the doorbell rang, as if what she had been about to say was of minor importance. Julia went into the hall to greet the rest of the guests, who had all arrived at the same moment. There were introductions where necessary, and especially to Karl and Eva. The manservant brought in the champagne. The conversation became animated, as people renewed acquaintance-ships, or began to learn about each other. It was a typical prelude to such a dinner party.

Normally Julia would have enjoyed it, but this evening she felt dull and listless. A headache was stirring, and she found she had to force herself to concentrate on what was being said. Her mind kept sliding back to her Oxford days, when she had first met Karl and Eva. Perhaps it was their presence, or the fact that the Sorbonne professor referred several times to Neil Grantham, that made her think of that last tragic Trinity term, of herself and Celia, of David – and of Richard.

'Richard?' she said aloud, startled. 'You mean Richard Kent?'

'Yes,' said the professor, looking mildly surprised. 'I was

144

saying that he and your husband must have been contemporaries at Oxford.'

'We were,' David agreed. 'And Julia was there too. Richard and I were both pupils of Neil's, and so was Peregrine Manville, Julia's brother, though he was a year ahead of the rest of us.'

'Ah, a brilliant man,' the professor commented.

'Yes.' David shook his head sadly. 'Poor Peregrine. His death was a tragedy. Undoubtedly he'd have got to the top of any tree he'd chosen to climb.'

'Actually – ' The professor was embarrassed. 'I – er – I was referring to Richard Kent.'

David was amused. 'Oh, neither he – nor I – was in the same class as Peregrine.'

'I'm not sure that's true of Richard,' Julia said, but so softly that the remark passed unnoticed.

The economist from OECD joined in the conversation. 'Kent's a political pundit now, of course – though with a capital "P" in his case, I admit. But they're all alike. Personally I distrust the lot of them. They pick up unconsidered trifles in the House or one of the London clubs – White's or the Reform or somewhere – and half the time they get hold of the wrong end of the stick. Er – I expect it's the same here in Paris,' he finished rather lamely.

'That certainly doesn't apply to Richard Kent.' The French professor was curt; he had begun to dislike the Englishman. 'I'm a political scientist and I specialize in European affairs. I have to keep in close touch with the British press and British commentators. Kent is very rarely wrong, and his analyses of current affairs are excellent. I'm not just discussing his television programmes, either. He's written some splendid books – and not merely popularizations. Some have been serious and highly respected academic studies. Don't you agree, David?'

'Splendid! Yes, indeed!' David was at his most urbane. 'But from my point of view decidedly left-wing. It seems to me he too often writes like a communist apologist.'

'You astound me! With all respect, in my opinion, I consider Richard Kent and his work extremely well-balanced.' The professor was obviously getting angry.

At last the Military Attaché had something to say. He came to the support of David. 'Personally, I can't stand this chap Kent,' he remarked bluntly. 'He always sounds too damned knowledgeable. One wonders who he's been pumping for information. And I suspect that if anyone wants to leak something in London – '

Eva glanced at Julia and intervened quickly, to avert disaster before the professor had time to put his expression into words. 'I was just about to ask Julia and David if they knew that Richard Kent was in Paris? We met him by chance in the rue de Rivoli the other day.'

David showed no surprise. 'He comes over occasionally, I know. I used to run into him at meetings and briefings in London – Julia met him there a few times, too – and I've caught sight of him now and then in Paris in the past year. I imagine he's here at the moment to set up coverage of next month's Summit Conference.'

'In a way, just like me,' Karl said cheerfully. 'But while I'll be preparing the ground for my Minister, Richard'll be preparing the ground for his interviews and commentaries, and getting material for articles – possibly for a chapter in a new book.'

But the professor had remained preoccupied with Richard Kent's supposed political leanings. He said, 'I did hear that he turned down the offer of a knighthood. Is that one of the reasons you think he's left-wing, David?'

'A knighthood? That was merely a rumour.' Once again, David seemed amused. Then the acid showed. 'Probably started by Richard himself. It would be good for his public image.'

Eva said quickly, 'Knighthood or not, I'm damned sure Richard's no communist. Liberalism's much more in his line.'

'In any case, he's a most attractive man.' The Military Attaché's wife, a brunette with little to say, commented. 'Every time I catch sight of him on the box, I wonder why he's remained single. Personally – '

'I quite agree,' interrupted the wife of the economist, a large lady who was a child psychologist. She spoke with enthusiasm. 'Like you, I can't imagine why he's never married. Perhaps he's too choosy, or perhaps he set his heart on a fair damozel and for some reason couldn't claim her.'

'Perhaps he's just got too much sense,' the economist said gloomily, filling a sudden silence.

There was mild laughter at his wife's expense. And to Julia's intense relief the manservant came in to announce that dinner was served. The subject of Richard Kent was temporarily abandoned.

★

The guests, with the exception of Karl and Eva, said their goodbyes shortly before midnight. By then Julia's threatening headache had materialized. Her temples throbbed steadily and she felt slightly sick. She yearned to go to bed, but knew that David would be angry if she suggested it before Karl and Eva left.

However, she did make an excuse to run up to the bedroom where she took a couple of paracetamol tablets and bathed her head with cold water. When she returned to the salon she hesitated outside the door and heard Karl speaking, quietly, but earnestly and with authority. She thought she heard Richard's name mentioned, but Karl stopped abruptly as she entered the room, and the odd silence that greeted her arrival made her aware that she had interrupted a conversation that was not intended for her ears. It was a curiously embarrassing situation.

'Ah, Julia,' said Eva. 'We were just talking about Richard, and David was – '

'I was saying we must have a kind of reunion,' said David. 'If Richard's in Paris for any length of time, we really should entertain him. A party with him and Karl and Eva would be fun, don't you think, darling?'

'Yes, of course.'

Julia spoke automatically, concealing her surprise. She was quite aware of David's occasional casual meetings with Richard, and knew there had been opportunities in the past when it would have been a pleasant gesture to invite Richard to their house – either in London or in Paris. She had even suggested such a move once or twice, but David had always objected. To renew such a close friendship once it had been severed was impossible, he had

147

said. What he had not said, but she had guessed, was that he had no intention or desire to get to know Richard again, however casually. Yet now he suddenly seemed to have changed his mind.

Julia suppressed a sigh. She failed to understand David. He was inconsistent and secretive; she knew that when it suited him he lied to her. Recently he had grown worse. Sometimes she wondered if he still loved her – she suspected he wasn't always faithful – or, for that matter, if she still loved him. But wondering about David was a useless exercise at any time – especially tonight, when her head ached and she needed to give attention to Karl and Eva.

'Sorry, Eva,' she excused herself. 'What were you saying?'

15

Except at weekends Julia and David breakfasted separately. He liked to leave for the office early, to read the overnight telegrams, to get some work done before the phone started to ring or the Ambassador, His Excellency Sir George Fauvic, demanded his presence at the double. Julia had no such urgent reasons for leaving the comfort of her bed. Their Algerian *femme de ménage* would let herself into the house, and start work without supervision. But Julia had not been brought up to pamper herself; a Scottish nanny, boarding school and punctilious parents had seen to that. She usually got up as soon as David left.

The day after their dinner party David, having already breakfasted, came into the bedroom to say goodbye. Julia, propped up with pillows, was drinking her early-morning tea, and reading *Le Monde*. Her headache and the malaise of the previous evening had disappeared.

'I'll try to get back by six tonight,' David said. 'You remember we're dining at the Residence?'

Julia nodded. 'I've a lunch date, too. At this rate, I'll have to start watching my weight.'

David laughed. 'It's one of the penalties of the diplomatic life, darling, as you should know by now. Luckily you seem to keep your figure without any great effort.'

He sounded in a good humour, and Julia said, 'I shall be writing to Rosemary, about her half-term break. Shall I give her your love?'

'Of course. Tell her I'm having to work like hell to prepare for this damned Summit, so she can't expect to hear from me. And Julia – '

'Yes?' There was something about David's tone that made her glance at him inquiringly.

'Tell her we're looking forward to having her here in Paris for the half-term.'

'Oh, David! You've changed your mind? Yesterday – '

'Well, she wants to come, and you want her to come.' He shrugged. 'But you'll have to cope with her, Julia. I really will be enormously pushed.'

'Of coure I'll cope.'

'Right. See you tonight then.'

With a blown kiss and a wave of his hand, David went. Julia finished her tea, had a quick shower and dressed, before going down to the small sitting-room, where the *femme de ménage* brought her the usual tray with orange juice, toast and coffee. She would have liked to telephone Rosemary, but she knew the school wouldn't approve. So, as soon as she'd finished her breakfast, she settled down to write to her daughter.

'. . . and good news, darling! You're to come to Paris for the half-term. Daddy and I will be very busy, but I'll try to arrange some entertaining things for you to do.'

Julia stopped. She'd have to check with David's schedule and her own before suggesting anything definite or specific, otherwise Rosemary would take the suggestion as a promise and might be hurt if it were broken. It wasn't going to be an easy few days, Julia thought half-resentfully, with the conflicting demands of Rosemary, her own parents – in both their private and public capacities – and David, who could be bloody-minded on such stressful occasions.

No. No promises, she decided, and cut the letter short with expressions of good wishes for various school events, and lots of love from David and herself.

★

It was half-past ten when Julia left the house. One of the advantages of living in the middle of the rue de Longchamp was proximity to the Bois, and she tried to make a practice of going for a walk there every day, regardless of the weather. This morning it was fine and bright, and she was looking forward to her outing.

She set off briskly, sniffing appreciatively at the smell of freshly-baked bread as she passed the *boulangerie* in the Place de Bagatelle, and smiling to herself at the old men sitting outside a café enjoying their coffees and *fines*. One of the most ancient lifted his cup to her and winked, which made her laugh. She cut across past the church on the Avenue de Bretteville and, crossing the Avenue de Commandant Charcot, was under the chestnut trees of the Bois.

She hadn't noticed the blue Renault parked fifty yards along the road from her house. As she came out of the gate the driver had started the engine and driven slowly after her. Now he was lucky enough to find a space for his car and, striding fast, he dodged through the trees and, as she reached the small lake known as the Mare Saint James, came out of a side path to meet her.

'Julia! What a pleasant surprise.'

'Richard. How – how nice to see you.'

Julia's mouth suddenly became dry, and she licked her lips. Eva had said Richard was in Paris, but she had had no expectation of meeting him like this, casually, in the Bois, in mid-morning. It was almost like an assignation.

'How are you, Julia?' Richard had turned and was walking beside her. 'You're looking well.'

The conventional, meaningless greeting annoyed Julia. She made no response and, when Richard asked after Rosemary and David, gave only brief answers. They strolled on together. Glancing sideways at Richard, Julia thought that her guests of last night had been right; Richard *was* an attractive man, perhaps more attractive now than when he had been young and an undergraduate. However, there was an air of amused detachment about him that she found hard to define, but which was nevertheless disconcerting.

She said, 'The Fischers told us you were in Paris, presumably for the Conference next month, which is why Karl's here, of course.'

151

'The Fischers? Karl and Eva?' Richard sounded mildly surprised.

'Yes. Eva said you bumped into them on the rue de Rivoli.'

'I did? I seem to make a habit of bumping into people, don't I? First the Fischers, and now you, Julia. And there was David in Bonn, a few weeks ago.'

'David? In Bonn?' Julia stopped walking, forcing Richard to stop too. She turned to face him. 'Would that be at the beginning of last month?'

'Yes. Didn't he tell you he'd met me? Actually it was in the Hofgarten. I was on my way from the University – '

'No, he didn't mention meeting you.'

Because she didn't want Richard to see her distress Julia started to walk again. David hadn't told her that he had met Richard in Bonn. How could he, when that week he was meant to be in Vienna? He'd lied to her. But why? Why bother to deceive her, unless – what she'd like to have known was if he'd been alone in the Hofgarten. But she was too proud to ask Richard the crucial question – Richard, who would immediately make the right deductions.

Richard broke the heavy silence that had fallen between them. 'Julia, I was wondering if you'd have lunch with me today, if you're not doing anything better?'

'Lunch, today?' Julia gathered her thoughts. 'No, I'm sorry. I can't.'

'Beause you don't want to? Or because you *are* doing something better?'

'Neither. I've got to attend a ladies' luncheon. Duty, that's all. I must be there.'

'What about tomorrow, then? I know an excellent little restaurant on the Île de la Cité. It's called *La Perdrix d'Or*. Please come, Julia.'

'It's rather a long way, and I'm not sure – ' Julia began to make excuses.

'I'll pick you up. Twelve o'clock. Okay?'

He didn't wait for a reply. He glanced at his watch, said he must be off, grinned at her, and went striding away. Julia watched him go. She felt oddly shaken, though she knew her feelings were absurd. On the very few occasions she and Richard had met over the years since the accident, their relationship had inevitably been that of casual acquaintances, who had once known each other rather well. It was, she thought bitterly, rather like a couple who had had a civilized divorced, except that she and Richard had never been married – never been lovers, even.

Not until she was putting her key into the lock of the house on the rue de Longchamp did she remember that she hadn't told Richard where she lived. Neither did she know how to get in touch with him.

★

This particular ladies' luncheon was being given by the wife of the First Secretary for Trade, who also lived in Neuilly, but off the Avenue du Roule, on the far side of the wide Avenue Charles de Gaulle – once the Avenue de Neuilly, and still called so by most of the residents of the area.

As she was unsure precisely where off the Avenue du Roule the First Secretary for Trade and his family lived, Julia picked up a taxi at the top of the rue de Longchamp. It was but a short trip, and she found that she was early for the luncheon, so she stood on the steps of the apartment block and surveyed the tree-lined street. As she did so she became aware of another taxi stopping a few hundred yards further along the road, and disgorging a young man of nondescript appearance. She had the distinct impression that she had seen him once or twice before in the past few days, perhaps during her shopping expeditions or walking in the Bois.

Shrugging her shoulders, Julia pressed the bell marked with the First Secretary's name and received an answering buzz. Once inside, she found that the luncheon was typical and as boring as she had expected. In her view, the diplomatic wives saw as much as they wanted of each other at official functions, without giving unnecessary parties, where conversation usually centred around children, domestic help or the lack of it, holidays and the latest cost of living survey. At least the last subject had some point, because their allowances depended on it. In the end, Julia made

153

the excuse of a non-existent appointment with her hairdresser, and left as soon as was decently possible.

It was a pleasant afternoon and Julia, now knowing the way, decided to walk home. She set off in the direction of the Avenue du Roule and, remembering her earliest impression, made a point of keeping a wary eye out for the man she had noticed earlier. Glancing back as she turned a corner, she had her suspicions strengthened. There he was again, about forty yards behind her, on the other side of the road. A little scared, she began to hurry to reach the more populated Avenue Charles de Gaulle. So did the man.

Once on the Avenue she wondered what action to take, and realized that she was only a few yards from L'Église St-Jean Baptiste. She turned into it quickly. At least this move would decide, one way or another, if he really were following her.

It was an unpretentious church and normally she wouldn't have bothered to visit it. But it was scrupulously clean and the smell of polish mingled pleasantly with that of stale incense. There were fresh flowers on the altar, and none of the candles before the various ornate statues had been allowed to gutter into a mess of wax. Clearly L'Église St-Jean Baptiste was well loved and cared for.

Julia sat down in the rearmost pew, close to the single entrance. Although it was mid-afternoon she was not alone in the church. An elderly lady in the funeral garb of a First World War widow – clothes which, even in the eighties, were not uncommon in France, a country which remembered its wars with intense feeling as if they had happened yesterday – knelt before a statue of the Virgin Mary. A priest, in long black soutane, came and inspected the red lamp that shone above the sacristy, and then went into one of the confessionals. A young girl was lighting a candle to a saint whom Julia didn't recognize.

Julia heard the door of the church sigh open and close. She tensed as she heard steps hesitate, and then the man came and sat immediately in front of her. As he knelt and buried his head in his hands, ostensibly to pray, she was able to inspect him more closely. He was in his thirties, of moderate build and with light-brown hair; he was essentially unmemorable, but Julia was able to notice one distinguishing mark – the top of his right ear was missing.

By this time Julia had begun to realize her vulnerability, and the briefing on security that all Embassy staff and their families had received came flooding back. Her heart began to pound, and she felt she needed reassurance. Breathing rather fast, she again looked round the church.

The elderly widow hadn't moved from before the statue of the Virgin. The young girl had lit her candle and was talking to the priest, who had emerged from the confessional. Julia wondered what they would do if she suddenly screamed and, when they came running to her, told them that the man in the pew in front had been following her for days. She realized that she could guess their reactions.

The man, of course, would deny the accusation, if he did not hastily disappear. The priest and the others would be kind, terribly kind. They would offer to send for her husband or a friend, or to put her in a taxi. The young girl might be prepared to see her back to her house on the rue de Longchamp. But they wouldn't believe her. They'd think she was hysterical, demanding attention. And when she'd gone they'd shake their heads, and agree that women of a certain age were apt to behave strangely.

Julia stood up, unconsciously squared her shoulders and walked out of the church. As far as she could tell there was no immediate sign of movement in the pew in front and luck was with her. As the church door closed behind her a taxi drew up in the traffic. She grabbed it, apologized for the brief journey, and was home on the rue de Longchamp in a very few minutes. Once safely behind her own front door, she was able to relax. The whole thing was stupid, she told herself at last. In retrospect, her suspicions seemed exaggerated. Maybe the whole thing had been coincidence. Maybe, she thought, he had even been attracted by her. Certainly he had made no move to accost or molest her in any way. The best thing for her to do was await developments, if any.

She decided not to worry David with the incident, and she didn't mention it to him when he came home. Neither did she mention her meeting with Richard.

16

Richard arrived punctually at noon. Julia was ready; she had considered her tactics and decided not to keep him waiting. In the same corduroy suit she had worn the previous day, she greeted him in the salon, and offered him her hand.

'This is very kind of you, Richard.'

'My pleasure, Julia,' he said, mocking her formality. 'It's very kind of you to accept.'

'Not at all.'

But she couldn't keep it up. She had to laugh.

'Where are you parked, Richard?'

'Just outside.'

Today Richard Kent wasn't driving a blue Renault, but a grey Mercedes with English licence plates. As he opened the door for her to get into the front seat she realized that the last time she had been in a car with him was that frightful morning when Celia was killed. She was sure Richard must be remembering the same thing, and she waited for him to comment. But he said nothing.

As they turned off the rue de Longchamp into the service road and a few moments later into the fast stream of traffic on the Avenue Charles de Gaulle and headed towards the Arc de Triomphe, Julia found that she was gripping the sides of her bucket seat, her body taut. She made herself relax, hoping that Richard hadn't noticed and, as a distraction, told him about the man who had seemingly followed her yesterday. To her surprise, Richard neither laughed nor treated the incident with scorn. On the contrary, he appeared most interested. He asked her to describe the individual, and she tried, though without great success. The man, in fact, had been nondescript, though she did remember the missing top of his right ear.

Richard seized on this.

'Are you sure it was the *right* ear?'

'Yes, I'm sure, but I can't see what difference it makes. You don't know anyone it could have been, do you?'

'No, certainly not.' Richard's denial was swift, and he continued quickly, 'Have you ever seen this chap before, noticed him following you or hanging round your house?'

'I've thought about that, and I'm not really sure. I had the impression I might have. But he really was a most unnoticeable little man.'

'Mmm. Probably a crank.' Richard was thoughtful. 'What did David have to say about all this?'

'I – er – I never told him. I – I was afraid it might worry him.'

Richard made no comment, though her excuse of concern for David was obviously forced. He concentrated on the heavy traffic as he edged the Mercedes around the Place de la Concorde, then drove along the Quais beside the Seine. In typically Parisian erratic bursts of speed and halting they reached the Place du Châtelet and turned right over the Pont au Change into the old heart of Paris. Julia's nervousness at being driven by Richard had by now completely dissipated, and she was beginning to enjoy herself.

'There's only one problem about going to *La Perdrix d'Or*,' Richard said as they bumped over the cobbles on the Île de la Cité, 'and that's finding somewhere to park in these narrow streets. But maybe we'll be lucky.'

In the event, after searching for five minutes, Julia spotted a slot in the rue du Cloître beside Notre-Dame. Beating a Fiat to it, Richard managed to park neatly. The car disposed of, they turned into a still narrower street, the rue Chanoinesse. Here they had to push their way through the locals hurrying home to lunch with long loaves of bread in their hands, past leisurely tourists with their cameras and shop-keepers putting up their shutters in preparation for their afternoon siesta. The air was a mixture of petrol fumes and the smell of good French cooking.

Richard said, 'Did you know that Abélard and Héloïse once walked along here?'

Julia shook her head. Richard had taken her by the elbow to

guide her, and she was conscious of the pressure of his hand. But it was only a minute before they reached the restaurant.

La Perdrix d'Or was painted brown and gold. From the outside it appeared chic, but shut, its windows heavily curtained so that a mere glow of light could be seen from the street. Inside brown and gold remained the dominant colours, even to the enormous menu with a partridge on the cover. The head waiter, who greeted Richard by name, led them to a corner table, and at once a bottle of champagne was produced in its bucket of ice. The cork was eased out, the wine tasted and poured. Julia watched, smiling.

'Richard, is this a celebration?'

'Yes. For me it is. I know we've seen each other occasionally over the years, Julia, but only infrequently and then on more or less formal occasions. Today, however, you're here, sitting opposite me, prepared to have lunch with me, when there's absolutely no pressure on you to do so. If this means anything at all, it means you must have forgiven me.'

'For Celia's death?' Julia understood at once. She looked down at her hands clasped in her lap. She said, 'I was quite badly injured at the time, and it was a dreadful shock when my mother told me Celia had been killed. My parents blamed you. My father was especially bitter. Richard, I didn't remember much about it; I didn't even remember that you'd been driving. I thought – but – it's all old history.'

Her voice trailed away. She was sorry now that Richard had mentioned the accident. It was impossible to explain what she had felt at the time, the horror of it, her father's attitude, her fear that Richard, too, might die. She had been ill and in pain, and she had done and said what was expected of her. Then she had married David. She was Mrs David Windfield.

Holding up her glass of champagne to him she said, 'I'm glad we're – friends again, Richard. I hope you'll come and have dinner with us before you leave Paris. David was saying we must make up a party – with Karl and Eva Fischer.'

For a moment Richard regarded her with a strange expression that she failed to understand. It was almost derisive, and certainly not entirely friendly. But at last he lifted his glass to toast her.

'Bless you, Julia. I shall look forward to dining with you and David and the Fischers.'

Julia buried her face behind the large menu, and asked Richard what he would recommend. He suggested onion soup, for which the restaurant was famous, veal stuffed with mushrooms and truffles, and a green salad, followed by crêpes and coffee.

While they waited for their first course to appear Richard said, 'I've been thinking about that chap who seemed to be following you. If you take my advice, you'll forget the whole thing. Accept that it's just one of those inexplicable incidents that can happen to anyone.'

'It's not as easy – ' Julia began.

'Ah, here's our soup.'

The waiter's interruption had clearly been so welcome to Richard that Julia was at a loss. After all, Richard had himself raised the subject of the incident, which had clearly interested, if not upset him, though he was trying hard not to show it. Or was she being over-sensitive? Had she imagined his attitude?

Richard began to talk about his work for the media, his books, his travels. He made it sound interesting and entertaining. Julia listened, asking occasional questions. The champagne, the excellent food, the ambiance of quiet luxury – and Richard himself – all served to dispel the disquiet she had felt.

Then, as they were eating their crêpes, Richard again seemed intentionally to strike a discordant note. 'Julia, are you happy?' he asked, out of the blue, and when she didn't answer immediately, he added, 'Is your life what you hoped for?'

Thankful for the addition to the first blunt question, Julia said, 'More or less. Much more than less. On the whole I enjoy the diplomatic round. The parties can pall, but I enjoy meeting different people, living in different countries. Rosemary would be in boarding school by now anyway, so our unsettled existence makes no difference to her. And as I've no particular talent and never wanted a career, I don't feel in the least thwarted.' Julia laughed. 'I must seem extremely old-fashioned to you, Richard.'

Richard's smile was wry. 'I wouldn't call you old-fashioned, my dear Julia. I'd use the word "defensive". Incidentally, how's your marriage?'

It was a moment before Julia appreciated the implications of the word defensive, and the insolence of Richard's last question. Then she replied, 'My marriage is fine, thank you, Richard – though it's none of your damned business!'

Julia sounded, and was, annoyed. One moment she was enjoying a happy, relaxed luncheon with an old – friend. In her mind she chose the word carefully; once she had been in love with Richard, desperately in love, but that had been a long time ago. The next moment she was being provoked by ridiculous personal questions. Well, two could play at that game.

'What about you?' she asked sweetly. 'Why have you never married?'

If Julia had expected some complimentary answer, Richard disappointed her. 'Marriage wouldn't be compatible with my way of life,' he said as if uttering a self-evident truth. 'Besides, I decided long ago that it wasn't for me, whatever I did. And over the years I've had no great difficulty in finding obliging girlfriends, though I prefer to live alone. Of course I suppose there are things one misses by not being married, but my choice is no bad alternative.'

His manner continued to irritate Julia. 'Haven't you ever been tempted?' she inquired. And suddenly she no longer wanted merely to pierce Richard's complacency; she wanted to know.

'No. Because I'd have expected a wife to go where I went – follow me to the ends of the earth at a moment's notice, if necessary. Such women are rare, and must love a great deal. I never found one who felt that way about me.'

Julia was silent. She could think of nothing to say. It was just like their earlier exchanges about the man who had followed her; Richard had successfully put an end to the subject of marriage, though he himself had raised it. Luckily the serving of coffee covered any apparent hiatus in the conversation, and afterwards Julia said she had some shopping to do, and refused a lift home. They parted near the Louvre, Julia promising to telephone Richard at the friend's apartment where he was staying, and arrange for him to come to dinner with the Fischers.

On the whole she had enjoyed the luncheon, but she had found Richard disturbing, and she was glad to be alone.

★

At five o'clock that evening David's secretary telephoned. She was an efficient woman, approaching retirement age and so no threat to wives. Julia liked her. David, she said, was very sorry, but he would not be back for dinner. He had been in conference most of the day and had a mountain of work to do before he could leave the office. He would pop out for a quick meal later, then work on till he was finished. Julia was not to stay up for him; it could be midnight before he got home.

Julia thanked her, and said that she quite understood. She wondered if she did. Naturally, this was by no means the first time that David had had to work late, though recently it had been happening more and more often. She thought – with little conviction – that he might be having a serious *affaire*. But such a thing would have been quite out of character; as far as she knew he had always been careful to avoid any protracted relationship that might become known and ruin, if not his marriage, his career. And, after all, there was this Summit Conference in about three weeks, which was bound to make extra work.

Julia had a pleasant evening, reading, listening to music and writing a couple of letters. She was in bed soon after ten and was thinking of turning out the light before lying down, when David returned. At once she sensed that he was tense but jubilant.

'Good news,' he said, sitting himself on the bed beside her. 'At least I hope it's good. I was talking officially to your father earlier today about his Paris trip. The Conference comes to an end on the Friday afternoon, and he suggested that he and your mother should stay over till the Monday and spend the weekend with us. Rosemary will be here, and the family'll all be together.'

'But that's marvellous!'

David grinned. 'I thought you'd be pleased.'

'Of course I'm pleased.' Preoccupied with thoughts of her parents, Julia didn't pause to ask herself why David, whose relationship with Hubert Manville was amiable but far from close, should seem so especially happy about the arrangement. 'And Rosemary will be delighted.'

'There are some snags.'

'Like what?'

'Security. After all, your father is the Foreign Secretary,

darling. It's all looked after at the Residence, but if he comes to stay the weekend with us, we'll have to put up his Special Branch chap, and the French will certainly demand to plant guards on the house. We'll have to play it down, keep their visit here as quiet as we can and not mention it to anyone. Otherwise we'll have the media wanting pictures of the Foreign Secretary with his beloved granddaughter. You can imagine – '

Julia shrugged. 'It can't be helped. It'll be fun having them anyway.' She hesitated, then said, 'Incidentally, talking of the media, I had lunch with Richard today.'

She saw David stiffen, and hurriedly began to explain. She was aware of being unnecessarily prolix, but couldn't stop herself. David, listening and saying nothing, made her feel guilty, though she knew she had no cause to be.

' – and I said we'd be in touch about arranging a party with Karl and Eva,' she concluded lamely.

'Fine,' said David. 'We must do that, though God knows when, with the present schedule. I must admit I resent giving up the little free time I do have.' He pushed himself off the bed and stood, smiling down at her. 'You never told me you'd met Richard yesterday.'

Julia made a helpless gesture. 'Last night you were in a hurry to get ready for dinner at the Residence, and this morning you were off early. Besides, it wasn't a definite date. I was a bit surprised when he arrived here.'

It was only half a lie, she told herself; she had been expecting – hoping – that Richard would come. But . . . When David put out a hand and slipped it under her nightdress to caress her breast she drew in her breath sharply. He bent over and kissed her with casual arrogance, knowing that he had aroused her.

'I'm going to undress, darling. Don't go to sleep before I come.'

'No, I shan't,' Julia said and, as she lay waiting for him to return from his dressing-room, she thought how she had misjudged him, and how stupid it was to imagine he might have a mistress. Yet, when he came to her she found it hard to concentrate on their love-making, and for once he failed to satisfy her.

17

'Bliss,' said David. 'A really wonderful, quiet evening. No going out. No one coming in. Not even a servant in the house. Just us. And no work. Nothing to do.' He grinned at Julia, and stretched himself luxuriously. 'I vote for a few drinks and early supper, and then bed. How does that appeal to you on a damp and drizzly night?'

'It sounds super,' Julia agreed.

At the beginning of the week she had suggested this evening as a possible date for the proposed party with Richard and the Fischers, but she couldn't blame David for refusing. Recently he had had almost no time to himself. And, as he pointed out, it was unlikely that the others would have been available at such short notice.

Yet Julia was irked that David would not make any effort to fix a definite date for the party. Once the Summit began there would be no opportunity, and afterwards the Fischers and Richard would be leaving Paris. It would be embarrassing to meet Richard at some reception, as they probably would, and make no reference to the invitation she had given him.

Since their luncheon together Julia had found her thoughts turning more and more frequently to Richard. She kept remembering incidents or scraps of conversation that she had thought long forgotten, and she wondered why after the accident she had been so ready to sever all connection with him. It had not only been Celia's death, and the subsequent reactions of her parents and David that had influenced her. Twenty years later she was able to admit, at least to herself, that it was partly hurt pride; she had as good as asked Richard to marry her, and he had turned her down.

'What is it?' David was asking.

'What's what?'

'You were frowning fiercely at something. Not happy, darling?'

'I was considering what we'd have for supper,' Julia lied quickly. 'There's a chicken casserole in the refrigerator. Shall I warm it up?'

'Sure. But let's get first things first, and have a drink right now.'

The pleasant, leisurely evening passed. At ten o'clock David suggested bed. Julia left him to make sure the house was securely locked, and went upstairs. She was entering the bedroom when the telephone gave its trilling summons. She picked up the receiver by the bed, but David had forestalled her and, as she heard him say hello, she was about to replace it. But it was late for a friend to call, and the possibility that it might be her parents or Rosemary's school on the line crossed her mind, so she hung on.

Then the woman spoke, in English but with the trace of an accent. Her voice was soft, scarcely more than a whisper. 'David, I want to see you,' she said. 'But don't use your car. It's too conspicuous. People notice it. Walk, and take care.'

'Now?'

'Yes. Right away. I'd not have phoned you at home if it weren't important, would I? Make any excuse you like, but come.'

Julia was unsure whether the demand was an order or an almost pathetic request or appeal. She heard the double click as the two receivers were replaced. The line hummed. She could hear David racing up the stairs; whatever interpretation could be placed on the call, he was taking it seriously. Julia had just enough time and presence of mind to replace her own instrument and move away from the bedside table as David came into the room.

'Darling, an absolute curse! You heard the phone? That was the Chancery, our duty officer. I'm afraid I've got to go in.'

'Now?'

'Yes. Right away.'

Suddenly Julia was aware that the conversation was repeating itself. 'Can't the duty officer cope?' she asked unkindly, forcing another lie.

'No. It's a "Most Immediate", from London. Some question of security, and the chap on duty isn't our brightest man.' David held out a hand in supplication. 'Darling, I'm sorry but I must go. Surely you understand?'

'Yes. Of course.'

'I shan't take my car. I've had more than enough to drink tonight, and if I got involved in some accident – ' He left the sentence unfinished. 'I'll walk as far as the Avenue and get a cab.'

It was a plausible excuse. A few months ago a Belgian diplomat, returning from a party, had knocked down a woman in the Place de la Concorde, and badly injured her. His diplomatic immunity had saved him from prosecution, but he had been posted home hurriedly. David must have remembered this, Julia thought, and seized on it as an excellent reason for not taking his Jaguar. Nevertheless, she was surprised at the ease with which he lied to her. If she hadn't listened to that phone call she wouldn't have doubted him.

'Okay, David. It's a shame when you were enjoying a free evening for once, but it can't be helped. I imagine you won't be long, if you can avoid it,' she said, hoping that David was too preoccupied to notice how stilted her words sounded.

'I'll do my best, but don't stay awake for me, darling.'

'I shan't.'

She had no intention of lying in bed, watching the clock, waiting for David's return. She intended to follow him, and see where the hell he went.

As soon as she heard him run down the stairs she pulled a raincoat out of her cupboard, and quickly tied a scarf round her head. It wouldn't be much of a disguise, but it was better than nothing on a wet evening. The front door slammed. As she had expected, David had delayed to pick up his own raincoat and umbrella from the hall cupboard, so she was not far behind him.

Indeed, when she came out of the house, she saw David, no more than a hundred yards away. Instead of going north towards the Avenue, he had turned south, and was walking fast. It was an unpleasant night, not cold, but with a steady, sticky rain, and there were few pedestrians on the rue de Longchamp. Julia held back, wondering if she were being foolish.

The question became more pointed when, after a few minutes' brisk walk, she realized that a Peugeot was crawling along by the kerb a short distance behind her. She stopped for a moment; it stopped too. When she moved on, so did the car. As she walked, she thought. She had no handbag. She had thrust her wallet, her keys and a handkerchief into her raincoat pocket, so that a long arm reaching out of the car window to snatch its prize – a favourite ploy on European streets – would have been unlucky. Or it could be an attempt at a pick-up, common enough in the Bois itself at night, but unlikely in the rue de Longchamp. Either way it was an added complication. Julia swore.

A couple, arms around each other, overtook her. For them she might not have existed, but she seized her chance and walked on, almost at their heels. And suddenly the Peugeot speeded up and passed all three of them. Then the driver brought the car to a complete halt, leapt out, slammed the door without bothering to lock it and ran, paying no attention to Julia or to her seeming companions, but apparently after David.

By now David himself had reached the Place de Bagatelle, and Julia glimpsed the light blur that was his raincoat cross the road and disappear beside the small church, which stood on an island in the middle of the Place. As the man from the Peugeot also crossed the road he was lit by the headlights of a passing car, and for a moment she saw him clearly. He was of medium build, and wore tight grey trousers and a dark blue or black anorak, its hood pulled over his head, shielding him against the rain and helping to conceal his face.

For some reason Julia felt a sense of urgency, as if something significant were about to take place. Brushing past the two lovers, she too started to run. The man had moved swiftly and with surprising silence – he must be wearing trainers, Julia thought. Julia herself, her heels tapping on the pavement, couldn't keep up with him, and when she saw the confusion of streets leading out of the Place, she feared that she had lost both him and David.

Then she heard what sounded like a muffled cry, close and frightening. It required all her courage not to turn and flee, but somehow she managed to steel herself. Her back against the church wall, she edged cautiously forward until she could peer around the corner of the building into an open shadowy space used as a car-park. It was dimly lit, but not so dark that she couldn't see her husband's pale face bending over a shapeless bundle on the ground.

The next moment David had straightened himself, and glanced quickly round as if to make sure he was unobserved. Julia ducked back, and waited. When she heard what she thought must be David's footsteps retreating into the distance, she risked another look around the corner of the church. David had disappeared.

Almost without volition Julia hurried to the still form on the ground. She knew whom she would find – the man in the dark anorak and tight grey trousers who had been following David. Obviously David had realized that he was being shadowed, had hidden in some doorway or recess of the church, sprung out and knocked the man down. By now Julia had abandoned her intention of following David to his destination. The situation had become so complex – so incomprehensible – that it no longer seemed important that she should know where he was going. But there was one thing she must do before she went home – make sure the man wasn't badly hurt.

Julia knelt beside him, and gently tried to move him, so that his face was free of a puddle of water in which it was partly submerged. To her horror his head lolled sideways as if unable to support itself, the hood of his anorak slid off and he was staring up at her, mouth open, eyes unseeing. She recognized him instantly; nondescript he might be, but there was no mistaking the misshapen outline of his right ear.

Julia got to her feet slowly. She was shaking. She was certain the man was dead – which meant that David had killed him. But why? And who was he? Why had he been following David? Questions thronged through her mind. Stumbling, she began to run back the way she had come.

At the corner of the Place she stopped, recovering her wits. There were other vital actions she must take. First, had she herself been unobserved? She, too, looked round nervously. The two lovers – the only people she had seen – had obviously and obliviously continued down the rue de Longchamp. Secondly, the man himself. She had no medical knowledge, and it could be that she was wrong. In common humanity she must notify the authorities in case he was merely badly hurt. Anonymously, of course. Fortunately, on the corner beside her was one of the new Paris phone booths, and she would need no change for an emergency call. She dialled 17 for *Police Secours* and spoke clearly and rapidly. Out walking her dog, she had found a sick man behind the church in the Place de Bagatelle in Neuilly. She put the receiver down before any questions could be asked. Her French accent was impeccable, so that no one would guess her nationality, and the call could only be traced to this booth. Having done her duty, she felt that she – and, what was more important, David – was safe and free from suspicion, and she hurried home.

Once secure in her drawing-room, Julia collected a brandy, curled herself up in an armchair and tried to consider her next move. She couldn't possibly ignore what had happened. But she was half afraid to face David with what she knew. She had to admit that, even after all these years of marriage, she had no idea how he might react.

She wished there was someone to whom she could turn for advice, and thought at once of her father. But she couldn't imagine him showing any sympathy for David, except possibly for her sake or for Rosemary's. After all, David had almost certainly killed a man. That in itself was shocking, because he was not naturally violent. It had to have been an accident. But even as an accident . . . What was more, the dead man was not some unknown assailant. There was a connection between him and them; the other day he had deliberately followed her, and he had been deliberately following David now. He couldn't be a mere crank, as Richard had suggested. Julia shivered; this was a night she would never forget.

At half-past one in the morning, having drunk more brandy than was good for her, Julia had a hot bath and went to bed. David had still not returned. Convinced that she couldn't sleep until he came, Julia tried to read. But the strain had been too great. The book failed to hold her interest, and very soon she was asleep.

Five hours later Julia awoke from a nightmare, sweating and

with a splitting headache. She remembered little about the dream, except that it had concerned her brother Peregrine, and had been very frightening. She lay still for a moment. Then, as the events of the night before returned to her consciousness she raised herself on an elbow and looked at the bed beside her. It was as neat as when the *femme de ménage* had made it yesterday morning.

Julia got up carefully and went into the dressing-room, where David sometimes slept if he came home late and wanted to avoid disturbing her. But the bed in there was equally tidy. Clearly David had been away all night.

18

It was eight-thirty before David telephoned. He was profuse in his apologies and full of explanations, all of which Julia knew to be equally false. What was more, she could sense the unease and tension beneath his spillage of words. He said how sorry he was to have spent the night at the Chancery; he hoped she hadn't worried about him; he knew he should have let her know, but at first there had been simply no time and later he hadn't wanted to risk disturbing her. It had been one hell of a night, he added.

'But the crisis – or whatever it was – is over now?' Julia had to force herself to speak civilly.

'No, not over, but under control, I hope.'

'Good,' Julia said, thinking that, in the circumstances, at least David's last remark had sounded credible and convincing.

'Julia – darling – '

'Yes?' she prompted after a pause.

But either David was for some reason unable to say whatever he had intended, or he had changed his mind. Instead, he merely remarked that he would do his best to get home early that evening, and wished Julia an abrupt goodbye. She put down her receiver slowly. She knew she could have interrupted him, pricked his damned arrogant confidence, told him that she'd followed him and knew about the man with the missing top to his ear. But she wanted to be able to see David's face when she confronted him. That way she believed it would be harder for him to lie. She assumed he would lie. But why? Why?

Suddenly she felt physically sick. Her head still ached from the brandy she had drunk the night before, and her stomach had knotted into a tight ball. She ran for the lavatory and retched into the pan, but she could bring up only bile. She sat on the seat. Misery overwhelmed her, and at last she wept – for David, for her marriage, even for the murdered man.

There was a knock on the bathroom door. *'Madame, le télé-phone! On vous appelle,'* called the *femme de ménage.*

'Merci.'

Julia dried her eyes, flushed the lavatory, washed her hands. Whoever was calling could wait; it was unlikely to be anything important – possibly a wretched, irrelevant invitation for drinks, or lunch or dinner. She announced herself in French as Madame Windfield, to be greeted by a laugh.

'Madame, c'est Monsieur Kent qui parle.'

'Richard! I – I thought it would be yet another invitation to some meal or reception or something – '

'And that's exactly what it is, Julia. Or have you turned me down before I've asked you?'

'No.' Julia tried to think clearly. Richard knew about the man in the church; she had even suspected he might have recognized him from her description. She could tell Richard about last night – not the whole truth, that would be impossible, but an expurgated version, without mentioning David. Richard had a lot of contacts; perhaps he could find out what had happened to the man and . . .

She tried not to sound over-eager. 'I'd love to come, Richard. Today?'

'Well, today isn't – '

'Richard, please.' Suddenly her mood changed. Why not insist? It could be vital that she should talk to him. 'I don't want a big lunch. Any little café'll do. But there's – there's something I want to tell you about.'

'Okay, Julia,' Richard responded at once. 'Look, the best thing would be for you to come here, to the apartment? Twelve o'clock. We'll have something light.'

'It doesn't matter. As I said, anything'll do.' Julia knew she was beginning to sound desperate. 'I'll be there. Thank you, Richard. I'm grateful,' she said as he gave her directions.

During the morning, as Julia busied herself over various small tasks, she was conscious that she was merely passing the time till lunchtime. She had no regrets. She planned what she would tell Richard. She would have to be careful. He was no fool and, in spite of her confidence in his judgement, she must not let herself involve David. But she felt certain that, whatever she said, he would be able to resolve some of her unanswered questions.

She left the house at a quarter-past eleven. It was not a pleasant day. The drizzle of the previous evening had turned to heavy rain during the night and, though that had ceased recently, the city was damp and dripping. Puddles were everywhere, and the gutters still ran with water that gurgled in the drains. The air was heavy and the sky leaden, promising more rain at any moment.

Julia had decided that it was no day for walking in the Bois but, balked of her usual exercise, she had set off for her lunch on foot. The rain, however, started as soon as she reached the Avenue Charles de Gaulle and, hoping that Richard wouldn't mind her early arrival, she thankfully took the last taxi on the rank. In fact the traffic was so thick and moved so slowly in the rain that it was only a few minutes before noon when she reached the rue Murillo, a short street lined with tall cream-coloured buildings, near the Parc de Monceau in the *Huitième Arrondissement*.

Following Richard's instructions she went through a black iron gate into a courtyard and pressed a large brass bell beside substantial wooden doors. Immediately there was a buzz and the click of the Paris *entrée*, common in older apartment blocks. The doors opened into a marble hall, where a lift, a mixture of glass and gilt, waited to carry her up to the second floor.

Richard stood in the doorway of the apartment directly opposite the lift. 'Welcome,' he said, taking her raincoat and umbrella. 'I'm afraid the interior of the apartment doesn't quite live up to the opulence of the entrance, Julia. Don't be too surprised.'

The salon was long and high-ceilinged, the curtains of heavy brocade, the parquet floor scattered with fine rugs. But it was the furniture and the arrangement of the room that caught her eye, and made it hard for her not to show surprise. One end of the salon might have been an office – desk, filing cabinet, computer screen, printer, typewriter; the other half could have been part of the smoking room of a London club.

Richard led Julia to one of the chunky leather armchairs. 'This establishment may look odd,' he said, 'but it's eminently practical, at least for a working journalist, like the friend who's lent me the place.'

'And you?' asked Julia. 'Is that what you call yourself, too?'

'I've been called worse.' Richard shrugged. 'What can I get you to drink, Julia?'

Julia asked for a glass of white wine, but the telephone rang before Richard could pour it for her. He was on the phone for several minutes, listening, saying only, 'Yes. Yes,' at intervals. When at last he brought the wine he said, 'Sorry about that,' but offered no explanation.

He sat himself in a chair opposite Julia, and stared at her, stretching his legs as if weary. He said, 'Do you want to tell me what the trouble is now, Julia, or would you prefer to leave it till after we've eaten?'

'Richard, I never said there was any trouble.'

'Nor you did.' He smiled, but said no more and waited.

'It's really rather embarrassing,' Julia said slowly. 'Yesterday evening, about ten, I decided to go for a walk. David was at the Chancery, working late, and I had a headache. I hoped some fresh air would clear it. It was raining, but it wasn't cold.' Julia sipped her wine, searching for the right words. She was finding it hard to deceive Richard, but she had to interest him without arousing too much curiosity; she didn't want to be cross-questioned. 'I saw that man again,' she said finally, 'you know, the one who followed me, the one with the funny ear. Richard, I know it was stupid of me, but I took a leaf out of his book and followed *him* and – '

Julia related the events of the rest of the night accurately, except that she omitted any mention of David, and she didn't suggest that she had believed the man to be dead. Richard listened without comment until she had finished. Then he looked at his watch, not casually, but as if he were preoccupied with the time.

For a moment Julia felt outraged. 'I'm sorry, Richard,' she said angrily. 'I didn't mean to bore you.'

173

Richard rose from his chair and took her hand. 'Julia, you know you never bore me – and you've told me a fascinating tale. But I'm expecting another phone call, which is why we're lunching here and not in some elegant restaurant. So, if you'll excuse me for a moment, I'll depart to the kitchen and put the quiche in the oven. Then you'll have all my attention, and you can tell me what you want me to do.'

Julia finished her wine, stood up and refilled her glass from the bottle that Richard had left on a side table. Her colour was high. She wished she hadn't come. She had expected Richard to be sympathetic, but – what did he mean by a 'fascinating tale'? Had he already realized that she wasn't telling the whole truth? And had she made it so obvious that she wanted him to take some action?

It was a long time before Richard returned. She heard him in the kitchen, and moving about elsewhere in the apartment. She thought she heard him talking, perhaps on another telephone. Eventually he reappeared, carrying a tray with bowls of soup.

'First course,' he said, setting a small table in front of her and producing a paper table napkin. 'Quiche, salad and fruit to follow.' He poured some more wine, sat opposite her and resumed the conversation as if there had been no gap. 'What did David say about it?' he asked.

Julia hesitated. 'I haven't told him,' she admitted at last.

'You've not told him? Julia! I know you said you didn't want to worry him about this strange chap, but obviously you were shaken by what happened last evening. Are you telling me you never mentioned it to David when he got home?'

'No, it wasn't that. He – he didn't come home. There was a crisis at the office, and he was there all night. I expect he snatched some sleep,' she added almost at random. 'There's a camp bed in the duty officer's room, I think. But when he phoned me he sounded so exhausted I didn't want to bother him with another problem.'

The telephone saved Richard from replying. He took the call in the salon, but stood with his back to Julia, muttering into the receiver, so that she couldn't hear what he was saying. After he hung up he took their soup bowls into the kitchen without speaking, and brought back the rest of the meal. As they began to eat, he regarded Julia with a curious expression that momentarily disconcerted her.

She felt she had to speak. 'Richard,' she said, 'you asked what I wanted you to do. I don't want to be a nuisance, but I just hoped that – with all your contacts – you might be able to discover what happened to that man.'

'Yes. I guessed that was what you wanted – and that's what I've done.' Richard continued to eat for a few minutes. 'Acting on your anonymous phone call, Julia, the police went to the Place de Bagatelle. They found the man. A karate chop across the throat had killed him. He'd not been robbed – his money and his papers were intact – so the motive for his murder is obscure.'

Julia pushed her plate away from her. She could eat no more. The food was choking her. It wasn't the man's death that shocked her, but the manner of it. She had assumed that David had hit him, and that he had fallen awkwardly, perhaps breaking his neck. But it now looked as if David had killed him deliberately . . . She felt the room begin to revolve.

'Julia! Julia, are you all right?' Richard was bending over her.

'Yes. Sorry.' She straightened herself. 'I – I felt a bit faint for a moment. It's nothing.'

'I'll get you some water.'

When Richard brought the water, Julia drank thirstily. Richard watched her, his face anxious. As the colour slowly began to come back to her cheeks he returned to his seat, but continued to fix his gaze on her. She would have given a great deal to know what he was thinking.

He said, 'Julia, I don't imagine there'll be any trouble about this man. He's a White Russian, though a French citizen, and a pretty shady character, known to the police.'

'What – what's his name?'

'Nick. Nick Panolov.'

'Poor man,' was the only comment Julia could think of.

'Yes.'

The monosyllable put an end to the subject. Richard cleared away the remains of lunch and made coffee. Afterwards he insisted on driving Julia back to the rue de Longchamp. He

175

refused her invitation to come in but, when he said goodbye as they stood on the pavement outside her house, he held her hand for longer than was necessary, until Julia felt bound to pull away.

'Thank you for lunch, Richard, and – and for your help.'

'My dear, I haven't done much. But – ' Richard hesitated for so long that it seemed unlikely he intended to say more. Then he added, 'It's possible I really could help, Julia, and I would, if it ever became necessary. Don't forget that.'

*

The *femme de ménage* had left – it was her half day – and the house was empty. Thankfully Julia went up to the bedroom. She took off her suit and, in her slip, got into bed. Her head no longer ached, but she felt exhausted. She curled herself up, and tried to make her mind a blank. She didn't want to think, not about Richard, or David, or the strange man called Panolov. And, after a while, she slept.

When she woke, it was getting dark outside. Julia rose and drew the curtains. She put on a dressing-gown and slippers, and went downstairs to make herself some tea. As she reached the hall she heard voices that she recognized coming from the salon. She hesitated. David was there, but with Karl Fischer. This was obviously an unsuitable moment to confront her husband, but she was unwilling to postpone the inevitable. Somehow she must get rid of Karl. She coughed loudly and the voices stopped abruptly, and then resumed but with far less apparent urgency.

'Hello, David. You're home early.' Julia was pleased how calm she sounded as she entered the room. 'Hello, Karl.'

With his usual exuberance Karl bounded out of his chair and came towards her with his arms spread wide. 'Julia, love! David told me you were having a rest, dreaming sweet dreams.'

'I was. But I'm awake now.'

Karl laughed as if Julia had made a joke, and she allowed herself to be embraced in his usual bear hug. But she turned her head aside when David came forward to kiss her. She thought he looked tired and tense.

176

'What have you been doing today, darling?' David said. 'I tried to phone you about one, but you were out.'

'I was having lunch with Richard.'

'Richard? But – '

'I wanted to ask his advice, about a – a private matter – and I'd like to speak to you about it, too.'

'Now?'

'Yes, now.'

Julia made no attempt to be tactful. She turned to Karl, making it quite clear that she wished to talk to David – and David alone. Karl, however, made no move to leave. He returned her gaze, his face expressionless.

David said, 'Julia, if there's anything you're prepared to tell Richard, you can certainly tell Karl.'

Julia's immediate reaction was astonishment – and anger. 'Do you really mean that, David?' she said coldly. 'I warn you, it's about last night and what really happened – not about the lies you told me. You see, I followed you to the Place de Bagatelle. Are you sure you want me to go on?'

'Quite sure!' David bit off the words. It was apparent that both he and Karl were shocked. 'Go ahead,' he said, resignedly.

'Very well.'

Julia began with the phone call she had overheard. David's only attempt at protest came when she mentioned a mistress, and even then Karl waved him down. Shaking his head, David went and helped himself to a whisky. He glanced at Karl, who asked one question when Julia finished, 'You're positive you gave Kent no reason to think that David was involved?'

'Yes. I'm positive!' Julia was getting increasingly furious, partly because inexplicably she felt she was being put in a false position. 'And what on earth has it got to do with you, Karl, anyway?' she demanded. 'Where do you come into this?'

Karl made no direct answer, and it was David who said, 'We'll have to tell her the truth. To start with, I refuse to have my wife thinking I've got a mistress secreted away somewhere.' He turned to Julia. 'Darling, I love you. I always have. I don't want anyone else.'

'Then who's this woman you went to last night?' Julia demanded.

'Come and sit down – and listen.' David persuaded her to a chair. 'The first thing you have to know is that, in addition to my normal diplomatic duties, I do a great deal of intelligence work, largely concerned with security – '

'Intelligence! Security! But you have special officers for such jobs. How are you involved?'

'Julia, it's a long story, and you must just accept the fact. Not everything in the diplomatic service is always quite what it seems. That's why I can't always tell you exactly what I'm doing or where I'm going. Anyway, this part of my work involves liaising with our allies. Karl here is a colleague with whom I often collaborate, as well as an old friend of ours. Our immediate problem is security for the forthcoming Summit in Paris – in which your father's going to play a prominent part. A lot of people would like to see the Conference not just fail but turn into a major disaster, so we're all scared of some kind of sabotage. I won't – I can't – go into details, but if you don't believe me, ask your father. And I won't tell you the name of the woman who phoned me last night.' David laughed. 'She's a colleague, too. She's intelligent and attractive, but in her late fifties. You don't have to be jealous of her, darling. Ask Karl about her.'

Throughout David's speech Karl had been lounging in a chair, apparently unperturbed. Now he said, 'He's right, Julia. It's all true. You've got to believe him.'

David added, 'Darling, of course it's true. I swear it! I won't say I've never been unfaithful to you, but – but not for ages. And I certainly haven't got a mistress.'

'And what about this man Nick Panolov?'

'That was awful – and an unexpected complication,' David admitted. 'He was shadowing me, and I had to know why. I didn't mean to kill him. I thought he was about to attack me. It was a complete accident, Julia, I assure you.'

And she did believe David, Julia thought, as she went to sleep that night. He had convinced her, partly perhaps because she wanted to be convinced – the alternative was too dreadful to contemplate – but also because his story rang true, explained so much. Even his final gratuitous warning that perhaps Richard was not altogether to be trusted hadn't made her have second thoughts. Richard was kind and gentle and generous – recently she had sometimes felt that she was still half in love with him – but it was David who was her husband, and she had been stupid to doubt him.

19

Moscow and Paris, Spring 198–

The years had been good to Vladimir Dolkov. He had survived – not a simple achievement during the succession of power conflicts in Moscow – and he had prospered. He was now a General in what had become the KGB, and enjoyed all the privileges that went with such a rank. He and Natalia had a large apartment to themselves, a *dacha* in the country, a chauffeur-driven car, tickets for the ballet when they wished, shopping in Granovsky Street, or in Section 100 of GUM, or sometimes even in the *Beryozka* – hard currency – stores. In short, as a Party member he was one of the élite, and as a senior KGB officer the cream of the élite. By any standards, he and his family lived well; Natalia had forgotten what it was like to queue.

What was more, they were happy together. Natalia had grown old gracefully, and Vladimir, always a big man inclined to heaviness, had been careful not to put on excess weight. He retained a moderate figure, and his back was straight. His hair was iron-grey now, but thick, and his face surprisingly unlined. He looked, and on the whole he was, contented with his lot.

His one serious regret was that he had no grandson. His daughters had made successful marriages, and he approved of both his sons-in-law, but they had produced only girls. And the photograph of the small boy he kept in his wallet was brown with age and soiled from handling, for the small boy had long ago become a man.

Vladimir had other photographs of Bird, as an undergraduate at Oxford and at later stages in his career, but these he kept in his private safe at KGB Headquarters, with the rest of the documentation he had accumulated. The photographs and papers were proof, at least to him, that Bird was indeed his nephew; the likeness to his dead brother, Alexis, had grown more striking as the years passed, and Vladimir had derived much secret pleasure from the knowledge that, by whatever name he was known, Pandora White's son was a Dolkov, and by Russian law a Russian.

Today, however, his pleasure was diminished. Vladimir Dolkov was disturbed. His current project – a major one, perhaps the biggest coup he could ever hope to conceive and plan – had started to go wrong. In any conspiracy there were always imponderables, he knew, unforeseen and unforeseeable occurrences that could ruin a scheme, however well devised. But this was absurd. As if he didn't have enough enemies abroad – and at home, within and without the Soviet intelligence and security bureaucracy – ready to thwart him, the very officers and assets engaged in the operation seemed to be at cross-purposes and liable to ruin everything.

'Damn Bird!' he said aloud, striding angrily the length of his large office.

'Yes, Comrade General,' his aide agreed.

Leonid Tchasky had no idea what his chief meant by 'Bird', but he had learnt that it was always wiser to agree first, and perhaps ask questions later. A man in his late thirties, intelligent and ambitious, he had also learnt that more often than not Dolkov was likely to talk sense. He could only hope that the exclamation did not mean that he himself had been to blame in some way.

He paused before speaking. Then, 'It's a pity about Panolov,' he offered tentatively. 'He was useful.'

'He was a fool!' Dolkov exploded.

Tchasky said, 'His orders were merely to keep an eye on Julia Windfield – '

'But not to get spotted! And certainly not to get killed by David Windfield!' Dolkov shook his head in exasperation. 'And then – the biggest irony of all – that she should go running to Richard Kent.'

'Panolov couldn't have foreseen that, Comrade General,' Tchasky said mildly. 'Still, as you say, he was stupid – '

The General continued as if Tchasky hadn't spoken. 'The trouble is that in Paris our right hand doesn't seem to know what our left hand's doing. They're making a stinking mess of the whole operation, and time is short. The Western Summit starts in two weeks' time, and if we miss our chance now, we may never have another one equally auspicious.'

Tchasky nodded his sympathy and understanding. 'It's regrettable you're not there yourself to direct matters, Comrade General. If only you could – '

He stopped, mouth open, as Dolkov held up his hand, so abruptly that for a moment Tchasky feared he had given offence. But slowly a smile spread across Dolkov's face.

'And why not, Tchasky? Why shouldn't I take charge myself, at least for the next few days? Tell me, don't we have a cultural mission going to Paris next Monday?'

'Yes, Comrade General. It's to arrange with the French for exchanges of ballet and theatre companies and art exhibitions. It's a small mission and everyone's been most carefully vetted; it was only judged necessary to send one of our people to keep tabs on them.'

'Maybe the judgement was wrong.' Dolkov grinned. 'I'll go with them, too – and you'll come with me. It'll give me a chance to sort out in person these fools who don't seem to know what the hell they're doing. We'll go to Paris as part of this cultural mission.'

Tchasky frowned. 'Are you sure that would be advisable, sir? You've been to the West before. You might be recognized.'

'So? My last visit was some time ago. And if I were recognized, would it matter? I've a perfect right to be in Paris on duty – or duty as cover for a good holiday, for that matter. No, Tchasky, we'll go. Arrange it. That's an order.'

*

Vladimir Dolkov stared from the window of the Ilyushin 62 as the aircraft gained height and Sheremetievo Airport receded behind it. His thoughts were already in Paris, and to the meeting he planned with his nephew. He had never met Bird, though he could have done so had he wished; opportunities had arisen on several occasions.

And naturally Dolkov had been tempted to take advantage of

182

them, but always in the past he had resisted the temptation. At first the difficulties had been enormous; any meeting would have had to be clandestine. In fact, he reminded himself, in the atmosphere of Moscow at that time it would have been dangerous – for him, for Natalia and the girls, and for Anna, who had been so helpful – to admit that his brother had spawned an English child. It had been vital to keep it a family secret, and his own hopes to himself.

Later, when Bird grew up and proved to be clever beyond expectations and destined for the British Foreign Service, Dolkov had been prepared to 'discover' the boy, and reclaim him as a true Russian who would work for his country. That matters hadn't turned out quite as he had wished or intended was not his fault. He would have called the accident outside Oxford an act of God, if he had believed in God. But, surprisingly, it had made no difference in the long run. It had merely meant a minor adjustment to his plans.

'Are you awake, Comrade General?' asked a voice beside him.

Dolkov opened one eye. 'No!' he said. 'Not now, Comrade Tchasky. And remember – don't call me "General". The name on my passport is Deresky, and I hold no rank. In Paris I'm Monsieur Deresky of the Ministry of Culture and Enlightenment, and you are my assistant. Get used to the idea.'

'Yes, Monsieur Deresky,' said Tchasky. 'I was about to say that we'll be landing at Charles de Gaulle Airport in twenty minutes.'

'Good.' Dolkov glanced at his watch. 'Nearly four hours in the air, I see. We're a little late, but not much. We shall arrive at the Embassy in splendid time for dinner.' He paused and, lowering his voice, added, 'The arrangements for later are all satisfactory?'

'Yes, sir,' Tchasky said. 'I will verify everything when we arrive, of course, both for tonight and for the reception for the cultural mission. I don't anticipate any difficulties.'

'Good,' said Dolkov. 'Let's hope you're right.'

'I hope so, too, sir,' Tchasky replied.

But Vladimir Dolkov paid him no attention. The seat-belt sign appeared as they prepared to touch down, and Dolkov couldn't help being gripped by an overwhelming sense of excitement.

★

It was near midnight when Tchasky knocked at the door, and entered Dolkov's bedroom in the Soviet Ambassador's Residence in the rue de Grenelle on the Left Bank. Both the KGB officers were staying at the Residence, but Dolkov's suite was ornate in crimson and gold, reserved for the most important of VIPs. Dolkov himself was lying on his bed. He was fully dressed, but he had been commencing a series of exercises in an effort to relax himself. Now he slowly rose to his feet and stretched.

'My car's ready?' It was a superfluous question.

'Yes, sir. And I've already picked them up in a separate vehicle and dropped them at the safe house.'

'What are they like?'

Tchasky shrugged noncommittally. 'He's a big man, who would like to appear as a jolly beer-drinking type, but I think that's only to deceive. In my opinion he wouldn't hesitate to slit his grandmother's throat, if he thought it expedient.'

'For thirty pieces of silver?'

Tchasky looked puzzled. He hadn't understood the allusion.

Dolkov grinned. 'And what about her?'

'She's more difficult to judge. But I'd say she's tough, definitely tough.'

'Fine. Then let's go. I think we've kept them waiting long enough.'

*

Tchasky's assessment of the Germans had been shrewd, Dolkov thought as he offered his hand to Karl and Eva Fischer. This was a couple who had proved themselves good communists over the years, but they had no intention of dying for the cause. Herr and Frau Fischer would always put Herr and Frau Fischers' well-being first.

'*Guten Abend*, Comrades,' Dolkov said. 'My German is a little rusty, I regret to say, and I understand you don't speak Russian.'

'Only very poorly, Comrade,' replied Fischer. 'My wife does, but I shall be happy if you would prefer English.'

At a signal from Dolkov, Tchasky moved to a table on which stood an array of bottles. 'English it shall be then,' Dolkov said to Fischer. 'Tell the Major what you and Frau Fischer would care to drink. Then come and sit down.'

'Must we drink alone? Won't you join us, Comrade?' Fischer asked.

'But of course. I'll have a brandy. And I expect the Major will have one, too.'

Vladimir Dolkov chose the most comfortable chair, and looked about the room. It might have been in a safe house anywhere. Plenty to drink, but the minimum of nondescript furniture, and no personal possessions. As anonymous as any slightly seedy hotel room.

'We can talk here without fear of being overheard in – er – in any way,' Dolkov said, knowing that the Germans wouldn't believe him. 'Now, first, tell me about your problems. What is it that's worrying you? And, more important, why are our plans failing?'

Fischer's grin was wry as he glanced at Eva. 'What's worrying us? The British – that's what's worrying us! No, I'm not joking, Comrade. They can't possibly know of our intentions, but they appear much more fearful than is customary for the safety of their delegation to the Western Conference in two weeks. The French are concerned about bombs, as they have every reason to be, but the British – it seems to me they may be expecting a more subtle attack. They're exceedingly wary, and they're taking extreme precautions. Don't you agree, Eva?'

'Karl's quite right, Comrade. There's no doubt about it.'

'But they don't fear anything specific, do they? An attack against an – an individual?'

'Perhaps,' said Karl. 'The Prime Minister and the Foreign Secretary are obvious targets. But no, Comrade, nothing specific, not as far as I know. Only – '

'Only what?' Dolkov was beginning to dislike the Fischers; for one thing, it irked him to be called Comrade so readily, but with no following rank, and the wretched man wouldn't come to the point – if he had one. 'Out with it!' he ordered.

While Karl Fischer hesitated, his wife spoke. 'We both distrust Richard Kent – and Julia Windfield, Comrade. Surely this isn't the moment for them to pick up their old and long-dead relationship, and yet that's what they seem to be doing. Why? To our certain knowledge he was once very much in love with Julia Manville, as she then was, and she with him. It's a personal involvement that we're afraid could cause trouble.'

'I see.' Vladimir Dolkov spoke thoughtfully. 'Yes, I suppose it could lead to complications. Indeed, Mrs Windfield has already been a nuisance, though it's unfair to blame her for Panolov's stupidities – or to blame Windfield himself, for that matter.'

'Panolov had his instructions,' Karl said. 'Admittedly he was inefficient as regards Julia, but we wanted an eye kept on her. Why he suddenly decided to follow Windfield, I can't imagine. Any more than I'd have imagined Windfield reacting with such violence.'

'Windfield's no fool,' said Dolkov. 'Don't make the mistake of treating him as if he were. The British don't pick fools for his kind of job, and they train them well.' He held his empty glass out to Tchasky. 'The same again, if you will, Comrade Major, and please help our guests.'

Tchasky did as he was told, and Dolkov decided that the time had come to give the Germans some encouragement. He lifted his glass.

'I drink to you, Comrades, and to the success of our enterprise.'

Fischer bowed in acknowledgement, then raised his own glass. 'To success.' He drank. 'It's never guaranteed, unfortunately, but I assure you that every detail has been carefully considered, and barring accidents – '

'Ah, accidents! Such as Panolov being killed.' Dolkov couldn't resist the jibe.

'Panolov wasn't important, and Kent believes there won't be any trouble over his death.' Fischer was firm. 'Windfield's perturbed about it, naturally – he never intended to kill him – but not perturbed enough to confess to it. Of course his people would cover for him, but it would be a black mark against him, and he wouldn't want that.'

'All right. But we mustn't forget it.' Dolkov spoke with equal firmness. 'It's the sort of minor incident that could blow up in our faces. Remember, his wife knows. Now – '

For the next half-hour they discussed the operation. If it were as successful as they hoped it would bring about the downfall of the British Government, rock the British people to their roots and cause such distrust of the British amongst their allies, especially the United States, as to make future co-operation impossible. Dolkov viewed the prospect with a deep but secret joy. The idea had been his originally, and circumstances had made the unthinkable at first conceivable, then achievable. Soon, very soon, he would know if he had brought off the coup of a lifetime.

He reminded himself that, if success was his, it would be largely due to the couple who sat opposite him. But it didn't make the Germans any more appealing; after all they were still Germans, communist or not. Dolkov's memory was long. He could never forget his elder brother's death at Stalingrad, or the way Alexis had been treated in Jersey by the Todt Organization. Yes, the Russians had had their revenge, and he knew he himself wasn't totally innocent, though some actions had been inevitable. But Boris and Alexis had been his brothers, his own – as Bird was.

Suddenly Vladimir realized that he had been silent for so long that the Fischers were staring at him anxiously. Collecting his thoughts, he said, 'Is there anything else you should tell me, Comrades? This reception for our cultural delegation at our Embassy tomorrow night, for instance. Will either of you be there?'

Fischer shook his head. 'No. My Ambassador wouldn't expect me to receive an invitation so, unless we're needed – '

'I see no reason why you should be. I shall be on home territory, as it were, and I've brought an aide with me, as you know. Besides, it's merely a social affair. I'm just taking the opportunity to meet one or two of the people who are involved in our operation. To see and speak to someone, however briefly, is worth more than a day with their file, as I'm sure you'll agree.'

Fischer expressed his agreement, though without enthusiasm. Eva asked suddenly, 'And would that apply to their relations, Comrade?'

'Relations?'

'Yes – parents, for example. I ask because it happens that Mr and Mrs Cornish are in Paris, and – '

'Cornish?' Dolkov couldn't place the name.

'David Windfield's mother. Recently married for the third time. In fact, as recently as last Saturday, and at present on her honeymoon. It was sudden and unexpected, I gather. No fuss. Just a few friends in some Registry Office in England. Apparently Windfield didn't know anything about it till she phoned him after the event.'

'Are they staying with the Windfields?' Dolkov leant forward in his chair. He swore in Russian, his English momentarily deserting him; surely this fool German understood? He checked his temper as he saw Karl Fischer's somewhat supercilious smile.

'Yes, Comrade, they *are* staying with the Windfields, but don't be alarmed. It's only for three nights. They leave the day after the reception.'

'In that case they're unimportant,' Dolkov replied, 'though anyone connected with Sir Hubert Manville, however remotely, is of some interest, I suppose.' He stood up and offered the Fischers his hand. 'I'll say good-night now, Comrades. My aide will take you back the way you came. And good luck!'

'Thank you, Comrade. Good-night.'

Dolkov had only to nod to Tchasky, who led the Fischers from the room. Dolkov gave them all a few minutes to get clear, then went out alone to his own car. Eventually, in his suite in the Residence, he undressed and got into bed. Tomorrow, he thought, as he drifted off to sleep, he would at last meet Bird; there were a lot of things those damned Germans didn't know.

20

Paris, Spring 198–

Vladimir Dolkov was nervous. For him, it was an unaccustomed emotion, and he admitted to it now only with reluctance. He was in his room in the Residence, half-loath to go downstairs to the car that would take him to the reception for the cultural delegation. The culture hounds did not rate a party at the Residence; instead, it was being held in the Soviet Embassy in the Boulevard Lannes on the edge of the Bois de Boulogne. The Ambassador had asked Dolkov to form part of the receiving line, but he had firmly refused. That way the meeting would have been too sudden, too – if the word was not absurd – public. No. He wanted, at least at first, to observe quietly and anonymously. Then he would choose his moment.

Nor, he reminded himself severely as the driver negotiated the evening traffic, must he forget that, whatever his personal feelings, Bird was not, could not be, of paramount important at this present juncture. Bird was merely an individual to be considered and assessed like all the others who were relevant to the operation. He had assessed Karl Fischer and his wife, Eva, the previous evening; tonight he would assess Julia Windfield when he met her, and David Windfield and Richard Kent. He smiled to himself as he thought of Bird. The car slowed and drew up before the new Embassy that had been completed next door to NATO Headquarters only a short while before NATO Headquarters left Paris for Brussels. Dolkov looked at his watch, and did his best to calm his nerves. It was time for action.

The receiving line had already broken up, and he was able to enter the reception room almost unnoticed. In many ways the room was incongruous in a modern building, but it reflected Russian taste for dark colours and heavy velvet, and managed to achieve an atmosphere of imposing grandeur. The Ambassador's wife, well-schooled, came forward to greet Dolkov, and asked if there was anyone he particularly wished to meet. Smiling, he shook his head, and she didn't insist. Instead, she waved him towards the buffet at the far end of the room, and let Tchasky, who had appeared at the General's elbow, lead him in that direction.

It was like any international diplomatic reception: groups of people forming and re-forming, drinking and nibbling, talking and listening, a mixture of languages, a variety of ethnic types. The occasional couple stood apart, heads bent in earnest conversation; this was an opportunity for business, for sounding out, as well as for sociability. And, as always, there were those who had stationed themselves permanently before the long table on which the food was set out, and were making their evening meal from the wide choice that was on offer.

Moving towards the buffet, Tchasky one step behind him, Dolkov took a glass of champagne from a passing waiter. They caught snatches of conversation as they crossed the room.

'Of course the Russians have no conception of modern art – look at the ghastly paintings they've hung here. Talk about socialist realism!'

'I agree, but you wouldn't be quite so sweeping if you'd seen the Costakis collection. I had that privilege some ten years ago. Splendid examples of Chagall, Malevich, Kandinsky, Rodchenko – '

' – *une grande artiste. Peut-être une seconde Margot Fonteyn.*'

There was the staccato of a language that Dolkov didn't recognize, and a woman's high-pitched voice saying in English, 'This is the first time I've ever been inside a Soviet Embassy. I think I'm a little scared.'

Then a deeper voice. 'Don't be silly, darling. We're with David.'

Dolkov and Tchasky exchanged glances and passed on. They reached the long table, behind which stood waiters in white coats easing corks out of champagne bottles, carving the hams and turkeys. The Russians might not entertain as often as some missions but, when they did, they vied with the Americans in the sumptuousness of their hospitality – and often surpassed them. Dolkov noted with appreciation the great mounds of caviare, black and red, and the bottles of Stolichnaya, the famous old vodka which was kept for export, and which even the élite found difficult to buy in Moscow.

Tchasky remarked, 'The lady who's scared of us is Madame Cornish, David Windfield's mother.'

'Is she, indeed?' Dolkov nodded his interest. He had just recognized Julia Windfield from photographs, and thought they had failed to do her justice. This evening, in a black dress, her corn-coloured hair piled high on her head, she looked particularly striking. 'Most attractive,' he murmured to himself.

Tchasky, who had followed the direction of the General's gaze, grinned. 'I've been looking, but I can't see her husband, or Kent, sir. Ah, there they are. Together. Talking to that tall, white-haired man, over by the – '

'Don't point,' Dolkov snapped abruptly, though his aide had made no attempt to do so.

In fact, Dolkov's sharp reprimand was an effort to cover his feelings. He turned his back, grabbed a shot of Stolichnaya and downed it in one gulp, Russian-fashion. For a minute, as the lethal punch of the vodka hit him, he had an excuse to fill his mouth with smoked salmon and brown bread, and avoid speaking. Then he picked up a glass of champagne. He had spotted Bird at the same moment as Tchasky. And, in spite of himself, he was shaken. The resemblance to his brother Alexis was strong, stronger than he had expected from the photographs he had seen. It was fortunate, he thought, that after all these years only a few people, all members of the family – himself, Natalia, Anna – remembered Alexis clearly.

He recovered himself, held out his champagne glass for a waiter to refill it and said, 'I'm going to circulate, Leonid. I'll signal if I need you.'

Dolkov strolled away, seemingly without purpose, but heading towards the small group that included Julia Windfield and her in-laws. Apparently they were discussing the pictures in the *Musée d'Art Moderne* with a couple from the Embassy of the

German Federal Republic. Dolkov had to wait for a gap before entering the conversation.

'Forgive me, but I couldn't help overhearing you,' he intervened finally. 'As far as I'm concerned I'm ashamed to say I've never been to the *Musée*. One morning in the Louvre was enough for me. Besides, I had to buy presents for my wife and daughter.'

There was laughter at this admission, and Julia Windfield said, 'I don't think we've met. Are you visiting Paris with the cultural delegation?'

'That is so,' said Dolkov. 'But still, one can only take in so much culture at a time.' He introduced himself as Monsieur Deresky, and the others responded with their names. There was a sudden silence. Dolkov reflected resignedly that now they knew – or thought they knew – who he was, the fact he came from the Soviet Union was enough to restrict their easy chatter.

But at last Julia asked what he had bought for his family and, when he told her, Mrs Cornish said, 'I think you were very wise to shop. Far more sensible than going to galleries – even for a member of a cultural delegation. The fuss they made about my shoes at that *Musée*. It's really a racket insisting on you buying those heel protectors.'

'Oh, come, Hope, they can't have you making holes in those wonderful floors,' her husband protested.

'People go to look at the paintings, not the floors,' said his wife firmly. 'Don't you agree, Mr Deresky?'

Mrs Cornish was making an effort to include the Russian in the conversation, but Dolkov's thoughts were far away. Hope, the last gift left in Pandora's box. It was a nostalgic reminder of his brother Alexis.

Mrs Cornish repeated her question, and Dolkov forced himself back to the present. 'I'm not so sure,' he said civilly. 'It seems a small price to pay to protect something fine.'

At this point an approaching waiter, offering to refill their glasses, gave Julia and the Cornishes an opportunity to slip away. Alone, Dolkov started across the room as if he had that instant sighted a friend to whom he wished to speak. He paused close by the Soviet Ambassador, who at once put out a hand to stop him.

'Ah, Monsieur Deresky, here is someone you must meet. Mr Richard Kent, from the United Kingdom. I wouldn't say the Arts were really his professional line, but – '

Adept at extracting himself from any situation that was likely to bore him, the Ambassador gave a slight bow and left them after a few words of conversation. Dolkov and Kent regarded each other with what appeared to be polite interest.

'And what *is* your line, Monsieur Kent?' Dolkov asked, from his apparent ignorance.

'Actually, it's quite similar to yours, Monsieur. The Ambassador was merely joking.' Kent smiled blandly. 'Of course, it depends how you define "Arts".'

'Naturally.' Dolkov was equally bland. 'Would you agree that politics is an art, the art of leading, or governing perhaps?'

'Yes. But ruling – defending – a country requires a good deal more than mere art, wouldn't you say?'

'Indeed. Much, much more.'

What an absurd conversation, Dolkov thought. He knows who I am – he's undoubtedly been told – and I know who he is. Yet here we are playing games with each other. Yet what else could be done in these ridiculous circumstances? It would have been unwise – impossible – to attempt to arrange a secret meeting, to talk openly, even if –

Momentarily Dolkov was distracted. Across the room, not far from where he and Kent were standing, there had been a commotion, a flurry of action. Earlier he had vaguely noticed a woman with grey hair, tall and striking in a red dress, looking in their direction. Now she was being supported and helped to a chair, as if she were faint or ill.

Kent's gaze had followed Dolkov's. With a stifled exclamation, he excused himself and, making his way hurriedly to the woman, he knelt beside her and took her hand. Someone had brought her a glass of water, which she sipped and gave back. Clearly she was feeling better, for she shook her head as if to apologize for the confusion she was causing; it was nothing serious. Kent had risen to his feet and was speaking to Julia Windfield and the Soviet Ambassador's wife, who had joined them in some anxiety.

Moments later Dolkov watched as Richard Kent and the

woman in the red dress left the reception. Only then did he realize that he was holding in his left hand the half full glass of champagne that Kent had thrust at him as he departed so unceremoniously. He drank from it before planting it on a passing waiter's tray.

'All goes well, Monsieur Deresky?' Leonid Tchasky was at his elbow.

'That woman who collapsed? Who is she?'

'I don't know, Monsieur.'

'Find out. But – ' As Tchasky turned away, Dolkov touched his arm. 'Be tactful about it, Leonid.'

Tchasky spent his life being tactful when circumstances demanded it, Dolkov admitted to himself. He reflected that the superfluous warning merely showed that he himself was tense.

'The lady is Mrs Kent, the mother of Richard Kent.' Tchasky had returned.

Vladimir Dolkov nodded. He was not surprised. Kent's behaviour had demonstrated that the woman was someone close to him, and she was too old to be a girlfriend. Dolkov regretted that he had had no opportunity to speak to her.

'This is becoming quite a family occasion,' he remarked. 'Windfield's parents, and now Kent's mother. Very odd. Why wasn't I told Mrs Kent would be here?' he asked softly.

'Evidently no one knew, sir. I gather she's staying with Kent for two or three days, while her husband is in Brussels at a board meeting of some bank. Kent just phoned for permission and brought her along tonight.'

'I see.' Dolkov was thoughtful.

'She'll have left Paris before the Western Summit begins, like Mr and Mrs Cornish, so she's not relevant,' said Tchasky.

'No.' Dolkov replied, but with no great conviction in his voice, and Tchasky glanced at him inquiringly.

Hardly thinking, Dolkov allowed a waiter to refill his glass and took a canapé of caviare from a hovering waitress. He told himself he must cease procrastinating, and complete what he had come for, before all the guests left; already the crowd was beginning to thin as people made their way towards the Ambassador and his wife to offer their thanks. 'Let us go and talk to Mrs Cornish,' he said.

'Mrs Cornish?' Tchasky's surprise was fleeting. 'Ah yes. And her son.'

Mrs Cornish showed no eagerness to renew her brief acquaintance with 'Monsieur Deresky'. As Dolkov and Tchasky approached she half turned from them, and seemed to be urging David Windfield to lead her in the opposite direction. But Windfield stood his ground, and she was forced to introduce him to Dolkov, who in his turn presented Tchasky.

'My son is a Counsellor at the British Embassy here,' Mrs Cornish remarked – proudly, perhaps – to cover the silence that followed.

'It's a pleasure to meet you, Monsieur Windfield,' Dolkov said, and meant it. 'A double pleasure, because I have already met your charming wife.' He retained his hold of Windfield's hand a fraction longer than necessary.

'And it's an honour to meet you, Monsieur – er – Deresky,' Windfield said seriously.

He had made no effort to withdraw his hand before Dolkov released it. Indeed, he smiled into Dolkov's face. He seemed assured and confident, but Dolkov felt the sweat on his palm. Windfield was less relaxed than he appeared on the surface.

Nevertheless, the man was good, Dolkov thought. Windfield knew who he was – like Kent, he had undoubtedly been told – and this couldn't be an easy meeting for him. But he had his emotions under control. Dolkov felt a surge of satisfaction.

Windfield's mother seemed to have accepted the presence of the two Russians as inevitable, and Dolkov let her dominate the general and innocuous conversation, mainly about Paris. He himself was content to watch her son. But he allowed himself only a few minutes with them before he made his excuses.

'I'm afraid we must leave,' he said. 'Goodbye, Mrs Cornish. Mr Windfield.' He looked directly at David. 'Perhaps we shall meet again.'

'I hope so, Monsieur.'

Followed by Tchasky, Dolkov made a point of thanking the Ambassador and his wife. 'A most enjoyable party – '

'You have met everyone you wished?'

Dolkov raised his eyebrows. He considered the question much

too blunt from a diplomat to a KGB officer. 'Not quite everyone,' he said softly. 'But enough.' And, as they left the reception, he added to Tchasky, 'A most satisfactory evening. A most satisfactory journey, in fact – especially our encounter with the Fischers. I shall almost be sorry to leave Paris tomorrow.'

★

The letter was handed to Vladimir Dolkov as he was enjoying a late breakfast alone in his bedroom.

'How did this arrive?' he demanded of the young Russian diplomat who acted as Social Secretary to the Ambassador, and whose office was in the Residence.

'It was delivered by a taxi-driver only a short while ago, Monsieur Deresky.'

'A taxi-driver?'

'Yes, sir. There was a slight altercation. The man refused to give it to the guard on duty, and he wouldn't enter the building either. However, he did agree to wait. I went out to talk to him – I speak French – and he gave me the letter when I explained that it was quite impossible for him to see you personally.'

'You questioned him?'

'Certainly. He said that a lady had appeared at the rank on the Champs-Elysées where his cab was parked, and asked him to deliver the letter. She paid the fare and added a generous tip. He said it was not unusual; taxi-drivers often delivered letters or parcels.'

'The lady? I suppose he'd never seen her before?'

'No. But he was observant, and could describe her. He said she was between forty and forty-five, short and big-breasted, but with fine legs. Her hair was reddish black, probably dyed, and she spoke French well, but with an accent.'

Vladimir Dolkov laughed aloud. 'The man was describing his wife, I expect, or his mistress. You should have offered him a bigger tip, Comrade.'

The young Russian looked surprised at such a rebuke from a member of a cultural delegation, but knew enough to make no excuses. He stood, waiting and wondering, while Dolkov studied the envelope. It was cream-coloured and of good quality. The name – Monsieur Deresky – was hand-written, in large, firm characters. Dolkov was intrigued, though he thought he could guess the writer.

Misinterpreting his silence, the First Secretary said, 'It's been through the X-ray machine, sir. It contains only paper. There's no danger.'

'I'm glad to hear it,' Dolkov said solemnly. He nodded his dismissal. 'If there's an answer I'll give it to you before I leave for the airport.'

As the door closed Dolkov took a knife from the table before him, carefully slit open the envelope and extracted a matching sheet of paper. It was an odd shape, because the address had been cut from the top. The letter was brief.

It read:

Dear Vladimir,

Bird has told me who you really are, so I feel I must write to you – and appeal to you. I am Bird's mother. I bore him and brought him up. I love him. Perhaps you love him too, or perhaps you merely want to use him. Either way I am full of fear, fear of losing him. He is mine, not yours. Please, please, do not let him come to any harm.

It is a very long time since I signed myself –

Pandora

Dolkov refolded the letter, replaced it in its envelope and put the envelope in an inside pocket of his jacket. He would have to consider his response, if any. The lack of an address was no obstacle; that had been omitted in case the letter fell into the wrong hands. He knew how to find Pandora. But there was an alternative: to ignore it, and let the events of the next few weeks speak for him.

There was a tap at the door, and Tchasky entered.

'The car's waiting to take us to Charles de Gaulle, if you are ready, sir.'

Vladimir Dolkov sighed. 'Yes,' he said. 'I'm ready.' And he thought that Bird's mother might indeed have just cause to be fearful.

21

Moscow, Spring 198–

Natalia Dolkova spoke softly to her husband. 'Will there be danger?' she asked.

It was many years since she and Vladimir had lived in an apartment with paper-thin walls where every word could be overheard by an inquisitive neighbour, and their present home was regularly 'swept' to make sure there were no unofficial bugs; whether they were subject to any official electronic surveillance was an open question, and one that Dolkov never asked. But they were a careful pair, and in any case old habits died hard. When they discussed anything that was strictly private, or possibly open to some misinterpretation, they turned up the radio and spoke in low tones.

'There's always danger for anyone connected with a conspiracy of this kind, Natalia, however slight or peripheral his connection with the opeation might appear to be.'

'But can't you do anything to minimize the danger, Vladimir? I feel so sorry for his mother.' Natalia returned the letter, which her husband had allowed her to read.

'There's no need to be sorry for Pandora. If you remember, she admitted to Anna that she never really loved Alexis. She had no wish to give him a son. In fact, as far as I can make out, she would have much preferred it if that German, von Blunthal, had made her pregnant.'

'Perhaps, Vladimir. But still, she loves Bird – and – and so do we, don't we? Surely you'll do whatever you can for him, if not for her?'

'Of course.'

Dolkov restrained his irritation. He crossed the room and poured himself a vodka, tossing it down his throat and following it at once with a bit of good black Russian bread. He was beginning to regret that he had ever shown Pandora's letter to Natalia, but on his return to Moscow she had been eager to hear every detail of his meeting with Bird, and the letter had seemed relevant. Now her insistence that Bird should be protected against every contingency was becoming unreasonable.

'Natalia, you must realize that Bird isn't of primary importance. Our duty – to our country and our own people – must come first. And that means that, if it came to the crunch, the safety of some others would have to rank before that of Bird.'

'Of course I understand, Vladimir Dolkov. I'm not a fool. All I ask is that you – you – '

'No one thinks you're a fool, Natalia. Let's not quarrel over this.' Vladimir went to his wife and put his arm around her shoulder. 'I appreciate your feelings for Bird. I share them. He's Alexis's son, and a Dolkov. But you're crying before he's hurt and, if all goes well with my plans, he won't be hurt at all – and neither will anyone else.'

'Yet you said there was danger.'

Vladimir suppressed an oath. 'I admitted a possibility, yes. But no more than that. And remember, Natalia, before you run gossiping to Anna, that if things should go badly wrong – and I emphasize *if* – I could be the one to suffer.'

'I'll remember,' said Natalia, surprised by his unexpected vehemence. 'Haven't I always remembered at times like this?'

'Good.' Vladimir nodded his approval. What he had told her was not precisely true, on two counts. First, there was no fear that he himself would come to any harm; he had so arranged matters that, in the event of catastrophe, others would take the blame. Secondly, anyone in Paris who was involved would certainly be in danger until the operation was complete.

*

In his office Vladimir Dolkov was re-running the tape of a programme that had appeared on the BBC a couple of days earlier. It was a weekly programme, a mixture of news, interviews and commentary. Inevitably, this week's edition dealt with the Western Summit that was to open in Paris the following week, the vital issues that would be discussed, the personalities taking part, the views of the pundits on what might or might not be achieved, the intense security which would surround the Heads of Government and their ministers and advisers. For Dolkov it was fascinating – and instructive.

'Amazing what you can learn from this sort of programme,' he remarked to Tchasky. 'Between them, the media and modern technology have made intelligence work a great deal easier.'

'Yes, Comrade General, but –' Tchasky hesitated, then decided to be bold. 'Even programmes which purport to give straight news and facts can be biased. Photographs can be faked to support dubious statements and – '

Dolkov interrupted. 'How long do you think I've been in the business, Tchasky? I know perfectly well you can't expect to have everything handed to you on a plate. But watch this.'

He rewound part of the tape, and once again two men appeared on the monitor screen. A voice-over said, 'In an exclusive interview, the Foreign Secretary chats with an old friend, Neil Grantham, about prospects for the Summit. As you will see, Sir Hubert is relaxed and jovial. He's clearly optimistic about the outcome – '

The promised interview ran on, and Dolkov and Tchasky exchanged glances, grinned, then shouted with laughter. They were laughing because it was obvious that the presenter, in his attempt to sound familiar with the great man and knowledgeable about his attitudes, had conveyed an impression that was clearly at odds with what appeared on the screen; Sir Hubert might have been relaxed, but undue optimism was certainly not evident from his replies. They were also laughing because they knew that with luck, any optimism on the part of the British Foreign Secretary would prove completely unfounded.

'Look at him,' Dolkov exclaimed. 'Watch that smile switching on and off. No! Let's hold that frame. Study it, Comrade. This is Sir Hubert, the politician, being interviewed on television by a man he doesn't like but who is a popular personality, and thus not to be treated with contempt.'

Tchasky stared at the screen and considered the two men more seriously. They were contrasting types. Grantham, the don who had become a political commentator and an adviser to governments, had wild red hair, white skin and bright blue eyes. He was sitting comfortably in his chair, legs crossed, wearing slacks and a jacket, with a blue sweater over his shirt and a red tie. To a British audience, he would seem to be asserting his nonconformity, his disregard of the Establishment.

This didn't appear to worry Sir Hubert. The Foreign Secretary was impeccable in a dark suit, white shirt and a Guards tie. A tall and elegant man, still strikingly handsome in his sixties, he had a reputation for ambition, hard work and high principles. He sat, stiff backed, and he was sufficiently aware of the tricks of the television interview to direct his responses to a point just above Grantham's right ear.

'Note those large silver-framed photographs on the table beside Sir Hubert,' Vladimir Dolkov said. 'The one at the rear – the one that's slightly out of focus – is of his wife and their three children when young. The nearer is of two of the children – the son and a daughter – in their late teens, I should think.'

'Peregrine, who was killed in a skiing accident,' Tchasky said as Dolkov paused. 'And Julia.'

Dolkov shook his head. 'Not Julia. Celia, also dead. But both of them important to us in their ways.'

'Both of them, Comrade General?' Tchasky frowned. 'I can understand why Celia was important. If she hadn't been killed Julia might have married Richard Kent, and – '

'No, I don't believe so.' Dolkov made no attempt to explain his reasons for this statement. 'But I agree we would be facing a different scenario, though just how different I wouldn't like to guess. However, one point's fairly certain. If Celia, who was Manville's favourite child, had lived, he wouldn't be as devoted to his granddaughter as he is. That's Rosemary, the granddaughter, in the third photograph. Incidentally, Tchasky, were you aware that Manville was furious when David Windfield refused to let the child be named Celia?'

'No, Comrade General, I was not.' Vladimir Dolkov's detailed knowledge of the Manville family and those close to them never failed to astound Tchasky. 'And Peregrine, the son?' he asked tentatively.

'Ah! Such a pity he was killed. I had great hopes of Peregrine Manville once. He was a brilliant young man. He could have risen to a pinnacle of power in his country and – though only a handful of people knew this – he was on our side, a confirmed communist. Karl Fischer recruited him during his first term at Oxford.'

Tchasky's eyes widened. 'Peregrine Manville! I had no idea. You – you have proof of this, Comrade General?'

'I have proof, Leonid. It's been of no use before, but now it'll serve nicely as part of the propaganda back-up.' Dolkov smiled in anticipation. 'Come on, let's watch the rest of the tape.'

Dolkov prodded the remote control unit and suddenly the two men on the screen became animated. Sir Hubert was speaking. His tone was measured, perhaps a little too clearly under strict control. His fingertips tapped on his knee in a compulsive rhythm.

Neil Grantham, on the contrary, had become almost over-relaxed, his expression innocent to the point of stupidity. Only his shrewd eyes betrayed him. This was a game he enjoyed, a game at which he was an expert.

'Am I right, Foreign Secretary? These threats against the Prime Minister's life are considered serious?'

'Any such threat must be taken seriously and every precaution will be taken to ensure the Prime Minister's safety in Paris. It would be foolish to do otherwise, wouldn't it?'

'Not for me to say, Foreign Secretary. As I understand it, the threats are pretty vague, and the source isn't known?'

Sir Hubert pointedly ignored the question mark in Grantham's voice, and wisely let the silence lengthen. Watching the screen, Dolkov and Tchasky again exchanged amused glances. They knew the source of the threats against the British Prime Minister; they had originated them.

' – so there's nothing to be learnt from the fact that you, Foreign Secretary, are flying to Paris on Sunday, and the Prime Minister is to follow tomorrow morning?'

'Nothing except that the Prime Minister happens to have a private engagement on Sunday evening.'

'Thank you for telling us that. It's very reassuring, Foreign Secretary. The public would hate to think that the attendance of the Prime Minister at such an important Conference was being delayed because of some obscure threats.'

'There's no question of that.' Sir Hubert was firm. 'But, as you say, the Conference is very important. Indeed, that's something of an understatement. If agreement – '

Grantham had made a tactical error, and given the Foreign Secretary an opportunity to pontificate at length. Vladimir Dolkov cut him off in mid-sentence, and the screen faded to black. He nodded his satisfaction. It would be a mistake, he knew, to underrate the British; Grantham had suggested that the threats against the Prime Minister were not as serious as the media, especially the tabloids, were inclined to insist. Nevertheless, anything which drew attention away from the intended Soviet operation was useful. Dolkov had long ago learnt the value of misinformation and misdirection.

'The explosions in Paris are still going well,' he remarked, continuing his train of thought.

'Indeed, Comrade General. That part of the operation's been well worth the money and effort we've expended on it. The French DST have caught the man who threw the grenade at the gates of the British Embassy on the rue du Faubourg St Honoré, and a girl blew herself up carrying a home-made bomb. But there's no chance of the French authorities establishing any connection between them and us.'

'Excellent!' Dolkov looked at his watch. He had promised Natalia he would be home early that evening; they were going to the ballet to see *Swan Lake*, one of his favourites. His car and driver would be waiting. He pushed himself to his feet. 'Not much longer,' he said. 'Only another week or so, Leonid.'

And then, he thought, he'd have brought off the coup of a lifetime.

22

Paris, Spring 198–

As an added measure of security, the Foreign Secretary and Lady Manville, with their accompanying entourage of secretaries, aides, advisers and two detectives, flew to Paris for the Western Summit Conference in an RAF aircraft. The jet touched down at Le Bourget – an airfield now normally used only for private flying, and of course the biennial Paris Air Show.

Again in the interests of security, the official welcome had been cut to an absolute minimum. These formalities quickly over, the Foreign Secretary and Lady Manville were free to greet Sir George Fauvic, the British Ambassador, and his wife, Kathleen, less ceremoniously. In fact, the greetings were especially warm and sincere, for they were all old friends. The two women were distantly related and, not having their husband's preoccupations with problems of State, were looking forward to a pleasant week in each other's company.

'Springtime in Paris,' said Mary Manville somewhat tritely. 'What could be more pleasant?'

The Ambassador was sour. 'We could do without these damned bomb scares. They disrupt our lives all the time. Now – '

He looked around, prepared to issue orders, but his wishes had already been foreseen. The aircraft was being unloaded as quickly as possible, and personal luggage, despatch boxes and briefcases stored in the boots of the convoy of cars that was waiting on the apron.

The Manvilles shook hands with the flight crew, and Sir Hubert began to make his way towards the large black limousine with the Union Jack flying from its bonnet. But the Ambassador stopped him.

'Sorry, Hubert, that's not for you. You're to go with the women in the unmarked Renault. More security, you know. We don't want anyone to blow you up before you have a chance to do your bit at the Conference.'

'What about you, George?'

'Oh, I'm expendable, I suppose. Anyway, there are lots of senior men who'd be only too happy to have my job. They'd do it just as brilliantly, I dare say. But you're irreplaceable, at least at the moment.'

'You flatter me. Maybe you'd better tell that to the PM.' Manville grinned, but he didn't argue. 'I'll see you at the Residence, then.'

But once in the car, driving down the Autoroute to Paris, he complained. 'This wretched security! I get so tired of it. It's infinitely worse than it used to be. I can remember the days when any minister, or the PM for that matter, could stroll through St James's Park by himself, without any fuss.'

Lady Manville gave a small sigh and grimaced at her friend Kathleen. She had heard all this before. She began to talk about their respective families, and the Foreign Secretary took the hint and remained silent as the women talked. His thoughts had turned to the arrival of the Prime Minister the next day, and the opening session of the Summit.

'What?' he said, suddenly aware that his wife was addressing him.

'We were talking about David, darling. Evidently he's doing awfully well as a Counsellor here.'

'I know. It's splendid, but I can't say I'm surprised. He's a clever chap, though I've sometimes thought there might be some kind of flaw in his make-up.'

'Hubert! What on earth do you mean by that?'

For once the Foreign Secretary had spoken without thinking, and he gave his wife a guilty smile. He was allowed to criticize his son-in-law to her, but to no one else. And, after all, Julia could have married someone far less acceptable. Windfield came from the same kind of background. He was intelligent and attractive, and should reach the top of his profession. Most people would have considered him an excellent husband and father. It was true that sometimes he appeared self-centred and ruthless, but such occasions were rare. Certainly, to Manville's knowledge, neither Julia nor Rosemary had ever complained.

Sir Hubert drew a deep breath. He had no right to complain either, he thought. But, for some reason he had never succeeded in analysing, he had always failed to find David Windfield totally sympathetic. On the face of it he had a great deal in common with his son-in-law but, left alone together, their conversation was apt to become forced and stilted, and dwindle into silence. They were both too well-mannered and too experienced to let uncomfortable gaps last for long, but the relationship was not easy.

Occupied with these reflections, Manville had scarcely noticed the route the driver had taken. He was mildly surprised to find they were already in the rue du Faubourg St Honoré, and turning past two gendarmes through the imposing wrought-iron gates of the British Embassy, which was also the Ambassador's Residence.

'We're first,' Kathleen Fauvic said, pleased. 'That was the idea, that the others should avoid the Autoroute and go the roundabout way. And now, dears, would you like tea in your rooms? Drinks at six-thirty. We'll be eating early. Just us, so no need to dress tonight. Sunday supper.'

'That sounds wonderful.'

'If I may telephone Julia – ' said Manville.

'Of course. As you know from your programme, you'll be seeing her at a *vin d'honneur* at the Elysée Palace tomorrow night, and I imagine you'll have met David during the day. They'll both be dining with us later in the week, and you're going to spend a few days with them after the Conference, of course. But by all means phone, whenever you like. I'd have asked them in this evening, but I thought you and George might want to work, Hubert.'

'You're right as usual, Kathleen – *Madame l'Ambassadrice*.' Manville gently mocked her concern for his duties. 'There certainly are papers I should go through with George, and questions of great international importance to be settled.'

'Meanwhile we women will get on with real things – the practical side of life?'

'*Mais, naturellement! La famille est – la famille est, alors, très importante.*'

The three of them laughed at this harmless *badinage*. Nevertheless, Hubert Manville's first action when he reached their suite was to reach for the telephone. He knew that Julia would be anxious to know that they had arrived, and that their plans for the weekend were firm.

The phone rang only once before the receiver was picked up. 'I was waiting for your call, Dad. You and mother had a good journey? No alarms?'

'All safe and well. No alarms, as you call them, thank God. What about you?'

They exchanged news briefly, and Julia said, 'We're looking forward to next weekend. I've not arranged anything. I thought you'd prefer to be free for once, and as lazy as you liked.'

'I doubt if it'll be possible to be as lazy as I might like, not with young Rosemary around. She's arriving on Thursday, I gather.'

'Yes. Her half-term break's from Thursday to Tuesday.'

'Good. At any rate we'll keep the weekend to the family, and hope the media don't make a nuisance of themselves. Or the security people. Do you know, Julia, I had an absolute row with the Security Service and the French about staying with you? They said they couldn't guarantee my safety in a private house, and it would be much wiser for me to leave Paris immediately the Summit's over.'

'I can imagine. We've had men inspecting this place for days. But you're going to stick to the original plan, aren't you, Dad? We'd be terribly disappointed – '

'So would your mother and I. No. I told them that if anyone wanted to plant a bomb or take a pot-shot at me he was as likely to do it in London as in Paris, and they'd better accept that fact. Anyway, one can't spend one's life being fearful of what might happen. But you really are quite happy about our visit, Julia?'

'Of course, Dad. Haven't I just said so?'

★

'One can't spend one's life being fearful of what might happen.'

Sir Hubert was repeating himself, and on this occasion with considerable greater vehemence. It was the following afternoon, and the end of the first session of the Conference. The Prime Minister and the Foreign Secretary had agreed to a meeting with the representatives of the British media in Paris. It had little meaning, other than as a political gesture of good-will, for they could say nothing of interest at this stage. Finally, as the questions tailed off, someone raised the question of security. But that, too, was stale news, and only Richard Kent persisted with the subject.

'Foreign Secretary, have you received a spate of threats directly concerned with this Western Summit, like the Prime Minister?'

'No, Mr Kent, I haven't. And I'm not aware of the details of any threats to the Prime Minister. In any case we don't compete in terms of threats.'

'But have you received any at all, Foreign Secretary?' Richard Kent continued, as the laughter occasioned by Sir Hubert's mild joke subsided.

Manville hesitated. 'No,' he said. 'Not recently.'

'In the circumstances, don't you consider that rather odd, sir?'

'Odd, Mr Kent? No, not particularly.' Manville was growing annoyed by Kent's insistence. 'I believe that even media people are threatened from time to time. May I ask when you last received a threat?'

'I was hoping you'd ask that, Foreign Secretary. Actually, it was last night – an extremely menacing phone call. Either I was to return to London at once, or else – it made me think I must be getting something right.'

Richard Kent had spoken casually, but he had gripped his audience. A murmur of surprise went round the room, and many of those present pondered the precise significance of his last sentence. True, journalists – especially political journalists – were accustomed to occasional threats, and inevitably some were killed in the course of their duties. But Kent wasn't a foreign correspondent nor, though he sometimes appeared in unexpected places, did he undertake especially dangerous assignments. Accidents apart, he was an unlikely person to be at risk.

Manville said, 'But you're still with us, Mr Kent. They – whoever they were – didn't frighten you away.'

'No, Foreign Secretary, but I'm taking precautions. I don't go down dark alleys by myself at night.'

This produced another laugh, as the Prime Minister nodded approval. Richard Kent sat down. A correspondent from one of the 'heavies' asked a question on a different topic, which was quickly answered, and a couple of minutes later the Press Secretary brought the interview to a close.

Sir Hubert Manville was thoughtful. He knew a lot more about Richard Kent than most of Kent's colleagues, because he had made it his business to follow Kent's career. Though he had never quite forgiven him for Celia's death, he had a respect, even a grudging admiration, for the man.

He was certain that Kent had not been shooting a line, that his story was true. Kent had indeed received a threatening call, but whether the reason was because he 'was getting something right', whatever that might mean, was another matter. Yet Manville had a strong impression that Richard Kent had been attempting to give him a warning of some kind. He tried to dismiss the idea, but he couldn't rid himself of it.

It troubled him so much that, later in the evening, at the *vin d'honneur* given by the French President at the Elysée Palace, after he and his wife had sought out their daughter for a brief greeting, he made a point of having what he thought of as a quiet word with his son-in-law.

'Richard Kent? Oh, yes,' David said. 'He's been in Paris for a few weeks, gathering material for a new book, I believe, and of course pontificating on the Conference, and its possible results.'

'He holds firm views about it? Most of the questions he asked me concerned security.'

David Windfield shrugged. 'He was on French television on Friday night in a *débat* with some other pundits. He rather harped on the nervy atmosphere in Paris at the moment, as if everyone were waiting for something dramatic to happen.'

'You wouldn't agree with him?'

'As you know, sir, there has been yet another series of bombings and bomb scares in Paris recently. These things tend to make everyone a little jittery. But the French police and the DST are extremely efficient, and I'm sure that if they had any knowledge – any intelligence – about dramatic plans relating to the Conference we would have been warned. I can't believe Richard knows more than they or we do.'

'It seems unlikely,' Manville admitted. He paused, considering. Then he asked, 'David, have you any idea why anyone should want Kent out of Paris enough to threaten him personally?'

'I wasn't aware that anyone had threatened him.'

'So he says.'

'I see.' Windfield's smile was supercilious. 'I wouldn't take that too seriously, sir. It's probably a gimmick to draw attention to himself, not unlike the rumour that he'd refused a knighthood.'

Manville stared at his son-in-law, nodded impatiently, and walked away. David had annoyed him. He knew the story of the knighthood, knew that it was more than a rumour. Kent had been sounded out about an honour – nominally for services to journalism – and had said he wasn't interested so, as protocol demanded, the matter had been quietly dropped. Windfield had no right to imply that Kent had started a false rumour to gain publicity. And, if he were so inaccurate about Kent on one subject, his other judgements concerning the man could hardly be trusted. It was not reassuring.

For a while Sir Hubert Manville mingled with the other guests. He was attentive to the men, charming to their wives. He listened politely to opinions with which he didn't agree, but expressed his own views only to those who actively sought them.

Eventually, finding himself again in a group with Julia, he drew her aside. She looked at him anxiously.

'Is anything wrong?'

'No, but I wanted to ask you something. Have you seen anything of Richard Kent since he's been in Paris? I'm told he's been here some time.'

To his surprise, colour rose in Julia's cheeks. 'I – I've had lunch with him a couple of times, and we met him at a reception. David said we should have him to dinner, and I invited him, though not for any specific date. That was lucky because David keeps on making excuses.' Realizing that she was offering unnecessary explanations, Julia stopped short. 'Why – why do you ask?'

Manville had already begun to regret his question. His daughter's reaction had been unexpected, and he was not sure how to interpret it. But clearly he had stumbled on a topic that embarrassed her.

He replied vaguely. 'It occurred to me that you might have some clue about the line he's taking over the Summit.'

Julia frowned and shook her head. 'I'm not sure what you mean by a "line", Dad. David thinks Richard's not to be trusted, but – oh, you'd better ask David, Dad.'

Sir Hubert hesitated again, before persisting. 'Why does David think Kent's not to be trusted?'

'I think David thinks he's – he's sympathetic to the Soviets.'

'But apparently Richard's a friend of yours, Julia. You must trust him yourself.'

Julia took this as a statement and didn't contradict her father. Instead she said again, 'Why all these questions about Richard?'

'It's like this. Kent says he's received a threatening phone call. Leave Paris, or else – you know. I'm interested in why anyone should want him out of the way.'

Julia, Manville knew, was an intelligent woman, but now she stared at him as if she were having difficulty translating what he said into a language she could understand. Then her chin came up and her mouth shut. She was clearly angry.

'How can you be so calm? You want to know *why* someone's threatening Richard? You don't seem to care a damn that he might get hurt, perhaps badly hurt – perhaps killed! Well, I care, even if you don't. You – '

'Julia!' Manville expostulated.

Fortunately, what might have turned into a bitter argument was interrupted by Sir George Fauvic with a couple whom he wished to introduce to the Foreign Secretary. Sir Hubert was forced to give them his attention, and Julia seized her chance to slip away. Neither was there any further opportunity that evening for Manville to continue the conversation with his daughter.

★

But Julia's outburst had worried Hubert Manville. While getting ready for bed that night he said to his wife, 'My dear, I think it might be advisable if you had a talk with Julia about her marriage. Apparently she's been seeing a fair amount of Richard Kent recently, and in my opinion she seems excessively concerned for him.'

Mary Manville stopped brushing her hair and laughed aloud. 'Oh darling Hubert, you can't mean that seriously. Mothers don't take their daughters to task about such things these days. If she wants to have an *affaire* with Richard Kent, I can't stop her.'

'You could try!' Sir Hubert was indignant.

'Why should I? She was desperately in love with Richard once. I never knew what happened between them, but I always thought she married David on a kind of rebound – quite apart from the accident. But an *affaire* with him now might get him out of her system for good. Otherwise she could well regret him always.'

Hopping from one foot to another as he put on his pyjama trousers, Manville said, 'I'm astounded at your attitude. What about David? An *affaire* could ruin the marriage.'

'I doubt that. Julia's a sensible woman and, even if David found out, he's far too ambitious to dream of divorcing the daughter of the Foreign Secretary.'

This was far too close to Sir Hubert's own thoughts. 'What a cynical remark, Mary,' he exploded. 'You don't usually criticize David. You shock me, you really do.' He paused, then added, 'Though I think you're perfectly right. All the same, I'm not having Julia risk her marriage. I refuse to let Rosemary have a broken home.'

As if this were the last word on the subject Hubert Manville disappeared into the adjoining bathroom. He failed to hear his wife mutter, 'Rosemary! I should have known it was your beloved Rosemary you were thinking about.'

23

Julia Windfield had found difficulty in deciding on her next step. It was unlike her to dither, but that was precisely what she had been doing all that Tuesday morning. Twice she had punched out Richard Kent's phone number on the keypad of her instrument, and twice she had replaced the receiver before the phone started to ring.

She had slept badly. Fears for Richard, prompted by her father's remarks at the reception the previous evening, had translated themselves into nightmares from which she woke in a series of cold sweats. David, snoring gently in the bed beside her, had given her no reassurance. She had told him what her father had said, but he had treated the matter with contempt.

'I doubt if there's anything to the story. Richard probably invented it. I've warned you, Julia. He's not to be trusted.'

David had left for the office early in the morning without making any further reference to Richard, leaving Julia in a quandary. What or whom should she believe, she asked herself bitterly as she picked up the phone for the third time. Now she let it ring, but there was no immediate answer. Angry with herself for worrying about Richard when no one else seemed to think there was any need to give a damn, she was about to hang up when the ringing tone ceased and she heard a slurred voice.

'Richard? Is that you?' Julia spoke sharply.

'Yes. Kent here. Who's that?' The words were still mumbled.

'It's Julia. Richard, are you all right?'

'All right?' She had the impression he was amused by her question. Then, 'Julia,' he murmured, 'what is it?'

'Are you all right, Richard? You sound odd.'

'Just walked into a door. It hurt me.'

There was a bang, not really loud, but enough to make Julia wince as it reverberated in her eardrum, as if Richard had dropped his receiver to his desk. Then she heard a heavy thud, followed by the gentle hiss of an open line. Julia pictured Richard lying on the floor, the receiver out of reach above him. She called to him two or three times but, when there was no reply, she didn't hesitate.

Inside five minutes Julia had taken her car from the garage and was speeding along the rue de Longchamp towards the Avenue Charles de Gaulle. A thin drizzle, sufficient to make windscreen wipers necessary, was hampering drivers, and she reached the Arc de Triomphe to find the traffic there almost solid. Frustrated by the delay, she drove with an unusual aggressiveness, causing several motorists to hoot at her indignantly. She paid them no attention, but in spite of switching lanes, giving way only when compelled, and forcing the car along, it was nearly twenty minutes before she drew up outside the apartment block where Richard was staying.

Julia had not considered how she was to get into his apartment if Richard didn't answer the *entrée*. In fact, she had no trouble; Richard might have been expecting her. The outer door was released as soon as she pressed the bell.

'Richard!'

'Julia!' At the door of his flat he seemed surprised rather than pleased. 'Hello,' he said at last.

'Richard!' Julia exclaimed again. She stared at him in horror. One of his eyes was half closed, his cheek was bruised, his lip split and his skin had a greenish pallor. Without thinking she put her arms around him and hugged him. Richard cried out.

'Oh, darling! What is it?'

Richard's breath was shallow. He swallowed. 'Sorry!' he said. 'I've got a couple of cracked ribs.'

'But how? What happened?'

'I suppose you've got to know, Julia, now you're here. I went to collect my car from the basement garage and was set upon. Not being as resourceful as I might, I failed to despatch my Panolov – actually there were three of them, which is some excuse – ' He

214

stared at Julia for a moment. 'In a word, I got beaten up.'

'Badly? Are you seriously hurt?'

'No, of course not. They were really very merciful,' Richard spoke lightly, trying to reduce the tension between them, though his words still slurred. He glanced at his watch. 'Julia, it was extremely kind of you to come to help, but I'm expecting a – a friend.'

Julia scarcely heard what he was saying. 'Dad said you'd been threatened. But why, Richard? What do these people want?'

'They clearly want me to leave Paris – and it's probably an excellent idea. Paris may be the most beautiful city in the world, but it hardly seems a healthy place for me at present. I wouldn't recommend it to – to anyone, either.' Again, his eyes met hers.

'Are you warning me now?' Julia shook her head in irritation as Richard made no reply. 'I don't understand. Who are these people, and why should they attack you in particular?'

Richard smiled, but still remained silent. They had been standing in the hall of the apartment and now, opening the front door, he gently pushed her out into the corridor.

'Goodbye, Julia. Again, thank you for coming. I'm sorry not to be more hospitable, but I really am expecting a friend at any moment.'

'Goodbye. I'm sorry I – I bothered you.'

Abruptly Julia turned away so that Richard shouldn't see the tears in her eyes. She hurried to the lift, subconsciously registering the fact that, just as Richard had shut his front door, his *entrée* buzzer had sounded. And when she reached the ground floor and opened the lift gate, she saw a girl waiting to enter. She knew instinctively that this was Richard's 'friend'.

The girl, who wore a trench coat over scarlet slacks, was in her late twenties. Tall, with straight black hair and blue eyes, she was striking rather than pretty, and the first impression she gave was of casual self-assurance. '*Merci, madame,*' she said, sweeping past Julia into the lift.

'*Mademoiselle.*' Julia acknowledged her.

Wishing she could suppress the intense emotion – it could only be jealousy, she realized – that the presence of the girl had engendered, Julia left the apartment building and went to her car. Don't be a fool, she told herself; don't be stupid and irrational. Richard owed her nothing, and she'd been wrong to let herself become involved with him again. She must do her best to forget him – and his little mysteries. But all the same she found she was shaking, and it was several minutes before she could trust herself to drive away.

*

Thursday was the last day but one of the Western Summit, and the day on which the Fauvics were giving a small dinner party for the Manvilles. So far the week in Paris had been peaceful. The wave of bombings had subsided, at least temporarily, and though security remained strict, there was a general impression that the worst was over.

It was not an impression that Julia was able to share. She was finding it impossible to relax. She slept only with the aid of tranquillizers, and woke unrefreshed and unwilling to make the effort that her days required. She had to force herself to behave normally, while she waited for some unspecified disaster that she was convinced was imminent.

It was about ten o'clock, well after David had left for the Chancery, that Miss Denison, Rosemary's headmistress, telephoned to say that Rosemary had measles and would be unable to come to Paris for half-term. What a pity, thought Julia. Rosemary would be disappointed, and so would they all, especially Rosemary's grandfather. But there would be other half-terms, other chances for the family to be together, if not in Paris, in some other foreign capital that Rosemary would consider exciting.

Miss Denison passed the phone to Rosemary so that she could speak to her mother herself. At sixteen she was a calm, self-possessed girl, used to being separated from her parents. Attractive, articulate and reasonably clever, she enjoyed school, appreciated the travelling that came her way because of her father's profession, and was secretly proud of the *cachet* of being the granddaughter of the Secretary of State for Foreign Affairs. She rarely made a fuss, and Julia did not expect too great a reaction to this bad luck.

But Julia was wrong. Rosemary complained bitterly, in a manner quite unlike her. She wasn't well. She was covered with spots and looked horrible. It was lonely in the sanatorium; everyone else was leaving for the half-term break. If she couldn't go to Paris, her mother could come to her. Why not? Why not? Rosemary began to cry.

At the other end of the line Julia gripped the receiver tightly, and did her best to be patient. She commiserated with her daughter. She promised her a wonderful holiday when term ended. She said she would ask Rosemary's grandfather and grandmother to take back some especially lovely presents for her. What would she like?

Rosemary sniffed, and said she didn't want a thing, except for her mother to come. Didn't her mother love her any more? Were Paris parties more important than a sick daughter? Didn't anyone care about her?

In any other circumstances Julia would have laughed and told Rosemary to stop play-acting and be sensible. Of course she was loved, as she knew darned well, but it was impossible for her mother to come to the UK at this juncture. After all, Rosemary only had spotty measles. She wasn't seriously ill. And she mustn't behave like a spoilt brat, must she? And at another time Rosemary would have laughed with her, and said she might be a brat but she wasn't spoilt.

But somehow today was different. For her part Julia had other worries and preoccupations. Rosemary seemed full of self-pity. Neither of them was behaving in character and Julia, who should have appreciated this, let her temper snap.

'Rosemary, listen. I cannot come over till after the weekend and that's final. There are other people to consider as well as you – your father, your grandparents, for example. Now, stop behaving like a baby and let me speak to Miss Denison again.'

'If you want to talk to her, then phone her yourself.'

The receiver in England was banged down, the connection cut. Julia swore under her breath. She waited. The headmistress believed that girls should have good manners and she would ensure that Rosemary called back to apologize for her outburst.

But it was ten minutes before the telephone rang, and then it was Miss Denison, not Rosemary, on the line. She admitted that Rosemary was unwell and upset, but made no reference to an apology. Julia replied coldly. She repeated that it was impossible for her to leave Paris before the following Monday, when her parents would be returning to England. She said goodbye, feeling that somehow she had been placed in a false position.

★

Julia greeted David with the news that Rosemary could not come to Paris as soon as he entered the house that evening. She expected him to be philosophical about the change of plan, if not indifferent to it. To her surprise he exploded with anger.

'For God's sake! Why does she have to get measles now, of all times? Hasn't she had them before? I thought she had measles that Christmas we were meant to spend with your cousins in Switzerland, which was why we couldn't go. Can you have measles twice?'

'There are different kinds,' Julia said mildly. 'German measles and – '

'Is she seriously ill?' David interrupted.

'No. Just sorry for herself.'

'Then why can't she come? We've both had measles and I'm sure your parents have.'

'Oh, David, do be sensible! Of course she can't travel – certainly not alone. I'm not sure if she's infectious now the spots have developed, but she's probably got a temperature. It's impossible.'

'Our bloody luck, that's what it is!' David wrenched off his tie. 'I need a drink.'

'We're already running late for dinner.'

'Too bloody bad!'

'David! The Fauvics are having a very busy week, too. It's good of them to arrange this dinner – '

'Rosemary'll have to join us later.' David spoke under his breath, but Julia caught the words.

She was becoming annoyed. 'What on earth do you mean? This is only the half-term break. Of course she'll be joining us when term ends.'

David had swallowed one quick whisky and poured himself another. The liquor seemed to steady him. Glass in hand, he turned to face Julia.

'Listen,' he said grimly. 'There's something you don't know, Julia – and it's important. I expect us to be leaving Paris soon, and don't be too surprised if we move at short notice. I can't tell you more than that for the moment – '

'But why? Your posting's not up. We've only been here – '

'It's connected with my other work. The intelligence side. There's been a bit of trouble.'

'You mean because of Panolov?'

'Panolov?'

'The man you thought was going to mug you. The man you – '

'Yes, yes. I – I'd forgotten his name. Yes, in connection with that – incident.' David finished his second drink quickly and put down his glass. 'Julia, you're not to tell anyone about this, or even hint at it – to your parents or anyone. There could be all hell to pay if – '

'Of course I won't tell anyone if you say not.'

'Good. I do say not.' David hesitated. 'I must go and change.' He went to Julia, put his arms around her and would have kissed her on the mouth, but she moved her head so that his lips only brushed her cheek. 'Darling,' he said, 'I love you. Don't worry. Everything will be all right.'

Easy enough to say, Julia thought cynically as David hurried from the room. But could she believe him? Would everything be all right? If there were any real trouble her father would make every effort to help, if only for her sake, but there were limits to what he could or would do. If there was a scandal, and David was kicked out of the Foreign Office, it could easily affect his own position in the Government . . .

In the car, driving to the Residence, Julia tried to question David, but he would not respond. He said he couldn't talk and concentrate on his driving, and in any case he'd already told her more than he should. There was nothing he could add, except that all the relevant decisions would be made before the coming weekend was over.

Julia arrived at the Residence in an unhappy mood. It required an effort to make casual conversation, when her mind was constantly reverting to what David had said. Richard had assured her that there was unlikely to be trouble over Panolov, but it seemed he had been misinformed. Or was it possible, she suddenly wondered, that Richard had betrayed what she had told him. If this were so, it would be her fault if David . . .

'Darling, what's the matter?' Mary Manville said. 'We've spoken to you twice, and you haven't answered.'

'I'm sorry.' Julia focused her attention on her mother. The ladies, leaving the men to their cigars and port, were having after-dinner coffee in the drawing-room. As an excuse, she added, 'I know it's silly, but I'm a little worried about Rosemary.'

'Very natural,' Lady Fauvic said. 'Such a shame she can't come to Paris while your parents are here.' She paused to sip her coffee. 'But actually I asked if you knew whether it was true that Richard Kent had been attacked and badly hurt, and that's why he's gone back to London. All I know is that we invited him tonight, and he sent apologies. I thought David might have heard something.'

'I – I didn't even know he had gone back to London,' Julia said, pleased that she could sound so indifferent. 'Certainly David hasn't mentioned it.'

'Such a clever man, Richard Kent,' one of the guests said. 'His last book was absolutely brilliant. And that piece of his in *The Times* this morning. I thought he was surprisingly optimistic about the outcome of the Conference.'

'He may well be right,' Sir George Fauvic commented, overhearing this last remark as the men joined the ladies. 'It *is* going remarkably well. We hope that tomorrow's communiqué will be more than just the usual anodyne stuff.'

Julia listened as they discussed Richard. She had told no one of her last visit to his apartment. Certainly he had joked about leaving Paris, but hardly in terms of a serious and immediate intention, and she hadn't seen or heard from him since. There was no reason, she knew, why he should have let her know that he had decided to go. Nevertheless, she felt hurt – and alone. His departure added an extra dimension to her general feeling of unease.

24

Shortly after noon on Friday morning Lady Fauvic used her own car to drive Lady Manville, accompanied by Sir Hubert's detective and the Manvilles' personal luggage, to the Windfields' house on the rue de Longchamp. The gendarme on duty outside the building saluted as they passed through the blank, black gates into the small forecourt.

The *femme de ménage* answered the doorbell; she greeted the visitors with the news that Madame Windfield had gone out to the local shops, but would be back in a few minutes.

'Silly girl,' Mary Manville said. 'I told her not to bother about lunch, that I'd be happy with a sandwich or a salad. I've eaten far too much in the last week, anyway.'

The detective, guided by the *femme de ménage*, set off to inspect the house, and volunteered to take the bags upstairs as he did so. In the meantime, Lady Manville, assuming the role of hostess in the absence of her daughter, led the way into the salon. In spite of her dismissal of Hubert's doubts concerning Julia's marriage, she was worried about her daughter. Julia, she thought, had looked tense and unhappy at dinner the previous evening.

'Well, if Julia's not here, let's help ourselves,' she said. 'Sherry, Kathleen?'

'Please. Medium dry.'

'It was very good of you to bring me over here privately like this.' Mary carefully poured two glasses of sherry, and brought them to where her friend was sitting.

Kathleen Fauvic shook her head. 'No bother, my dear. As you know, it was all arranged. George thought that if you and Hubert arrived here separately and with as little fuss as possible, you might escape some media interest and have a more peaceful weekend.'

'Which Hubert certainly needs. He's been working tremendously hard lately.'

'I know. George, too. But it seems to have been worth it, doesn't it? The Summit's really been a great success, apparently – even more successful than they expected – and there's been no trouble of any kind.'

'And that's a relief. I must admit I've had the odd qualm about this Conference, Kathleen.'

'Haven't we all?' said Lady Fauvic quickly. 'But it's over now, thank God, so enjoy your weekend.'

Mary Manville smiled. 'We'll do our best.'

Julia came in as they were talking. She apologized for not being there to welcome them. 'You must blame David,' she said. 'He phoned a few minutes ago to say he's asked a couple of friends in for dinner this evening. I was hoping it would be just family, and I'm sure Dad was, but David decided not.' Julia couldn't hide her annoyance. 'So I had to do some extra shopping.'

'You see, it wasn't your lunch she was worrying about, Mary.' Kathleen Fauvic laughed.

'No, evidently not,' Mary Manville said lightly, but she glanced keenly at her daughter. 'More sherry, Kathleen?'

'Thank you, no. If I can collect Hubert's detective, I must go. I've got a luncheon date.'

Mary tried to dissuade her but she persisted and, when she had left, Mary said, 'Julia dear, come and sit down, and let's have a glass of sherry together. You're looking ragged. Surely two more for dinner can't make that amount of difference.'

Julia poured herself a sherry, though she would have preferred a strong gin, and sat down opposite her mother. 'Not really,' she said. 'Most of the food can easily be stretched, but we're having stuffed vine leaves for the first course, so I had to buy some extras. There's also the question of help. Usually when we entertain I have people in to serve and so on, but it's impossible at such short notice.'

'Does it matter? We'll only be six. Hubert's detective won't expect to eat with us.'

'Well, there's nothing I can do about it now.'

Lady Manville sighed. It was unlike Julia to make a mountain out of a molehill. She wondered if she should mention Richard Kent's name, and decided against it. If Julia wanted to talk, she would. It was useless to try to force her confidences.

'Who are these extra guests, anyway?' she asked instead. 'They can't be all that important if David only invited them at the last minute.'

'Oh, it's not like that, mother. They're just the Fischers. Karl and Eva.'

'But how nice! I was afraid they were going to be people we'd never met.' Mary Manville was genuinely pleased. 'I've always had a soft spot for Karl and Eva, ever since the accident. They couldn't have behaved more sensibly or helpfully. If it weren't for them, you might have suffered considerably more than you did, Julia. And they were so sympathetic about dear Celia. So far in Paris we've only been able to snatch a few sentences with them at a reception.'

'That's just what David said. Apparently Karl phoned to ask if there was any chance of seeing you and Dad over the weekend, and David decided that dinner tonight would be best.'

'I think that was a good idea. We'll be able to have a proper talk. I can't imagine why you're making such a fuss about it, Julia. I'm sure Hubert will be perfectly happy with the arrangement. We'll look forward to it.'

Indeed, Mary Manville was proved right. When the Foreign Secretary was delivered, with his detective, at the Windfields' house in the late afternoon, he expressed unreserved pleasure at the opportunity to meet the Fischers informally once again.

And Julia was left to blame herself for having been angry with David at upsetting her plans for a peaceful family evening, when clearly no one else minded in the least.

*

That evening Julia was busy in the kitchen. The *femme de ménage* had laid the dining-room table before she left, and prepared all the vegetables. It was to be a simple meal. Only the main course was hot, which meant there would be little for Julia to worry about, and she could enjoy her own party.

David had warned her that he would be late home; there was a lot of post-Conference work to be completed. But, glancing at the clock as she took off her apron and prepared to join her mother and father in the salon, she was surprised to find that he was not yet back. She couldn't believe that he had returned without her hearing the car.

Nevertheless, there he was, pouring himself a drink. He turned as she came into the room and, glass in hand, went to kiss her.

'Darling, I'm sorry I'm so late.'

'I didn't hear you arrive.'

'That's because I came by taxi. Absolutely infuriating, as I was telling your parents. I was driving perfectly happily up the Champs-Elysées when a wretched Renault charged out of a side street and hit me. We had to go through the whole bit, of course. Police, protestations, arguments, general fun and games, until finally we filled in all those wretched questions in the *Constat aimable*. At least I had some satisfaction. The Renault had to be towed away, but I could drive the Jag to a garage, where the chap was very good and got me a cab.'

'But what a nuisance, dear,' Mary Manville exclaimed.

'Fortunate you weren't hurt, David,' said her husband. 'These French drivers!'

'They're usually extremely disciplined, Dad,' remarked Julia. 'You were unlucky, darling. What a shame!'

David accepted their commiserations, then said that he must go and wash, if they'd excuse him. In the doorway he hesitated, and turned back.

'Julia, I've had a thought. It's never easy parking in the street here in the evening. Would you phone Karl? He shouldn't have left yet. Tell him he can put that huge Mercedes of his into our garage. Without the Jag there's plenty of room. It might save him a hassle.'

'Yes. All right.'

Julia went to the telephone. Eva answered at once, and said Karl would be grateful. 'I'm glad you caught us. We were just about shutting the front door. See you soon.'

'We'll be expecting you. I'll warn the gendarme.'

She slipped on a coat and went out through the kitchen and the garage, opening and leaving open the garage doors and the gates that fronted on to the rue de Longchamp. It was a fine evening, but chilly, and she didn't envy the gendarme pacing steadily up and down the pavement outside the house. She made a mental note to take him a mug of coffee later.

Returning to the house she met the Manvilles' detective, who promised he would shut the gates and garage doors once the Fischers had arrived. But when she mentioned coffee for the gendarme he wasn't particularly sympathetic.

'The *flics* take good care of themselves,' he said.

Julia laughed. She was feeling happier and more optimistic. The Summit was over, she reasoned to herself, successfully and without incident; her parents had arrived, prepared to enjoy a family weekend; they had regretted Rosemary's absence, but they hadn't minded about the Fischers. Even David, who might have been furiously angry over the damage to his Jaguar, seemed in a better humour. Perhaps his fears of having to leave Paris in some kind of disgrace might not be realized after all. She herself had been worrying too much, about David and Rosemary – and Richard Kent. She must learn to be more relaxed.

★

The Fischers arrived. The Manvilles were clearly pleased to see them, and the evening promised well. Out of deference to Sir Hubert they avoided politics and the Conference, but chatted about Paris, about Karl's and Eva's movements since they had last met, about the unfortunate Rosemary. If David was unusually silent, only Julia noticed.

The meal was leisurely and informal. David poured the wine, and Eva insisted on helping Julia in the kitchen. It was after eleven before dinner was finally over. Julia looked into the study, where the detective had eaten, intending to ask him if there was anything more he would like but, to her amusement, found him asleep in an armchair, tie loosened, collar undone, snoring gently, the remains of his meal on a tray beside him.

'So much for security,' she said to herself, returning to the kitchen with the tray.

The kitchen was empty, but Eva had made the coffee and left it ready to be taken into the salon. Julia poured a mug to take out to the gendarme. It was a different officer, and he hesitated, looking up and down the street, before accepting it. Julia divined his thoughts, and told him to come through the gates and into the forecourt to drink it. She told him that some German friends, who had come to dinner and parked their Mercedes in the garage, would be leaving before too long.

'My husband will be seeing them out and locking up,' she said. 'But perhaps you'd check the gates when they've gone.'

'*Mais, oui, madame. Merci. Vous êtes très gentille.*' The gendarme saluted her.

Julia returned to the house. The door of the dining-room was shut, but she could hear the murmur of men's voices from behind it. The coffee tray had disappeared from the kitchen and she assumed that Eva had taken it in to her mother in the salon. In fact, she found Eva there alone.

'Where's mother?' Julia asked.

'I think she went into the dining-room. Where have you been?' Eva's eyes were bright, her ugly face alive with excitement like a child's at a party.

'I've just taken some coffee out to the gendarme.'

'You've *what*?' Eva spoke so sharply that Julia stared at her in surprise.

'Just taken some coffee to the wretched gendarme who has to parade up and down outside in the cold. Is there anything wrong with that? It's a fine night, but – '

She stopped, realizing that Eva was no longer listening. Eva had gone to the window and, pulling back the curtains, was staring out towards the street. Then, without a word of explanation, she ran from the room, calling 'Karl! Karl!'

In spite of her astonishment, Julia automatically poured herself a cup of coffee and drank it. She took neither cream nor sugar, and thought it tasted bitter. She made a face – Eva makes her coffee too strong, she thought – put down her cup and stood up, intending to draw the curtains that Eva had left open. Without warning, she was overcome by a wave of giddiness. She ran her hand over her face, but the gesture didn't help. She was aware of her heart thumping, and was suddenly acutely fearful. She started across the room in search of help – David, her father, her mother – but stumbled and fell across the sofa. And there she lay until she sank quietly into a deep, drug-induced sleep.

★

In the forecourt outside the house the gendarme had drunk his coffee appreciatively. It tasted somewhat unpleasant, but it warmed him and, anyway, you couldn't expect the English to make good coffee. He wiped his moustache and wondered what to do with the mug. He had no wish to disturb the occupants of the house, so eventually he put it on the ground close to the garage entrance.

As he straightened himself he staggered a little. Then he found himself staring at the coffee mug. He was not a stupid man, and instinctively his mind made the connection. He realized he was breaking into a cold sweat. By now he wasn't sure whether he was feeling unwell, or merely imagining his symptoms. He started towards the gates but, before he had time to reach for his radiophone, he found himself lying on the ground inside the metal-backed railings. Soon he was asleep, and he knew nothing of being man-handled into the back of the garage, of the needle jabbed into his arm or the cords that trussed him. It would be some hours before he, like Sir Hubert's detective, learned what had happened to him.

25

In an apartment on the other side of the rue de Longchamp, directly opposite the Windfields' house, the two SIS officers who were keeping watch stared at each other. They had seen Julia bring the mug of coffee to the gendarme, who had disappeared through the gates to drink it. But it was odd that he had not reappeared.

'Go and see what's happening,' said one of the officers.

'Why not?' said the other, starting for the door.

That they were there at all was due to Richard Kent. Kent had faced a great deal of opposition from his superiors to his proposal for twenty-four-hour undercover surveillance by the SIS of the Foreign Secretary and his family while they were in Paris during and, particularly, after the Summit Conference. It was argued that their safety was in the hands of the Special Branch in liaison with the French police, and that any further action was unnecessary, especially after the Conference was over. But Richard had persisted, in spite of a lack of evidence that more than routine dangers were involved.

Richard had admitted that his suspicions were based largely on hunches, but the hunches were not entirely without foundation. The curious behaviour of the Russian, Panolov, who had seemingly been told off to keep some sort of watch on both David and Julia, was intriguing and the fact that the Russian had on occasion appeared to concentrate on Julia, rather than her husband, was odd. Even more fascinating had been the presence in Paris just before the Summit of Vladimir Dolkov, apparently posing as a culture hound and art connoisseur. And there had been other oddities – remarks of Julia, for example – and similar straws in the wind. He was sure he was right, but it had proved impossible to convince either his own Director or the PM, who himself expected to be the central focus for an attack, that any important resources should be diverted from other tasks.

In the end, Richard had been allowed to take what action he thought fit, as long as he sought no co-operation from the DST or other French authorities, and he had been given permission to assemble a team of three with a couple of cars for the operation – quite inadequate, Richard thought. Every schoolboy knew that it took at least ten people and four cars if unobtrusive surveillance were to be maintained.

But still, Richard thought, it was better than nothing. And luck had been with them. By chance a member of the SIS Paris Station lived in the apartment opposite the Windfields' house, and had been coerced somewhat unwillingly into providing them with an observation post, not high enough to see over the blanked railings, but useful nevertheless.

This evening Kent himself was sitting in his car, an unmarked Renault, a hundred yards down the rue de Longchamp. One of his team – a girl called Maureen Grant, whom Julia would have recognized as the woman she had met in the hall of Richard's apartment building – was beside him. They were in radio communication with the two men on watch, who had reported the disappearance of the gendarme.

'I think the Germans are on the point of leaving,' the voice from the apartment said suddenly. 'Their Merc is edging through the gates. No apparent hurry. Still no sign of the gendarme.'

The SIS officer who had gone down to the street to investigate broke in. 'The big man's driving the Merc. Little woman beside him. No one else in the car that I can see, but there could be. They're heading towards the Bois. Orders?'

'Okay.' Richard made up his mind. 'Continue to watch the house. If anyone else leaves, follow in your car. As a last resort, cry havoc and raise hell. We have the Merc in sight and we'll go after it.'

There was little traffic on the rue de Longchamp at that time of night. Richard waited until the big Mercedes had driven by, then, letting a Peugeot pass, he made a U-turn and followed at a safe distance. Neither he nor his companion spoke until Karl reached the southern end of the rue de Longchamp and turned right towards the River Seine and the Pont du Puteaux. Then Richard exclaimed, 'Thank God for that!'

The girl gave him a quick glance, and frowned. 'Why?'

'Why? Well, they're not going straight home, as you'd expect after a party. That could mean I'm right. They're up to something. I was afraid we might be on a wild-goose chase.'

Richard was used to making harsh decisions, but it hadn't been easy to decide to follow the Mercedes himself. He distrusted Karl and Eva Fischer intensely; he was convinced they were working for the Soviet bloc, probably directly to Moscow Centre, though he had never been able to prove it. But the temptation to let them go and make some excuse to enter the house on the rue de Longchamp had been strong. He yearned to know what had happened or was happening there. All the indications – including the mysterious disappearance of the gendarme – seemed to him to point to some operation directed against the Manvilles, an operation in which the Fischers were playing a major role. Abduction was an obvious option, so he, in turn, must play percentages, and follow them – and his hunch.

By now they had crossed the Seine, and were in the suburb of Puteaux. They turned right off the main street and suddenly Maureen broke in on Richard's thoughts. 'Careful. They're stopping. No, they're turning into that – that garage or service station. It looks shut – '

'We'll have to drive past. Try to see what they're doing.'

As they passed Maureen said, 'The doors of the big building next to what seems to be the office are open. It's probably the workshop. The Merc's going in there.'

'Damn!' Richard accelerated, then braked hard as they came to a crossroads. Behind him a car hooted reproachfully, but he paid no attention. He swung round the corner and parked. Maureen had the door open before they had stopped moving. She walked back to the corner, where she stood in the shadows and watched the forecourt of the garage, while Richard used the radio.

Nothing had changed on the rue de Longchamp, he was told.

No one had entered or left. There were still lights on all over the house, in the salon and upstairs. The gendarme had not reappeared.

Richard swore, not knowing whether to be encouraged or despairing. He turned the car, assuming that when the Mercedes left the garage it wouldn't come down this side street. He waited, cursing his limited back-up facilities.

Time seemed to creep slowly by. Richard tried not to look at the digital face of the car's clock. In fact, less than ten minutes had elapsed before he saw Maureen detach herself from the darkness and sprint towards him. He had the engine running and the door open before she reached the car. She flung herself into her seat.

'Quick, Richard! Quick! The Merc's gone, the way it came. It shot off. You'll never catch it. But another vehicle left just before it. You'll overtake it easily, it's just one of those Volkswagen minibuses that people convert and use for camping. Turn right.' Richard nodded and acted immediately. Maureen added, 'As far as I could see, one man driving – not Fischer – and a woman beside him.'

Richard's mind raced. The Fischers had delivered something – someone – to the garage and were now probably on their way to the apartment where they were staying, and where they would establish their alibi. To judge from the time spent in the workshop one or more people could have been transferred from the floor or the boot of the Mercedes to the minibus. And they could travel in comfort – or discomfort – in an innocent Volkswagen for a considerable distance.

At the thought of Julia, Richard said fiercely, 'They've got to be stopped. If necessary I'll ram the damn thing – and to hell with the consequences. You've got a gun, Maureen?'

'Of course. You?'

'No. You know I rarely carry one. And if we get to needing two weapons, we'll have lost the battle.'

★

231

Julia Windfield was not in the Volkswagen. She was lying on the sofa in the salon of her house in the rue de Longchamp, gradually wakening from her drug-induced sleep. David was kneeling beside her, holding her hand. He had put a cushion under her head and, though the room was warm, had covered her with a rug.

'Darling, are you all right? Would you like something? A glass of water?' he asked.

'What's happened, David?' Julia made an effort to move but he pressed her gently back. 'Where's everyone?'

'They've gone, darling.'

'Gone? What on earth do you mean? Gone where?' She pulled her hand away from his and this time David couldn't prevent her from sitting up.

'Julia, are you sure you're all right?'

'I feel as if I've got a bloody hangover. It – it must have been the coffee. Eva put something into it.' She gritted her teeth. 'David! What's happened?'

David rose from his knees, and sat down on the sofa beside her. He had to tell her the truth, and he had to put it bluntly. He said, 'Darling, I'm afraid this is going to be an enormous shock to you, but the fact is the Fischers have smuggled your parents out of the house and are passing them on to some – er – friends. These friends will take them to – to Moscow.' He held his breath as he waited for her reaction.

'Moscow? David, are you crazy?' Julia stared at her husband in disbelief. It was a bad dream, a nightmare. She felt inclined to laugh.

'No.' David's voice was suddenly hard. This was, he knew, the crux, the point of no return for Julia and himself.

'Listen, darling,' he said, 'and try to take in what I'm telling you, because it's vitally important. This was a most carefully planned operation. By Monday it will be realized that Sir Hubert and Lady Manville have disappeared. Rumours, which are about to be spread around, will hint that they've gone to Russia. Soon these rumours will be confirmed, and the headlines will read, "BRITISH FOREIGN SECRETARY DEFECTS WITH FAMILY." It'll be a scandal to rival Burgess and Maclean. Even Philby will seem small beer. And you can imagine the repercussions, the waves the announcement will cause throughout the West.'

'You're mad, David. It's not true! It's a pack of lies! If there's any truth in it at all, it means they've been kidnapped. Dad would never defect. None of his friends will believe it for a moment.' Half-drugged as she still was, Julia could hear herself; her voice sounded shrill and stupid.

'Oh yes, they certainly will. When he starts making statements, appearing on radio and television, being photographed with the Soviet hierarchy – '

'But he won't. Even if he is in – in Russia, he'll refuse. He'd rather be killed – and I suppose you'll say that would be the alternative. Don't be silly, David. You're sounding like a character from some cheap spy thriller.'

'I dare say I do, Julia. But nevertheless your father will do as he's told. It's not his own death that matters. He's very fond of your mother, for instance. He wouldn't want anything to happen to her. And he's even fonder of Rosemary. He won't be able to watch either of them being maltreated – ' David stopped; he didn't want to sound too brutal.

'You – you – ' Julia could find no words. 'Anyway, Rosemary's in England,' she said weakly.

'I telephoned Miss Denison this afternoon to say that, measles or not, some close friends of ours would be collecting her tomorrow and taking her home with them for the rest of the half-term break. She'll be flown out of the country the same day.'

'David! How could you.' Julia paused. By now the shock of her husband's words was beginning to make her forget the after-effects of the drug. 'You've never liked Dad, have you?' she said. 'But Rosemary!'

'She'll be quite all right. They all will. Your father will play along. He'll have no choice.'

'And what about me? Do you expect me to play too?' Suddenly she remembered. 'Where's Dad's detective? What have you done with him? And the gendarme outside?'

'Oh, they've both had a shot in the arm and they're having a good long sleep. They'll be found eventually, but not till Monday, we hope. They won't have come to any harm. No one will.'

Julia shook her head helplessly. She wanted to scream. She raised her fists to beat David until he admitted that what he had been telling her was a joke – that none of it was true. But in her heart of hearts she knew that it was, and the enormity of what was happening overwhelmed her. She felt powerless to act, or even to think with any clarity.

'Is that what you've planned for me?' she asked, not really caring.

'Oh no, darling. I love you. You must believe that.' David was deadly serious; he had to convince her. 'I want you. I need you to come with me.'

'To Moscow? You mean you're going to Russia too?'

'Yes. I've no option, have I? I've aroused a lot of suspicion in certain quarters, mainly thanks to our dear friend Richard Kent. Damn him to hell!' David looked at Julia. This was no time to reveal his true feelings towards Kent. 'I'd have to get out anyway, even without this operation. I tried to warn you.'

'Warn me? All you did was tell me lies. You're a shit, David, a shit – as well as a traitor.'

'Yes, I'm well aware of that,' he admitted in an attempt to be disarming. 'But – I love you, Julia. I don't know what I'd do without you. You'll come with me, won't you? Please.'

'What happens if I refuse?'

'I – I can't leave you behind to spread your version of events, and cast doubts on the whole story. You must realize that.'

'You'll kill me, then?' she asked calmly.

'No. I want you to come willingly but, if I must, I'll take you with me by force. However, for that I'll need help, and it'll be known when we arrive. You may not be allowed to see Rosemary or your parents for – for some while.' David shrugged. 'Darling, it won't be entirely up to me, but I promise you that if you co-operate I'll do my utmost to see you don't regret it. I swear it.'

'And I must decide immediately?'

'We need to pack and snatch a few hours' sleep. Then I'll collect the Jaguar. Incidentally, I didn't have an accident this evening, as you've probably guessed. I had to arrange matters so that Karl could park his car in the garage.' Carefully David kept the relief from his voice; from Julia's expression he believed he had won. 'We'll leave tomorrow morning about nine, as if we were going shopping. With luck, there won't be a hue and cry till Monday, but we need to get out of France and behind the Curtain, as they call it, as soon as possible.'

'Yes. Yes, I suppose we do,' Julia said slowly.

The effects of the drug had almost completely worn off now, and Julia was absorbing the full import of David's story. Her mind was beginning to work clearly once again. She could conceive of no means of helping her father and mother. But David had made one mistake; he had said that Rosemary would not be collected from school until the next day. So there was still time – somehow she must save Rosemary. Once she had done that, maybe she could find the strength to defy David – and his friends.

★

'I think they've spotted us,' Maureen Grant said.

'Yes. I'm afraid so. They're going much too slowly for the Périphérique. It was a smart move on their part to come down here and then turn north.' The Volkswagen had returned across the Seine and woven its way through the Bois de Boulogne to join the Périphérique – the motorway that encircles Paris – at the Porte de Passy, as if it was intending to go south. 'I can't do anything here without chancing a major pile-up and getting the police involved.'

'So what now? They're inviting us to pass them.'

'Sure. But as soon as we've committed ourselves they'll change lanes and go out the exit behind us. We'll slow down too, and see what happens.'

In the slow lane and at a dignified speed they continued in convoy around the Périphérique. Even at that time of night there was a steady flow of vehicles thundering along, through its tunnels and underpasses. Again and again, Richard's Renault and the Volkswagen he was following were overtaken.

Then, without warning, the driver of the Volkswagen accelerated, and went up the exit ramp at the Porte de Clignancourt. Richard swerved after him.

'Where the hell are they going?' Richard said. 'This doesn't even lead to an Autoroute. Hang on, we may be in for trouble if he's called up help.'

But there was no sign of any such assistance. The Volkswagen proceeded at a moderate pace through the *banlieue* of Paris towards St Denis, seemingly oblivious of the Renault or any other vehicle.

'I know,' said Richard suddenly. 'They're making for the N1 and the little airport at Beauvais. I'm sure they didn't expect to be followed or they'd have gone direct. Any moment now they'll try to throw us off the trail.'

As he spoke the Volkswagen turned at the last moment into the complicated one-way system around Montmagny. This was an area that Richard knew well, and he realized that, as long as he could keep the Volkswagen in sight, its driver had perhaps made a tactical error. Here, at this time of night, the streets were quiet. If the right moment came –

Almost at once Richard saw his opportunity. The road was narrow, with high factory walls on either side and no one in sight.

'This is the showdown,' he said, 'for better or worse, Maureen.' He accelerated violently and sped past the Volkswagen, swerving sharply ahead of it to force it to a halt. 'Give me your gun. You stay down till I call.'

He jumped from the Renault, clutching the small black automatic, and aimed it directly at the figures behind the windscreen of the Volkswagen. He fired one warning shot, shattering the glass, then took shelter behind the open door of his own car. Answering shots came immediately, so he took careful aim and fired twice more. His care was rewarded; he saw the driver drop forward over the wheel and, after a moment, the Volkswagen's near-side door opened and a slim woman emerged slowly.

'Hands on head!' Richard shouted. 'Throw me your gun!'

The woman obviously understood some English for she raised her hands to her head, then very slowly moved one to point to the figure in the driver's seat.

'Get his gun then!' said Richard. 'Now. Slowly.'

He stepped forward to cover her as she obeyed, emerging with a revolver.

'Drop it!' Richard ordered. 'Is he badly hurt?'

The woman stared at him silently, then nodded. 'God!' mouthed Richard. 'If I've killed the bastard! The French authorities – the international rumpus – '

This was the tricky moment, Richard realized. If the man weren't dead and had another weapon concealed in the minibus . . . watching the unmoving driver intently, he waved the woman towards him and called to Maureen. She came from the Renault to pat the woman down, finally signalling that she was clean.

Time was running out on them, Richard knew. The street would not remain empty indefinitely, and the rue de Longchamp was waiting. But he still moved slowly and carefully to the open door of the minibus.

The neat hole in the centre of the forehead slumped over the steering-wheel left no doubt. In terms of French law, Richard himself was a killer, no matter how justified the man's death. It was more imperative than ever that they get clear as soon as possible.

First, get rid of any unnecessary complications. Richard turned to the woman and pointed. 'Go!' he said. 'Go! Now!'

He breathed a sigh of relief as the woman turned on her heel and, at first slowly and reluctantly, then more quickly, made off into the distance. He glanced back at the body in the minibus; fortunately there was very little blood.

In the meantime, Maureen Grant had crept to the rear of the vehicle. She waited seconds till Richard joined her with the automatic. When he nodded she swung the doors wide.

Richard held his breath. He hoped against hope that there was not another conspirator concealed in the van. God knew what might happen then – a hostage situation, with its inevitable publicity, or even immediate death for the victims of the abduction –

In fact, all they found were the British Foreign Secretary and his wife strapped to bunks, and apparently sleeping peacefully.

'What d'you think?' asked Richard at once. 'Hospital or the Embassy? Hospital will mean a lot of explanations, but – '

Maureen had been examining Sir Hubert and Lady Manville. She felt for their pulses and opened their eyes. 'As far as I can see they're just drugged,' she said. 'After all, there'd have been

237

no point in putting their lives in danger. I vote for the Embassy.'

'Okay,' said Richard. 'We'll drag the driver's body on to the pavement, get his prints on his gun and drop it beside him. Maybe that'll confuse matters. Then I'll drive this thing, and you bring the Renault. We've been lucky so far, but let's get out of here before anyone comes. God knows what the French'll make of it. But as long as we can keep it out of the headlines – '

26

'You must know I can't agree to that. Not without instructions – '

Sir George Fauvic spoke testily. He was not accustomed to being dragged from his bed in the middle of the night to welcome the drugged bodies of the British Foreign Secretary and his wife, and to be told by an SIS officer that they had been kidnapped and rescued, and that a member of his Embassy's staff – in this case, David Windfield – and *his* wife could be lying in their house either dead or drugged. He had demanded that a doctor be called, and Richard had acquiesced reluctantly, as long as the Embassy medical man could be trusted to keep his mouth shut. The initial confusion was soon over, largely thanks to the good sense of Lady Fauvic, but Sir George had still had no time to dress, and he felt this put him at a disadvantage in what was proving to be a difficult interview. He tightened the belt of his silk dressing-gown before again confronting Richard Kent with a certain amount of disfavour.

'And what about the French authorities?' he added. 'If you don't want the police or the DST, surely the *Quai* – '

Richard was trying to restrain his temper. Largely because of his personal involvement with the Manvilles, the last few weeks had proved a tremendous strain on him. He was mentally and physically tired. In the circumstances, he was in no mood for a stupid argument with a diplomat.

'Look, sir,' he said finally and quietly. 'We may be on the verge of another major espionage scandal. We might be able to avoid it. At least let me play it my way for an hour.'

'Exactly what do you propose to do?'

'Frankly, sir, I've no idea. A lot will depend on what I find when I get into the house.'

The Ambassador opened his mouth to reply, then shut it again. There had been a bleak quality in Richard Kent's expression, a coldness in his voice. It warned Sir George, who was no fool, that Kent knew or guessed more than he had reported.

'Very well,' he said at last. 'Do as you wish – '

'Thank you, sir,' Richard said.

'But I hope you've appreciated that if you're right about the situation there's a fair chance you'll disappear into that house and not be seen again, like the unfortunate gendarme.'

'I've thought of that, sir,' said Richard. 'I'll take every care.'

There was something oddly chilling in his tone, and the Ambassador reverted to a previous subject. 'What about London?' he asked. 'Surely we should both report through our own channels. Are your people in the picture?'

Richard hesitated. 'Not completely, sir. But give me an hour, as I say. That should be enough to resolve the position. My people in the apartment opposite the Windfield's house will keep you informed of my movements. If I don't reappear within that time I'll have failed, and you must use your own judgement.'

Richard was thankful that Sir George had not been able to read his thoughts, for he too had made up his mind. He had decided that if David and Julia were both dead, or – less likely – that David was dead and Julia alive, he would do his best to arrange a scenario which would compromise neither of them. He would do it for Julia's sake, and Rosemary's – and because it was his duty, as he saw it. If, as he feared, he found Julia dead and David alive and apparently in control of the situation, he would still cover for them. But first he would kill David.

Sir George had mellowed slightly by this time, and he now regarded the SIS man with something approaching approval. 'You're quite right, of course,' he said. 'A public scandal would be a highly undesirable outcome. You must do your best – and I'll wait for an hour before taking any action. Is there anything more I can do to help?'

'No, sir. Maureen Grant will come with me to the rue de

Longchamp, but she won't enter the house unless I call her. I think I'm best alone on this one.'

Sir George nodded heavily. 'All right then,' he said at last. 'Good luck.'

'Thank you, sir.'

★

Richard Kent drove from the British Embassy to the rue de Longchamp in an almost total silence that Maureen Grant respected. She was sensitive enough to perceive that the present operation had more than usual significance as far as he was concerned. So, if he chose not to talk, she had no objections. She was happy to leave him to his thoughts until, stating the obvious, but as if slightly surprised by it, Richard said, 'Here we are.'

Maureen Grant took the microphone and spoke to the watchers in the apartment opposite the Windfields' house. Their report was negative. No one had arrived or left. There was still no sign of the gendarme, and they were wondering what would happen when his relief came on duty and found him missing. In the house, lights had remained on both upstairs and downstairs throughout the night.

'Okay. Then I'll go. Let H.E. know I'm on my way,' Richard said. 'Assuming all goes well,' he added to Maureen, 'I'll either be back, or I'll call you into the house within an hour. All right?'

'Fine!' Maureen said. 'Good luck, sir. Do you want the automatic this time?'

'Certainly not.'

Richard grinned at her as he got out of the car. Maureen Grant didn't often call him 'sir'. But his grin faded as he walked the hundred metres along the street to the Windfields' house. He tried the gates. They were locked, as he had expected, so he rang the bell. When no one answered he pressed his thumb on the bell-push, and kept it there.

★

'Who the hell can that be?' David, in the salon, was thoroughly startled.

241

Julia shrugged, hiding her sudden excitement. Any contact with people from outside gave reason for hope. Earlier she had naturally thought of the phone, but David had watched her closely, and even when she had finally made an opportunity, she had found the line dead.

'Hadn't you better answer the bell?' she said. 'With so many lights on it's obvious that someone's awake.'

'Someone – you – could be ill!'

David spoke savagely, and Julia thought, 'Oh, God, he's afraid.' She felt a rush of pity for him, but it was brief. Here was a chance, and she must make the most of it.

She said, 'Really, David, you'd better answer. It could be anything – even a – a drunk. But if you don't answer he might get unpleasant, and then – '

'Ye-es, you're right, I suppose. But come with me, Julia, and don't try anything stupid. Understand?'

'I understand.'

Holding her so tightly as to hurt her upper arm, David pulled Julia into the hall. 'Yes, who's that?' he demanded through the Entryphone, trying to sound like someone angry at being woken from sleep.

'It's Richard Kent, David. Please let me in. We must talk.'

David's grip on Julia's arm tightened again, so that she winced. 'Go away, Richard,' he said. 'It's the middle of the night, and Julia's none too well. Mild food poisoning, I suspect. Surely whatever you want can wait till morning?'

'No, David, it can't. Time's short. It's either talk to me now, or talk to the DST in a few hours. You're in trouble, chum, deep trouble, and I'm prepared to do my best to get you out of it – not for your damned sake, but to help avoid an almighty scandal that'll do us all a lot of harm.'

Richard waited, praying that his judgement of David was accurate, that a mixture of curiosity and bravado, if nothing else, would induce him to open the door. Once inside what he did would depend on what he found. He had already learnt something – that David was alive, and sure enough of his position to prevaricate.

'All right, Richard,' the metallic voice said. 'I'll come and let you in. Why not? I take it you're alone?'

'Yes – and thanks.' The laconic response hid Richard's relief.

Moments later David opened the gates. Richard had stood well back, so that David was able to glance up and down the street.

'It's all right, David,' Richard said. 'I told you I was alone. This is between us. I want to talk.'

'I can't imagine what about. However – '

At David's gesture, Richard went ahead. The front door of the house was ajar. He pushed it open and entered the hall. At once he saw the suitcases at the foot of the stairs.

'Planning to go away, David?'

'Yes. Julia and I are going on – holiday.'

'Where *is* Julia?'

'In the salon.'

Again David gestured, and let Richard precede him into the long, elegant room. Julia was standing with her back to the far window. She came forward slowly. She was pale but seemed composed.

'Hello, Richard.'

'Julia.'

Richard gave a stiff small bow. He was so deeply thankful to see Julia alive and unharmed that for a moment his mind was blank. Then he thought how ludicrous the situation was.

Clearly David had had the same thought because he said, 'Okay, Richard, let's stop playing games. Put your hands against the wall and spread your legs. Just like in a cops and robbers movie.'

'I'm unarmed,' Richard protested, but the atmosphere changed dramatically as David produced a lethal-looking revolver. Richard did as he was told.

Julia watched impassively as David patted Richard down, and assured himself that Richard wasn't carrying a weapon. The great resurgence of hope she had experienced when their unexpected visitor turned out to be Richard Kent was beginning to fade. She wondered why Richard had come seemingly unprepared to do anything but talk, when it was clear from what he'd said that he knew David was fully committed. What was more, he must realize, too, that he was almost the last person likely to persuade David to change his mind.

'All right, Richard,' said David. 'Sit down. There.' He pointed to an armchair. 'Now tell us why you're here. And be quick. Julia and I are leaving early. I expect you've guessed where we're going.'

'Oh yes,' Richard said quite calmly. 'Moscow, I assume.' He looked at Julia. 'Willingly or unwillingly?'

Julia hesitated. 'Does it matter?'

David intervened. 'Richard, isn't it obvious that Julia's a free agent? She could walk out of here right now if she wished.'

'You mean if she knew her parents were both safe in bed at the British Residence?'

David's head came up with a jerk. 'But they're not! You're lying!'

'Oh no, I'm not. They were drugged here, and taken away by Karl and Eva Fischer in their Mercedes, obviously with your connivance. They were transferred to a Volkswagen, in the care of another couple, but by a mixture of good luck and judgement they were intercepted.'

'I can guess what you mean by good luck and judgement. You've been hounding me, Richard. Damn you!' said David.

'It's true?' demanded Julia. 'Mother and Dad are safe?'

'Yes. And so's Rosemary, who hasn't got measles or anything else. She thinks that spending her half-term with her headmistress and a policewoman to guard them is terribly exciting. Of course, what she doesn't know is that her father's a traitor.'

Richard addressed his last sentence to David, and neither of them so much as glanced at Julia, who sank into a chair and buried her face in her hands. Richard watched David closely. He knew that the moment of danger was at hand. David still held the automatic, though he wasn't aiming it at anyone. But it was possible that if he became desperate and his reason snapped, he would shoot all three of them. Richard edged forward in his chair.

He said, 'David, no one wants a great spy scandal – not another. It won't do my masters any good – or yours either, I guess.'

'What do you suggest?' David asked abruptly, the knuckles of his hand with the gun white with strain, and his breathing shallow. 'Assuming that what you've been saying isn't a pack of lies.'

'You can take it all for Gospel. Unless you'd like to phone the Ambassador?'

'You forget I've got the gun. What's to prevent me killing you, and taking Julia to Moscow?'

Julia lifted her face. 'I won't go with you, David. Not now I've got a choice. I'd rather die if I have to.'

Her voice had risen hysterically, as she uttered the blunt ultimatum. And it acted as the kind of goad to David that Richard had feared. David's reaction was immediate. He turned towards his wife and fired wildly and mindlessly. Julia screamed as the bullet went through her shoulder, and the shrill sound made David hesitate for a fraction of a second, before he swung round in a murderous attempt to aim with greater deliberation at Richard.

But the momentary hesitation had been suffstment for Richard to anticipate David's action. He propelled himself out of his chair and flung himself headlong towards his adversary. His outstretched hand was able to grasp David's ankle and pull him off balance as the gun went off.

The bullet made a furrow through the carpet, missing Richard's head by a centimetre and, as Richard jerked on David's ankle again, David fell to the carpet. The gun arced away from his hand.

The two men rose to their feet simultaneously. They eyed each other like wrestlers in what each knew to be a momentous personal confrontation. In a way they had always been rivals, even during their earlier friendship at school and at Oxford. At first it had been Julia standing between them, then Celia's death, and finally irreconcilable ideologies had separated them for ever. In that moment they both knew how deep their enmity went.

It was David who made the first move, and Julia screamed again as he dived suddenly towards the revolver. Richard leapt for it, too, but David reached it a fraction of a second before Richard.

He had no time to fire a shot before Richard was upon him. The two men fell to the ground as they struggled, Richard trying to claw his way to David's gun hand, David trying to prevent him.

In fact, the struggle was brief, and its ending conclusive. There was the sound of a shot, muffled by the two bodies and slowly, as it seemed to Julia, they rolled apart. She stood and stared down at them, holding her shoulder tightly. For a moment neither of them moved. She thought they were both dead, and moaned softly.

Then, after appreciable seconds, Richard pulled free the arm on which David was lying and knelt beside him. Carefully he prized the gun from David's clasp, removed the clip and the round in the chamber and slipped the weapon into his pocket.

'Richard! Is David – ' Julia said shakily.

'David's dead.' Richard had been examining him, and spoke gently. 'It was an accident, Julia.' He got to his feet.

The after-effects of the drug, the stabbing pain in her shoulder, and the mental and physical shocks she had suffered were taking their toll on Julia. She staggered towards him and Richard caught her as she fell.

'No,' she managed to murmur. 'He meant to kill you.'

Richard didn't argue. There would be time later to agree on their story; it would bear little relation to the truth. Quickly he inspected Julia's wound, folded his handkerchief into a pad and made her press it hard on the hole where the bullet had entered her shoulder. He took her by the hand.

'Come along,' he said, as if to a child. 'There are people outside waiting to help. Everything's going to be all right.'

Finale

Richard Kent was breakfasting with Neil Grantham in the latter's rooms in College. Richard had left London after an early cup of tea to drive up to Oxford. Now he felt he needed sustenance before he and Grantham attended David Windfield's funeral in the Cotswold village where David's mother and stepfather were living.

The scout, having brought in coffee and arranged dishes on the hot plate, had left the two men alone. They ate in companionable silence.

Then Grantham said, 'You know, I'm far from sure why we're going to this funeral.'

'For old time's sake, Neil.' Richard shrugged. 'And for my part I suppose there's an element of something like *noblesse oblige*.'

'For heaven's sake, Richard, you're not under any kind of obligation to Windfield. In my opinion, he treated you despicably over that car accident all those years ago. He could have stood by you, given you some moral support, at least. Instead, he seized his chance to marry Julia, and – '

Grantham stopped speaking. Richard was shaking his head in contradiction, though for a moment he said nothing. He poured himself more coffee, as Grantham waited impatiently.

'Why? Am I wrong, Richard?'

'In a way. In the first place you're assuming I'd have asked Julia to marry me.'

'So? You were in love with her, weren't you?'

'Yes, but – Neil, there's an awful lot you don't know, I'm afraid.'

'Really?' Grantham speared a piece of sausage and chewed it fiercely. 'And you're not prepared to enlighten me?'

Richard hesitated. All his training had taught him to keep secrets, and he had kept these personal ones for so long that he didn't find it easy to speak out, even to someone he trusted like Neil Grantham. Nevertheless he had told Sir Henry Manville; he had thought it right in the circumstances that the Foreign Secretary should be aware of the whole truth. So why not tell Grantham?

'Neil,' he said at length, 'you've heard of Vladimir Dolkov, the KGB General?'

'Of course. I gather the SIS suspect it was he who masterminded the plan to kidnap the Manvilles and abduct them to the Soviet Union.'

'Well, Dolkov is my uncle.'

'*What?*'

Grantham's expression was such that Richard had to laugh. 'You can't be more flabbergasted than I was when I first learnt about it.'

'But it can't be true! How on earth – '

'Oh yes. It's true all right. You know my mother was in Jersey during the war. She went there to look after a relation, and got caught by the German occupation. To cut a long story short, she took pity on a Russian – a prisoner who had escaped from the Todt Organization in the Island. She gave him shelter, and eventually they became lovers. His name was Alexis Dolkov. He was Vladimir's younger brother – and my father.'

'Good God!' Grantham ran a hand through his shock of red hair, still as thick as ever. 'When did you find out? Where? How? What happened?'

'In Oxford, just before my Schools, my final examinations. A woman phoned me, here at the College. She said she was a friend of my mother's, and asked me to dinner at the Randolph. After the meal, she told me bluntly that my father was not John Ingram, as I'd always believed, but Alexis Dolkov, the brother of her own first husband. She said that Alexis was dead, but that the third brother, my Uncle Vladimir, who was a Soviet KGB officer, was very interested in my welfare. After all, I was his nephew – and, according to their law, a Russian.'

'I suppose it was obvious where all this was leading?'

'Of course. Anna Basnova – that was the woman's name – made no secret of it. I was to work for Mother Russia. Why not? I was "one of them".'

'What did you do?'

'My first reaction was to try to refute her whole story, but she produced photographs of Alexis, and there was no denying that I looked like him. She also told me to ask Pandora – as you know, that's my mother's real name, though she prefers to be called Poppy. Anyway, by now I was half beginning to believe the Basnova woman.' Richard sighed helplessly. 'Neil, I won't even try to describe how I felt.'

Grantham nodded in sympathy. 'You must have been shattered.'

'I was. I was angry, too. It was stupid, but what really riled me at the time was that Anna Basnova kept calling me "Bird" – the family's pet name for me when I was a child. Short for "Dicky bird", of course, though the Dolkovs don't seem to have realized that. Her use of the word infuriated me. I considered it the ultimate impertinence.' Richard grinned ruefully. 'In the end, anger gave me courage. I told her to go to hell, and walked out.'

'But did she take no for an answer?'

'She had one more go at me, but by that time I'd talked to my mother and my stepfather. Poppy admitted the Basnova woman was right about Alexis Dolkov, but they both agreed with me that in no circumstances must I let myself be blackmailed. So I was very firm, and the Russians never approached me again. I assume Uncle Vladimir decided to cut his losses, or at least realized that he'd never be able to trust me completely. To give him his due, he never seems to have tried to do me any harm.'

'Good for him. Because he must have been disappointed.'

'Yes. I imagine he had high hopes for me from the beginning, and subsequently hopes for Peregrine Manville and David Windfield, my closest friends. We were all thought to be "high-fliers", and maybe he hoped we'd form an Oxford trio of traitors, like the Cambridge crowd. But, as you say, Neil, he was disappointed. One out of three wasn't a particularly good score, given such a base. Admittedly Peregrine was recruited, but he got himself killed before he'd been much use, and I was a complete loss.'

'A good thing, too. Far better to work for the SIS than the KGB.'

'That was thanks to you, Neil. I know you kept your eyes open for them. So you made the right noises in the right places, and gave me the right introductions, and luckily they decided my murky past was irrelevant. Incidentally, I did come clean about the whole thing to them, and I got the impression they felt the connection might be useful at some future moment. A pity the FCO proper wouldn't have taken the same view.'

'At least I know now why you suddenly decided not to be a diplomat, Richard. It's a point that's always puzzled me. But I can see it wasn't practicable once you knew about the Dolkovs – quite apart from the accident.'

Richard hesitated, as if he were about to add something but had then changed his mind. He reached for the butter and marmalade, and attended to his toast. Grantham regarded him curiously.

'Anyway, you've not done too badly in the end,' he said, 'though I suppose it's not what you'd hoped for.'

'Not really. I saw myself as a senior diplomat in Washington or Paris, or even Moscow, married to Julia, perhaps with a small family – everything that David was and had.'

'Except that David was a traitor.'

'In a funny kind of way, that was my fault. If Vladimir Dolkov hadn't followed my career with such concern, neither Peregrine nor David would have attracted his interest, and he'd never have drawn them to the Fischers' attention as potential recruitment material. So at least to some extent I'm responsible for what they became.'

'Rubbish!' Grantham spoke sharply. 'They could have said no, as you did. I just don't understand either of them.'

'I believe Peregrine agreed partly because he thought it would be exciting, and partly to spite his father. They didn't get on well. As for David – ' Richard sighed again. He glanced at his watch. 'Neil, we'd better be off. Look at the time. We can't be late for a funeral.'

'We won't be. We can easily spare another quarter of an hour. Tell me about David, Richard,' Grantham pressed. 'You were closer to him than anyone. I accept what you say about Peregrine, and as he was killed we'll never know what might have happened. It could have been only a brief flirtation as far as he was concerned. But David – '

'David was blackmailed by the Fischers,' Richard said flatly. 'Neil, I got away with that "accident" comparatively lightly. Everyone swore I wasn't drunk and I was badly injured, so I received a certain amount of sympathy. And, of course, I got tremendous support from my family. But God knows it was no joy, even for me. For David it would have been infinitely worse. His stepfather had died recently, and his mother wouldn't have been much help. He was worried about money. And he was tight. His driving would have been called criminally irresponsible, and he'd probably have gone to gaol.'

'Yes, but – Richard, are you telling me that it was *David* who was driving that morning, not you?' The thought was a second shock for Neil Grantham, and he stared at Richard unbelievingly. 'But that's not possible. Julia would never have lied for David.'

'Not intentionally, no. But remember she was seriously hurt and, when she was recovering, still shaken by Celia's death, she was assured I was driving. There was no question about it. I didn't deny it, and no one doubted it. After all, the police had found me behind the wheel. Karl and Eva must have set the scene for them and, once David had acquiesced, there was no going back for him. He'd put himself completely in their hands. Later they presented the bill.'

'What a risk for them to take.' Grantham shook his head slowly. 'They weren't to know you'd lose your memory.'

'It was a fair risk, Neil. If I'd denied that I'd been driving, who'd have believed me? Not many people, in the circumstances. In fact, when my memory started to return, I could scarcely believe it myself. I told my parents, and they agreed with me that it was too late to try to prove the truth – even if I'd wanted to. And Julia was married to David by then. Of course, at that point I didn't know about the Fischers' little plans, and I couldn't foresee the future. If I had?' Richard shrugged. Smiling wryly he stood up. 'Come on, Neil. I've talked enough. It really is time to go now.'

★

251

The funeral was intended to be private. Only family and close friends were expected to be present. Inevitably, however, David Windfield's death had aroused public interest. Indeed, with the help of the media, it had created a minor sensation. After all, the shooting of a senior member of the staff of the British Embassy, and the wounding of his wife in their Paris home by would-be thieves – that had been the cover-story, easily devised – could hardly be expected not to make the headlines. The fact that David was the son-in-law of Sir Hubert Manville, the British Foreign Secretary, and Lady Manville, and that the Manvilles had been in Paris at the time staying with their old friends, the Ambassador and his wife, added spice to the tale, and multiplied the radio, television and press coverage.

Neither had David's mother helped to damp down the publicity. Hope Cornish, as she now was, received the news in the middle of her honeymoon. She and her new husband had been lifted off their cruise ship and flown to Paris. Here she had insisted that her son's body should be returned to England and buried in the village where the Cornishes intended to live.

As they had bought the house only a few months earlier, in anticipation of their marriage, the villagers would not have been particularly interested in the funeral if it had not been for the media. But the presence of television cameras and crews, news photographers, radio and press reporters, had made it almost a public event. The little church was full, and the congregation – plus the sightseers – overflowed into the churchyard.

It was a brilliant day, and the sun coming through the stained-glass windows made Rosemary Windfield shift in her seat to avoid it shining directly into her eyes. She was sitting in the front pew beside David's mother and Robert Cornish. She hadn't wanted to sit with them. She would have much preferred to be with the Manvilles, who were across the aisle, but for once Sir Hubert had been firm.

'No, Rosemary, you can't sit with us. David was your father and, if your mother had been well enough to come, on such an occasion as this both she and you would have sat with the Cornishes.'

Rosemary began to protest, but something in her grandfather's tone of voice made her desist. Instead she said, 'Okay, but I wish they wouldn't talk about Dad as if he were some kind of hero. He wasn't, was he?'

'No. He was just an – an – unfortunate man. But when someone whom one has loved dies, Celia, especially if they die in unhappy circumstances, one remembers their – their finest qualities.'

Rosemary was silent. She had noticed that her grandfather had called her 'Celia'. He did this sometimes when he was absent-minded, and she knew he was thinking of her dead aunt. In fact Hubert Manville had been thinking both of Celia and of his son, Peregrine.

Now, in the church, as he automatically sang 'Land of our fathers, we pledge to thee' – a hymn so inappropriate that he could have wept – he thought again of Peregrine.

Richard Kent hadn't attempted to soften the facts. 'It's best you should know the whole truth, sir,' he had said, 'in case the Fischers seize their opportunity and start mud-slinging when the West Germans put them on trial.'

But it was hard to realize that Peregrine had been a traitor, saved only by his death from God knows what. To call it a young man's folly was no excuse. David, Julia's husband, Rosemary's father – that was bad enough, Manville thought miserably – but Peregrine . . .

He had offered the Prime Minister his resignation as soon as he had learnt about David, but it had been refused. If he had known then about Peregrine he would have insisted; at the first suitable moment he would insist. He felt dirty, dishonoured. Glancing sideways at his wife as they knelt after the hymn, he prayed that she would never learn about their son.

They stood again while the coffin, covered with white roses, was borne down the aisle. As he turned to watch it he caught sight of Richard Kent towards the rear of the church, and was instantly reminded of how much he owed him. If it hadn't been for Richard, whom years ago he had pursued so vindictively because of Celia's death, he would probably be in Moscow now, with Mary and Julia and Rosemary, forever branded a defector, a traitor.

Vladimir Dolkov's plot to kidnap the Foreign Secretary and his family had been brilliant, he admitted. The possibility had always been present, he supposed, since the wretched David had married Julia, and he – the father-in-law – had become Foreign Secretary. But circumstances had played into the Russian's hands. The private weekend at the Windfields' house, with a minimum of security in the relaxed aftermath of the successful Summit, had provided an ideal opportunity. As far as he could make out, he reflected, most secret operations were a combination of careful contingency planning and the seizure of the right moment.

Suddenly he became aware of the pressure of his wife's hand on his arm. The Cornishes and Rosemary were following the coffin, and they must join the procession next. As they walked together down the aisle he saw Richard Kent again, and once more thought of what might have happened not only to himself and to those he held most dear, but to the country. The Government would certainly have fallen, the Americans would have lost all faith in Britain, and the consequences for the Western Alliance could have been catastrophic.

As he came out of the church into the sunshine Sir Hubert Manville shivered, and his wife's grasp on his arm tightened reassuringly. They still had to get through the wake at the Cornishes' house.

*

Richard Kent and Neil Grantham had refused Mrs Cornish's offer of hospitality. Now they hurried to get away, but a reporter forestalled them.

'Mr Grantham, Mr Kent. Would you care to make a personal comment on David Windfield's death?' The newsman walked backwards in front of them, his accompanying photographer seeking a good picture.

'No!' Richard said sharply. He had been more affected by the funeral than he cared to admit.

Grantham replied for both of them. 'What can we say, except that it's been a tragedy for his family and his friends, and indeed for his country. There aren't many men like David Windfield.' And, as he got into the car beside Richard, he added, 'For which may God be thanked.'

They drove in silence for some time, each preoccupied with his own thoughts. In Blenheim they stopped for a quick drink and a sandwich. Richard was eager to get back to London, and Grantham had a College meeting which needed some preparation. They parted in Oxford, in the High, promising to meet again soon.

Much as he liked Neil Grantham, Richard was glad to be alone. He slipped a cassette into its slot and, to the sounds of Dvořák's Fifth Symphony, headed for London. Traffic was heavy, and it was after three when he reached his family's home in Hampstead.

His mother and stepfather had left that morning for a holiday on the Swiss lakes, but as Richard turned into the drive his heart lifted when he saw that a sitting-room window was open. He put the car in the garage and went to the front door. Julia had been listening for him, and was waiting.

'Darling, I'm sorry I've been so long,' he said.

'It doesn't matter. You're here now.'

Richard put his arms around her, and Julia lifted up her face to be kissed. She was pale and there were dark shadows under her eyes, but her smile was bright. She had recovered from the bullet wound she had received, but the shock of David's death and the nature of it was still with her. Richard hoped that now and in the future he would be able to help her to forget.

'Was everything all right?' she asked anxiously.

'Yes. Your father looked a little wan, but your mother was clearly supportive. Rosemary was calm and very self-possessed. She's an attractive child, Julia. And – and it was a rather touching ceremony.'

'I couldn't have gone.'

'Of course not. But it's over now, darling. In the past. All of it. It's time to think about us.'

'I know,' Julia said. 'I know, Richard darling. We've waited too long already.'